MATCHMAKING CAN BE MURDER

Center Point
Large Print

Also by Amanda Flower and available from
Center Point Large Print:

Assaulted Caramel
Lethal Licorice
Premeditated Peppermint

**This Large Print Book carries the
Seal of Approval of N.A.V.H.**

MATCHMAKING CAN BE MURDER

An Amish Matchmaker Mystery

AMANDA FLOWER

CENTER POINT LARGE PRINT
THORNDIKE, MAINE

This Center Point Large Print edition
is published in the year 2020 by arrangement with
Kensington Publishing Corp.

The text of this Large Print edition is unabridged.
In other aspects, this book may vary
from the original edition.
Printed in the United States of America
on permanent paper.
Set in 16-point Times New Roman type.

ISBN: 978-1-64358-573-4

The Library of Congress has cataloged this record
under Library of Congress Control Number: 2019956994

For Pastor Rob & Nancy Seymour

ACKNOWLEDGMENTS

Thanks so much to my wonderful readers who loved the Amish Candy Shop Mysteries, which made this series possible.

Thanks always to the great team at Kensington, especially my editor Alicia Condon, and thanks too to my super agent Nicole Resciniti.

Special thanks to author Suzanne Woods Fisher for her advice as to how to use the Amish proverbs throughout the story. And to my dear friends Mariellyn Grace and David Seymour while writing this manuscript.

Finally, to God in Heaven, thank you for letting my biggest dream come true.

When you get to your wit's end
you will find God lives there.
　　　　　—AMISH PROVERB

CHAPTER ONE

If someone had told me that in this season of my life I would be living in a little ranch house all by myself with just a couple of ornery goats as company, I would have laughed. This life wasn't the one I'd planned. Growing up in my Amish district as a young girl, I dreamed of love, of a husband, and of children. I'd had two of those, just not for as long as I would have wanted, and the third was not to be. But as the saying goes, "If you never taste the bitter, you won't know what sweet is."

Even though I didn't have children of my own, the Lord saw to it that I would help young people in a different way. He gave me the gift of recognizing love and affection. I knew, knew down to the very center of my bones, when two people were meant to be together. And I knew when they were not. My niece Edith Hochstetler had not yet found that unshakable love. She hadn't found it with her first husband and I knew, as sure as I knew my dear Kip was waiting for me at heaven's gate, that she had not found it in Zeke Miller.

I brushed dirt from my garden-glove-covered hands. Having only lived on my little hobby farm for a few months, I was finally in the process of putting my garden in. Planting the flower bed was the perfect way to convince Edith to come over. An avid gardener, she never turned down an opportunity to get her hands in the dirt. This was a characteristic that I was counting on because it was time that she and I had a little chat about her future.

For the garden, I'd collected a number of rocks from my brother's quarry, and I planned to nestle them in among the plants. My mother always had a rock garden in her home, and so would I. Tradition is important, even more so if you're Amish. Every season has its own rhythm and duties, from planting to farming to harvest and on and on. Some of my *Englisch* friends would hate the monotony of it all. Had they been raised Amish, they would find comfort in knowing what was expected of them next.

Edith ran Edy's Greenhouse, a nursery that was just on the edge of the little village of Harvest where we lived. It had been her father's business, *Gott* rest his soul, and he'd named it after his daughter, Edy, as he liked to call her. No one else in the family had been able to get away with calling her that. She ran the greenhouse herself now.

Her brother Enoch had chosen another life. Her business was the main reason that she shouldn't marry Zeke Miller. The greenhouse did very well. Edith had a gift for plants and growing things that had been passed down to her from her father.

12

Zeke knew there was money in that business and more to be made if he got his hands on it. If she married him, that business would become his. As her husband, he would be the head of it, not Edith. It was the Amish way for the head of the house to be the head of the family business too.

And that was why I had asked her to come help me plant my garden—so we could have a heart-to-heart talk away from the prying eyes and eavesdropping ears in the greenhouse. This was a conversation that no one else should hear.

I wiped at my brow and knew I had a smudge of dirt now in the middle of my forehead. It itched. I didn't bother to wipe it away. The dirt would add to the impression that I needed help putting in the plants and clearing the earth. The smudge gave the dramatic effect that I was going for. Edith wouldn't be any the wiser.

My two goats, Phillip and Peter, walked around me in a large circle like lions stalking their prey. That would be if lions were as silly as these overly rambunctious creatures. They were Boer goats. Phillip was black and white, and Peter was brown and white. I'd adopted them when I moved back to Ohio after years in Michigan caring for an invalid sister. I bought them to help me clear the overgrown land around my home. Goats were the very best at clearing land. They would eat almost everything, but, surprisingly, wouldn't eat grass. That was good. I wanted the lawn to stay

13

intact. Phillip and Peter were doing a good job of chewing through the overgrown weeds and plants. They ate everything in sight, including the invasive multiflora roses that were the bane of any Ohio farmer due to their propensity to spread like wildfire and blanket the landscape with their treacherous thorns.

I found the goats circling suspiciously and picked up my spade to encourage them to move away from the freshly tilled earth. In all my sixty-seven years, I had never come across such ornery animals. I shook my finger at the goats. "This will be my flower garden, and if I see either of you in it, I will send you packing!"

Phillip and Peter shared a look.

"I know what you are thinking, but the garden is off limits. You—"

I would have said more, but just then there was the clip-clop of hooves and the rattle of a farm wagon on the other side of the house. Phillip and Peter took off. They loved to be first to greet visitors to my home.

I jabbed the spade into the lawn, rubbed a little dirt on my cheek to look frazzled, and made my way around the side of the house at a much slower pace than I usually tended to move.

As I walked around my ranch house, I reviewed what I was going to say. Somehow, I needed to convince Edith that it was better to wait for love than grasp at the first man who showed interest.

There was a reason I had never remarried in the twenty years since I'd lost my Kip. I knew what true love was and would not accept anything short of it. I wanted my niece to find the same. I wanted all the young people I helped to find it too.

I removed my garden gloves and tucked them into the front pocket of my apron and touched the top of my head just to check my prayer cap was on straight and my snow-white hair, only a shade or two lighter than its original blond color, remained tucked tight at my nape. I had always hated my white-blond hair until it turned completely white, so it was not a great hardship for me when I started going gray. However, I could do without the wrinkles on my neck and the aches and pains when I rose in the early morning each day. I came around the side of the house just in time to see Phillip and Peter gallop like a couple of colts with their floppy ears flapping in the wind as they approached a petite blond Amish woman standing by a wagon. The back of the wagon was full of blooming plants.

Edith stood on her tiptoes, which only gave her an inch more on her five foot height. "*Aenti* Millie!" she cried. "Your *gees* are attacking me! Again!"

Gees was the Pennsylvania Dutch word for goats. It always made me laugh when the word was said around *Englischers* because I suspected they thought we were talking about geese.

"Phillip! Peter! You leave her alone, you rascals! Leave Edith be! If this keeps up, she won't take you to the greenhouse."

Peter stopped bouncing, but Phillip got in a couple more hops before he settled down on all four hooves. He was the more excitable of the two.

I snapped my fingers, which was a signal to the goats that I meant business, and they ran toward me, then began pulling weeds from the grass with their square teeth as if that had been their plan all along. I knew better.

"Rapscallions," I muttered. It was an *Englisch* word I had heard while living in Michigan and I had come to like it quite a lot. It was one of the better names I could call the goats when they were really being troublemakers. My sister had lived in a predominantly *Englisch* community in Michigan. I'd learned all sorts of interesting words during my decade there.

Edith lowered herself from her tiptoes, keeping an eye on the goats the entire time. "I do appreciate your lending me your goats for a few days to clear the land behind the greenhouse. The weeds back there have gotten out of control."

"It's no trouble. Did you bring the wagon today to take them to the greenhouse?"

She nodded. "If you don't mind, *ya*. The work is long overdue, and it's something I can do to make a difference. I just need to do *something* to make things better at the greenhouse."

16

"What do you mean, child?"

She shook her head. "It doesn't look right for a greenhouse to have a messy yard. That's all. I would have taken care of it months ago if I had been allowed." Her face fell. "Things have been so challenging this season."

I wanted to ask her what she meant by that, but before I could, she gave me a big hug.

"It's so *gut* to see you. I wish that we could spend more time together. It's just . . ." She trailed off.

"It's *gut* to see you too, my dear." I hugged her back and worry filled the back of my mind. A skill I had as a matchmaker was empathy for others. The emotion I felt most from my niece at that moment was sadness.

Of all my nieces, and I had many, Edith was the most dear to me. When I lived in Michigan to care for my sister, she came and stayed with us for a summer to help out. She was the kindest, most considerate girl, and I saw her more as a daughter than a niece. That may have been because her mother died young, just like my Kip. My sister-in-law's death left my younger brother Ira Lapp with two young children to rear by himself. Because I had no children of my own, it made the most sense for me to be the sister to pitch in. I never regretted doing that. Some believed that I put life on hold to help Ira and then my sister in Michigan when she became ill.

I never saw it that way. The only regret I had was failing Enoch, Edith's twin brother. I hoped that I could make amends for that mistake soon.

I shook sad memories from my head and smiled at my niece. "And how are the children?" I asked.

"They are *gut, Aenti* Millie, and growing like summer weeds." She said this with a mother's glow.

"Dandelions, I hope. Those are my favorite weeds."

"*Aenti*, there are a lot of *Englischers* who come into my greenhouse just to ask me how to get rid of their dandelions."

"And if an *Englischer* does something, it is right?" I shook my head. "They are missing out on one of *Gott*'s great gifts. Next time they stop by and ask that, ask them to dig up their dandelions and give them to me."

She laughed. "All right."

"And how is Zeke?" I asked tentatively.

She licked her lips. "The wedding is next week."

That wasn't what I'd asked, so my eyebrows went up. "I know that."

Zeke and Edith had only been betrothed since the winter. Typically Amish weddings happened in the autumn, but they didn't want to wait that long because of the children, or so my niece had told me. We Amish do not have a long wait period between betrothal and marriage. When the decision is made, we get on with it. I knew things

18

were much different in the *Englisch* world. My *Englisch* friends have had children who were engaged for a year or more. That would never do for the Amish.

"I've been thinking about what you said the other day. That I should only marry again for love. The greenhouse can sustain the children and me until I find love, or it will as soon as I make some changes."

"What kinds of changes?" I asked.

She played with her bonnet ribbons as she spoke. It was a nervous habit she'd had ever since she was a little girl. "It's just so frightening to be alone, and I have been alone these long three years raising the children the best I can without their father. The judgment of the community is heavy on my shoulders. I know there are many who believe I should have married long ago. They don't believe it is right to raise children with only one parent. Then Zeke came along, and he was charming and helpful at first. He wasn't afraid of the hard work at the greenhouse or that I had children. The district thought it was a *gut* match. You were the only one who didn't."

"Only because I wasn't sure that you loved him. If you loved him, Edith, my thoughts would be different."

"The community convinced me that I did. They said it was the best thing to do for the children."

"If that's not how you felt, you should not

have listened to them. It's far worse to marry the wrong person than to live alone."

She nodded and dropped her bonnet ribbons so they fell to her shoulders. "I know this. I should only marry for love. You have told me so many times." Finally, she looked up and met my gaze.

"And have you found love? With Zeke?" I asked, searching her dark brown eyes, which were the same color as mine.

She shook her head. "I don't love Zeke. I—I don't want to marry him. I—" She smoothed her white apron over her plain blue dress. "I thought over what you said about him, and everything is true. He does only want to marry me for the greenhouse." Tears sprang to her eyes. "I don't want to make another mistake like the one I did with my first husband, Moses, and marrying Zeke would be the greatest one yet."

I blinked. Had I heard her right? "You're sure?" I had been trying to convince her not to marry Zeke for weeks, and now, I hadn't even had to put forth my latest argument.

"I only agreed to marry him because I was afraid of raising the children alone." She took a shuddering breath. "I mean to tell him when he comes back from Millersburg today. He's doing a roofing job there. I will tell him when he returns to Harvest. I have to tell him today. I can't wait any longer. It's killing me."

It would seem that my ploy to get Edith's help

with my garden wouldn't be necessary at all. I certainly hadn't needed to smudge so much dirt on my face. I must look ridiculous. I suppressed my smile. I knew this was difficult for her to admit, and it would be even more difficult to tell Zeke. "You're doing the right thing."

She nodded. "But it will be so hard to tell him, to tell everyone that I changed my mind."

"It is your mind; you have a right to change it. If it is not love, it is not *Gott*'s will for you."

She nodded and squeezed my hand tight.

"Zeke will understand in time." I patted her arm. "All will be well."

At the time, I honestly believed that was true.

CHAPTER TWO

Edith was a good girl, and even though it was a Saturday near the end of May, one of the busiest days of the year for her at the greenhouse, when people bought the most plants and needed her sage advice about how to care for their gardens, she stayed for a while longer and helped me put the garden in. We worked in silence most of the time. I could tell she needed the quiet to sort out the thoughts in her head over what she was to say to Zeke that evening. I did not envy her the chore, but I would have done it for her if I could.

When she climbed back into her wagon an hour or two later, I reached up and squeezed her hand. "You will be fine, my dear. *Gott* is with you in all things."

She nodded, but her body was as tense as a clothing line stretched from tree to tree.

Phillip and Peter were in the back of her wagon, tethered to the sides. They butted heads. A small part of me ached to see them go. I knew they would be back in a few days after they had cleared the land for Edith. But it would be a long, quiet night on my little farm without them.

"You will feel better when you can put this behind you," I said.

She smiled down at me from her seat in the wagon. "This is true. It's best to get the worst done as soon as possible, so that you can move on to the *gut* again."

"That is right." I grinned. "It seems to me that you have been listening to my favorite sayings all these years."

Her smile fell into a frown. "I have always listened to your advice, *Aenti*, and if I have made the wrong choices along the way, that is my fault and my fault alone." She flicked the reins on her wagon and the horse backed up and turned the wagon around in the driveway. I watched her go. The cries of the goats when they saw me staying behind pierced my heart. I would visit the greenhouse the next day to see how both Edith and the goats were getting on. I prayed Edith accomplished her difficult task before fear caused her to change her mind.

I brushed my hands on my skirts. It was time to head into the village for the Double Stitch meeting. I walked back to the house and tried to put these worries behind me. As the saying went, "Every moment of worry weakens the soul for its daily combat." It was a saying I often repeated to Edith and Enoch when they were small. This one made me laugh a little to myself, considering we Amish were pacifists.

I drove to the village in my secondhand buggy, which was hitched to my mare Bessie, a gift from one of my brothers. She was a light brown Haflinger with a bright white star on her forehead. I was one of ten children. There were only four of us left in the world—two of my brothers and one sister—and now that I was back in Ohio, we all lived within an hour's buggy ride of each other.

I inhaled deeply as I came to the outskirts of the village. The apple trees that had been in full bloom just a week ago were leafed out with bright green leaves. We were on the edge of summer, and the village of Harvest was getting ready for it. It was the busy season of the year in Holmes County. Busloads of *Englischers* would descend on the village, which was just what community organizer Margot Rawlings was counting on. From what I had heard, she wanted everything to be bigger and better in Harvest this year. If she was behind the idea, I didn't doubt that it would happen. She was as stubborn as a bull and as clever as a fox.

On the village square, Amish men and a few *Englisch* ones were pruning and mowing and making sure that the grounds were perfect. In the middle of the gazebo, I saw Margot with her short brown curls, barking orders.

I flicked the reins and asked Bessie to pick up the pace. I didn't want to get pulled into the fray with Margot. The best way to avoid that was to avoid eye contact. I parked Bessie and the buggy at a hitching post next to the big white church on the square. That was the place where Raellen, who'd organized our meeting that day at a new café in the village, had told me to park. I counted the other horses and buggies at the post, and it looked like most of the ladies from Double Stitch were already there.

I climbed out of the buggy and hurried down the sidewalk to the café. It was the first time I had been there, but the café was easy to find. It was a freestanding white brick building with a bright yellow sun painted on the side of it that was facing the church. A matching yellow awning hung over the front door. Giant planters of yellow tulips sat on either side of the door. It was bright and shiny and decidedly not Amish.

The last time I lived in the village, the café had been the local hardware store. I had gone into that store with my father and then with Kip many times. The shop had been Amish-owned, like most of the businesses in downtown Harvest, but the café that took its place was clearly an *Englisch* business. On the sidewalk chalkboard, the specials of the day were listed. Most of them were salads and soups with squash, kale, and berries of which I had never heard. These foods weren't typical, not for me, anyway. Amish cooking was heavy on meat, potatoes, and pies of every kind. I wondered why Raellen, one of the members of Double Stitch, had picked this place for our meeting. Part of the motivation would be just to get out of the house. As a mother of nine, Raellen was always looking for breaks from her children and husband. I couldn't say I blamed her. The sheep farm that she lived on with her family was in a constant state of upheaval. It seemed to me that every time I was there, either a sheep or a child was upset about something. Raellen, the Lord bless her, took it all in stride, and I thought she must have been given the greatest patience *Gott* had ever bestowed on any woman before or since.

I looked through the front window and noted that the decoration inside wasn't very Amish either. Where our culture called for plainness, the café was anything but plain. The wallpaper was flowered and the tablecloths were covered with a colorful swirl pattern. Even so, many of the features from the old hardware store were still intact, such as the exposed brick wall and some of the pine shelving along those walls. Now instead of tools and nails, the shelves held brightly colored dishes. On another chalkboard on the wall, the specials and the soup-of-the-day were written out.

I opened the front door and a bell chimed. Raellen Raber, my bubbly next-door neighbor and mother of nine children, was already seated with two of the other members of Double Stitch, Iris Young and Leah Bontrager.

Iris was the mother of one fifteen-year-old

son. She was a beautiful woman with auburn hair, delicate features, and skin that already held the sun-kissed glow of working outside. She had been very popular with the young men in the district until I introduced her to Carter Young, an industrious young man who had moved to Holmes County from Geauga County to help his grandparents with their farm. Carter's grandmother had implored me to find Carter a match, so that he would stay in Holmes County permanently. Usually, I don't make matches without the young man and *maedel*'s consent, but the moment I saw Carter and Iris together, I knew they were meant to be. After Carter, there was no other man worthy in her eyes, and there shouldn't be. Carter was her perfect match.

I bit the inside of my lip when I saw Iris. I knew that Carter worked at the same construction company as Zeke. We never spoke of it, but it was even possible the two men were friends. What would Iris think of Edith and even of me when Edith ended her engagement to Zeke Miller?

Leah waved at me from the table. She was my age, and it startled me at times how much she looked like her mother, who'd passed on years ago. Just like her mother, she had steel-gray hair pulled back into an Amish bun and bright pink cheeks that seemed to be in perpetual blush. In my mind, when I think of her, I still see my old schoolmate, who used to sit with me at recess and make patchwork dolls to sell in her father's general store. The store was no more, and Leah, a mother of five and grandmother of eleven, lived in town over her husband's Amish gift shop, where they sold Amish-made trinkets and toys to *Englischers* visiting Harvest. As Harvest became a more and more popular destination in Holmes County, their store rose in popularity too. Leah was always happy to get away from the hustle and bustle of a busy day at the shop.

I smiled and waved back. Other than my quilting circle, there was only one young man in the café, tapping away on his keyboard.

Leah waved again. This time a little more enthusiastically. "Millie, what a blessing that you are here."

I made my way across the wooden floor, which was so old that it dated back to my father's childhood. The table was a large circular affair that could fit as many as eight people around it or in our case, five busy quilters. In a quilting circle, you don't want to be too close to the next person. If you were, you were bound to accidentally elbow your neighbor in the ribs, or even in the teeth if the stitching really got going. Every member of Double Stitch took the craft very seriously. It wasn't long before elbows would start flying. The table was covered with coffee mugs, cookies, quilting squares, and threads of every color of the rainbow.

"I'm happy to be here."

"And I'm glad that you are here because I want to talk to you about my granddaughter Pippa."

I nodded, understanding at once. Pippa Bontrager was Leah's eighteen-year-old granddaughter. She was to be baptized into the Amish church in a few months, and she'd come to me two weeks back asking me for advice and requesting help to find her a match. As of yet, I hadn't found the right Amish young man. I knew that sweet Pippa was anxious about it, but it was Leah who was the most frustrated.

"You said that you'd find her a husband."

"Oh!" Raellen said, leaning in. She was a tiny, dark-haired woman with a slim figure despite the nine children she'd had over an eleven-year span. I thought that she had been able to keep her figure by chasing after her brood. Raellen's was the next farm over from mine, and she was my closest neighbor. It wasn't uncommon to see her running after one of the children on their family farm or after one of the many sheep in her husband's herd of fifty strong. The family cleaned, hand spun, dyed, and sold the wool in local shops throughout Holmes County and the neighboring area. "Are you looking for a match for Pippa, Millie?"

Leah scowled at the group's notorious gossip. "Mind your own stitches, Raellen Raber."

I sat at the table and ignored Raellen's question. "I never said that I would find her a husband. I don't promise anyone that I'll find him or her a spouse. That's not a promise that I can keep. I simply told her that I would look for a young man who I believe is compatible with her, her best match and her best chance for a long and happy marriage."

"Well, you had better find someone quickly. She's been moping around our gift shop for days, staring out the window."

I was about to offer some sage advice about not putting so much pressure on Pippa to marry. She was only eighteen. I knew that wasn't a popular Amish position. Many Amish, like Pippa, want to marry young so that they can make their homes and start their families, but it's never a *gut* idea to marry before a person is ready. There was a reason that I hadn't found the right match for Pippa yet. It might have to do with Pippa. I didn't say any of that to Leah. I didn't want to come across as rude. "The right match for her will arrive when she is ready."

Leah looked as if she wanted to protest, when someone slapped a hand down on one of the tables. "Millie Fisher, as I live and breathe, is that you?"

I spun around and faced the counter, which was lined with bar stools made out of old barrels. I blinked. "Lois?" I jumped out of my seat.

The woman behind the counter had a round face, spiky red hair that was just on the edge of purple, and two pairs of glasses: one pair was on her head and the other was hanging from her neck on a beaded chain. She wore three gold rings with large glittery gems on each hand, but no wedding band.

I hurried over to her and gave her a mighty hug. "I can't believe it. Lois Kenny?" I asked. "What? How?" I couldn't even finish the sentence.

She hugged back, saying, "Believe it. Oh, Millie, it's so good to see you!" She laughed and stepped away, still holding on to my arms. "And you called me Lois Kenny. I haven't heard anyone call me by my maiden name in decades. I'm Lois Henry now. It was the last name of my third husband, God bless his soul. He passed away five years ago. I didn't keep the last name of my fourth husband since that marriage didn't last more than six months. I knew I should never have married a man I met at the poker table at the Rocksino."

I blinked at her. "Rocksino?"

She laughed again. "Don't you worry about it. It's not a place you will ever see, and I have no plans to go back. There are too many old goats wandering around the game floor looking for a woman to take care of them in their old age. I have no interest in that. Four marriages are enough for me. I'm done."

Behind me Leah cleared her throat.

I spun around. "Oh, I'm so sorry. I just got so

caught up in the surprise of seeing Lois again. Let me make introductions. Lois, this is Raellen, Leah, and Iris. We are members of Double Stitch Quilting Circle."

"I know Raellen, of course. She's a good friend of my granddaughter Darcy Woodin, who owns this place. Darcy is in the back, whipping up some delicious treats for all of you. We were just tickled when Raellen said that she wanted to have a quilting circle meeting here."

Raellen beamed. "It's the most central location for all of us, and I always want to help an old friend."

"Don't we all," Lois said.

Raellen beamed. "I never knew you were friends with Darcy's grandmother, Millie."

I smiled at Lois. "I am indeed. We've known each other for a very long time."

"That's true," Lois said. "I know all Millie's secrets."

Iris's mouth made a little *O*. "You have secrets, Millie?"

I rolled my eyes at Lois. "She's teasing."

"Am I? What about that time Mr. Lewis's cow escaped—"

I stepped on her foot lightly, and she barked a laugh. "It's just like old times already! My, this is such a treat!"

I couldn't help but smile. Seeing Lois again was such a gift.

"I know Raellen, of course," Lois said with a smile. "I'm happy to meet all of you and so thankful that you chose our little café for your get-together."

Leah cocked her head. "How do you and Lois know each other, Millie?"

I could read the expression on Leah's face. I supposed that I should have expected it. Lois and I made an odd couple of friends. I was Amish in plain dress and no makeup. She was *Englisch* with wild short hair, jewelry, and makeup to spare. Right now she was sporting teal eyeshadow over her blue eyes. "Lois and I grew up together on the same road. Our families had neighboring farms, and even though my family was Amish and hers was *Englisch*, the two families were very close. We were the same age, born just a few weeks apart, and spent all the time we could together."

"Getting into trouble," Lois added.

I snorted. "You spent time getting into trouble. I spent time getting you out."

Lois slapped her dish towel on her hip. "It's so good to see you, Millie," she said. "What has it been, twenty years?"

"I think so. The last time was when you came from the city for Kip's funeral."

She nodded. "God rest his soul. He was a good man, and the perfect match for you." She grinned. "But being a matchmaker, you would know all about that. Did you ever marry again?"

I shook my head. "*Nee.*"

"Ah, you were wiser than me then. You found a good one and called it quits. I had to find a real bad one before I gave up on love."

"Don't give up on love," Raellen said with shining eyes.

Lois laughed. "From the mouths of babes." She waved me into a seat at the quilting circle table. "Sit with your friends. We will catch up later. I need to help Darcy in the kitchen. We will be out in a moment with your food. Let me get you a cup of coffee. You still like your coffee black?"

I thanked her and settled into one of the two empty chairs at the table. I knew the other chair was there for the last member of our group.

Raellen clapped her thin hands. "What a small world!"

"Even smaller in Holmes County," Leah said.

"When everyone arrives, I have some interesting news to share." Raellen glanced at me.

I frowned. Gossip, I would guess; it was Raellen's favorite pastime.

"Where's Ruth?" Iris asked.

I was just about to ask the same question when Ruth Yoder, a square-shaped woman with steel-gray hair and a take-charge demeanor, walked through the door with her quilting basket on her arm. Ruth saw herself as the leader of our little band of quilters because she was the bishop's wife. No one bothered to tell her the circle

34

didn't need a leader. It wasn't worth the lecture. Typically, we all worked on our own projects when it came to piecing the tops. The only time we worked as a group was when we were ready to do the hand quilting. At that point, we used the large front room in my small house and stretched the quilt from wall to wall on a quilt frame.

"Millie Fisher," Ruth snipped. "You have got to do something about those goats! They are a nuisance, through and through. I was just at your niece's greenhouse, and they chased me right off the property. What on earth are they doing there?"

"Phillip and Peter are helping Edith clear some land. I'm sure they just saw your friendly face and wanted to play. A little play would not hurt you, Ruth."

She harrumphed and stomped over to her chair at our table. "Why on earth are we meeting at an *Englisch* café? That's what I would like to know. There are plenty of Amish places in the village where we could meet."

Raellen opened her mouth as if she was about to answer.

"Hello, Ruth!" Lois, with her purple hair unnaturally glistening under the electric lights, greeted the last member of our group with a big smile on her face as she brought a tray laden with generous slices of blueberry pie.

"Lois Kenny! We are coming to the end of days!" Ruth cried.

CHAPTER THREE

I was distracted from Ruth's startling remark by the tray of pie and the sweet scent of blueberry. It took all my strength not to grab the biggest slice before anyone else had a chance. "You made blueberry. That's my favorite."

"Oh good," Lois said, looking pleased. "I remembered right. I saw that blueberry pie back there and told Darcy we just had to give it to you on the house."

"I can pay for it," I protested.

"No, no, consider it a gift from an old friend."

All the time that Lois and I had been talking, Ruth Yoder stared at Lois openmouthed. She then opened and closed her mouth, but no words came out.

"Oh, Ruth, you are going to want to close your mouth or a fly might get in there," Lois said with mock sweetness. "Not that there are any flies in my granddaughter's café, mind you."

"What are you doing here, Lois? I thought you moved away to Cleveland years ago," Ruth said.

"I did, and now I'm back. I'll leave you ladies to it." My childhood *Englisch* friend winked at me before she walked away.

I, for one, was glad that Lois was back. I glanced

36

at Ruth; my guess was the bishop's wife was less thrilled.

"Well, this has been an exciting meeting so far," Leah said. "What other surprises are in store?"

Immediately, my thoughts turned to Edith.

As the ladies set in to their quilting, I took the liberty of taking a piece of blueberry pie, already planning to have a second if there was any left. I crossed my fingers that there would be.

I asked the other ladies if they would like a slice. All of them passed except for Raellen. "I want one the same size as yours," she said.

I did as she asked and handed her a plate with the large slice of pie, a napkin, and a fork. She tucked her quilting beside her on her seat before she took the items from my hands.

I was just about to put a forkful of blueberry pie in my mouth when Ruth said, "You really must do something about them, Millie. I thought they were temporary."

I blinked and lowered my fork, unsure what she was talking about. As part of my mind was always on Edith that day, I wondered if she was referring to my niece's predicament. But I knew better than to mention Edith first. "Who?"

She let out a sigh of exasperation. "The goats!"

"Oh," I said and then took my bite unconcernedly. Ruth had been demanding that I get rid of the goats from the moment they'd arrived on my little farm.

"I have half a mind to talk to my husband about your goats. They are a nuisance to the community."

I laughed. "There is nothing in the *Ordnung* that preaches against goats, and the only person who finds them a great nuisance is you."

"Millie Fisher! This is not just my opinion. Those goats of yours just about bit through the sleeve of my coat."

"My husband doesn't like it when the goats get the sheep worked up either," Raellen said.

"I just gave you a piece of pie," I reminded her.

She laughed. "That's right. I take it back."

Ruth grunted in annoyance at our banter. She had very little time in her life for banter. "The bishop will not be pleased that you aren't taking my concerns seriously."

"I hear you, Ruth, and you are right," I acquiesced. "The goats are rambunctious. I'm sorry if they frightened you."

I wasn't very concerned that she would speak to her husband, the bishop, about my goats or, if she did, that Bishop Yoder would take her seriously. He was nearly twenty years her senior and had seen every trial that the district could possibly face in his time. A couple of exuberant goats weren't much of a concern. I wasn't worried about him enforcing his wife's demands.

Besides, Ruth's bark was far worse that her bite. I had known her since we were school girls in pigtails, and she always thought she should be the boss of everything. That didn't come from being married to the bishop, although her marriage to Bishop Yoder did put a feather in her cap.

Even so, Ruth and her husband were a good match. He needed her with his quiet ways, and she needed him with her loud ways. In some marriages balance is the key; in others it is commonality that keeps the bonds strong. Every marriage is different. It was my gift to notice what was needed most to make the match successful.

"I'll remind Edith to keep them corralled while they are at the greenhouse," I said. "We can't have them chasing customers away."

She sniffed. "What customers? I was the only person there."

I felt a pang in my chest. "You must be exaggerating. The greenhouse is very popular on a Saturday in May. It's where everyone in the county goes for their plants."

"It *was* very popular, and it *was* where people went for their plants. It's not that anymore on either count."

"What do you mean?" I asked.

"The greenhouse isn't doing well. Anyone can see that. Haven't you noticed that they don't have a booth at the farmers' market any longer?"

My mouth fell open. "*Nee*, I don't usually come down for the market. If they lost their booth, Edith would have told me."

"Well, they don't have it, and it's clear that she didn't tell you that."

Ruth shook her head. "When are you getting rid of the goats?" she asked, returning to the issue she was most concerned with. "You never said that you were going to keep them after you cleared the land."

I cocked my head at her. Even with my mind reeling over what she'd said about the greenhouse, I had to defend my boys. For that was how I thought of Phillip and Peter. I knew that it went against my upbringing to regard animals as pets rather than livestock, but my boys were *gut* company for me despite their tendency to get into trouble. "Why shouldn't I keep them? I'm quite fond of those goats, even if they are ornery rascals. They keep me on my toes. It is something I need at my age, living here all alone."

Ruth folded her arms. "That's the first problem. You shouldn't be living way out there alone. Any one of your nieces or nephews would have taken you in when you moved back to Ohio. Why would you choose to live by yourself? It's not natural for a woman to live alone. It's not what the Good Lord intended. Women were created to be companions to men."

I narrowed my eyes.

"Now, Ruth," Raellen said. "Don't you forget that the Apostle Paul said being single and serving the Lord was a righteous life."

"Lots of women live alone," I said. "Some by their choice and some because that is the life they are living. There is nothing wrong with it." This was an argument that I'd had with Ruth many times. I let her say her piece because I had known Ruth all my life. It was better to let her get her opinions out and be done with them.

"*Englisch* women. Not Amish women."

"Oh, Ruth," Iris said. "Don't you be so hard on Millie, and this close to Edith's wedding too." She opened her quilting basket and pulled out a stack of fat quarters and a pair of fabric scissors. "Is Edith ready for the wedding?"

"She's ready for her future," I said vaguely. I didn't want to tell the women that Edith planned to break her engagement with Zeke that very day. She could even be doing it this very moment, while we were speaking.

Just then, another member of our district, Joelle Beachy, came through the door, her face as pale as paper. "I saw all of you in here, and I simply had to share the news."

Ruth jerked back. "What news, Joelle? Spit it out."

Joelle started at Ruth's tone. In her forties, Joelle Beachy was a mother of two and, like me, widowed years ago. She had graceful hands with long tapered fingers. With those graceful hands, she was a far more talented quilter than anyone in our group. Her quilts, many of her own original

41

design, usually placed at the Holmes County fair, where the quilting competition was the toughest in the country, counting both the Amish and *Englisch* communities. In fact, she'd won the grand prize twice. In addition to being a quilter, she could embroider and knit as well. Being able to do one did not mean that you could do them all. I had never been able to embroider.

I didn't have the patience for the painstaking work, especially not for cross-stitch, which was the most difficult of them all, in my opinion. Life was too short to spend that much time in a chair sewing. I knew if I'd said that aloud, Ruth would say it was my overexposure to *Englisch* life in Michigan that made me think such things. According to Ruth, anything wrong in this world was *Englisch* related.

"Joelle, you look like you might faint dead away," Raellen said. "Whatever has gotten into you?" Raellen started to get up from her seat.

"You have a seat, Joelle," I said and pushed an untouched glass of water her way. "Then you can tell us what happened."

She shook her head. "I can't stay!"

"What news, Joelle?" Ruth's patience was paper thin.

"Edith isn't marrying Zeke Miller. The wedding is off!"

Behind us there was a crash and a young *Englisch* woman with the curliest blond hair I had ever seen dropped an entire tray of pie. Broken plates, pie crust, and bright raspberry filling covered the floor. The filling looked like blood smeared on the wide-plank floor.

"Darcy, what happened?" Lois asked, running in from the kitchen.

"I—I—" She fled into the back.

Lois watched her go, but instead of following her, started to clean up the mess. Iris and Leah jumped out of their seats and helped her. I wanted to get up too and help, but it seemed that I was frozen in place by Joelle's announcement.

Raellen's hand flew to her mouth. "Poor Edith. Did he break it off? I always thought Zeke Miller was a fickle man."

"No," Joelle said. "She was the one who ended it."

CHAPTER FOUR

What?" Ruth asked. "How do you know that?" Ruth sounded offended. She always wanted to be the very first to know anything that was happening in the district. She wasn't happy that big news like this was coming to her secondhand.

Joelle wrung her hands. "I saw Zeke's mother at the market, and I asked her if she was looking forward to the wedding. She said that there wasn't going to be a wedding. I asked what happened, and Zeke's mother said it was Edith's fault. She said her son returned from work this afternoon and wasn't home ten minutes before Edith told him that she wasn't going to marry him."

"Did Edith give a reason why?" Raellen asked, leaning in.

Joelle shook her head. "Not one that Carolina Miller knows. Carolina wasn't too happy about it." She winced. "She believes Zeke was set aside for another man. She said some very unkind things about Edith."

"Like what?" Ruth asked.

I pressed my lips together. "I would rather not hear them. I don't want to dislike Carolina, and I know whatever she said was spoken out of pain and hurt."

"Of course, it was," Ruth said. "If Edith just carelessly cast aside Carolina's son for another man, of course she felt hurt."

I felt my face grow hot. "Joelle said that Carolina didn't know the reason, and there was no mention of another man. I know for certain that's not what happened. There is no other man in my niece's life." I couldn't keep the sharpness out of my voice. The last thing I would want for Edith at a time like this were rumors like that flying around the district. The possibility that she had been unfaithful to Zeke would certainly ruin her reputation and possibly her business.

"But Carolina said another man would be the only reason Edith could have to leave her son. Everyone knows that the woman needs a father for her children. It would be easier for her if she had a man's help." Joelle shook her head as if this predicament was unbearably sad. I couldn't help but wonder if she wasn't thinking of her own situation and raising her two children alone.

"I am telling you Carolina is wrong, and she should not say such things," I said. "Even though her son is grown, she is going to defend him. I know Edith better than any of you, much better than Carolina, and she wouldn't do anything so deceitful as to take up with another man. She just wouldn't."

Ruth narrowed her eyes at me. "You don't look too surprised about this news. You don't look shocked, worried, or upset. You knew!" She pointed her finger at me. "How could you know this and not say anything to us about it? We asked you about Edith's upcoming wedding."

I arched my brow at her. "And I said nothing about the wedding. I only said she was ready for her future. I did not lie."

"A lie of omission," Ruth muttered under her breath.

I pretended that I didn't hear her say that.

"What will Edith do now if she doesn't marry?" Iris asked, wiping raspberry filling from her hands with a paper napkin. While Ruth and I had been arguing, the other women had cleaned up the mess. "She has three children. They need a father."

Joelle shifted from foot to foot and her face turned red.

Realizing that she might have offended Joelle, Iris began to blush too. "I know that you have children with no father too, Joelle, but your situation is different. Your father and brother are living with you. The children have the influence of a man in the house. Edith's father has passed on, and Enoch . . ." She trailed off and glanced at me. No one liked to talk about Enoch in my presence.

I shifted in my seat. "There are many men in Edith's family too, even though they might not live in her home."

Iris pressed her lips as if to hold back words,

and wrung her hands. She sat back in her seat. I glanced over my shoulder. The mess was gone and so was Lois.

I shook my head. "Just like Joelle, it's better if Edith raises the children alone with the support of her community than with the wrong person. She has the greenhouse to support her financially, and she has done an amazing job managing it these last three years since her first husband died."

"I just told you the greenhouse is not doing well. I think your niece has pulled the wool over your eyes, Millie Fisher."

"Not the wool from my farm," Raellen joked, but no one at the table laughed.

"Besides, the death of her first husband was no great loss to the community," Ruth said.

"Ruth!" Raellen and Iris cried in unison.

"How can you say such a thing, Ruth?" Iris asked.

"It's true. Moses Hochstetler was involved with some very dark dealings. I will let you know that my husband prayed for him and his soul but gave a sigh of relief that we wouldn't have to deal with the likes of him in our district any longer. He would have likely caused a rift in the entire community. That's the very last thing we want. We need our community to grow together and stay committed to each other. It's church members like Moses Hochstetler that make that difficult."

I bit my tongue. No one knew how Moses came

to his end. They only said that it was an accident. However there were rumors that the *Englischer* he had been working for was a criminal who killed Moses because Moses tried to cheat him. I wouldn't have put that past Moses. He was the sort of man to cheat. Even so, every loss of life is terrible. I had prayed every night that Moses would turn his life around. I had prayed for Edith too. I still prayed for my sweet girl. It broke my heart that she was connected with something so sordid and had to live with the pain of her first husband's mistakes. One day she would have to explain those mistakes to her children. She would also have to tell them how their father died or how the police thought he died.

Now, I prayed for Zeke. I was relieved that Edith wouldn't marry him, but I knew he would need comfort in this season of disappointment.

Joelle looked around the table. "I have to go, but I was glad I saw you so that I could tell you the news. Please keep Carolina and Zeke in your prayers."

"And Edith too," I said quietly.

She blinked. "*Ya*, Edith too. I must be off." She hurried out the door.

"She's off, so she can tell more people what she heard," Leah said with a frown. "She is almost as big a talker as you are, Raellen. Everyone in the district will know by tomorrow's Sunday morning services."

"That's not fair," Raellen said.

"But true," Leah argued.

"How come you didn't tell us about Edith and Zeke first?" Ruth asked me.

"It's not my place and it's not my news." I raised my eyebrows at her, hopeful my words would work as a reminder to her that we as Amish are committed to keeping the confidences of another person in the faith.

"What will Edith do now if she doesn't marry?" Iris asked.

"She will go on as she has been for these last three years. It's better that she raises the children alone with the support of her community than with the wrong person," I repeated.

Iris arched her brow as if she wasn't so sure of that.

"Were they a good match?" Leah asked. "Edith and Zeke?"

I pressed my lips together and would say no more about it. It wasn't my place to tell others about a couple's future. It's not that I can see the future; I just know when a marriage will be solid and when it will be rocky going.

"*Gott* has a way of sorting these things out," I said and glanced at Raellen, who had been very quiet much of the time. I couldn't help but feel suspicious. "Was this the news that you had wanted to tell me when you first arrived, Raellen?"

49

She jumped in her seat, knocking into the table next to her. She caught her plate before it fell to the wooden floor. "*Nee.*"

"You have news too, Raellen?" Ruth asked.

As she said this, I immediately regretted bringing up the fact that Raellen had something to tell me. I had a deep-seated feeling that whatever news Raellen wanted to share, it would not be welcome to me. Out of the corner of my eye, I saw Lois come back out of the kitchen, but the blond girl, who I could only assume was Darcy, didn't reappear. Lois's mouth was pressed into a tight line.

Raellen licked her lips. "It's not about Zeke Miller."

I frowned. "Edith?" I asked.

She let out a breath. "In a way." She glanced at me. "Millie, your nephew Enoch Lapp is back in the village, and I heard tell that he's here to stay."

There was an audible gasp in the room, and I felt my heartbeat race.

CHAPTER FIVE

The next morning was Sunday of a church week. Many *Englischers* don't know this, but most Amish districts only have church every other week. On the off weeks, it is supposed to be family time to study the scripture. We don't have brick-and-mortar churches either. Instead, the church meets in the home of a district member. All the owners' possessions and furniture are moved aside so that benches can be brought into the home for the congregation. It was quite a production, and, in my district, the moving of the furniture took place the Saturday evening before church, so Sunday morning could be saved for worshiping. Because my home was so small, I would never be able to fit the entire district inside. The only Sundays that the church could meet on my property would be when it was warm enough to set up the benches outside.

It might have been warm enough that very Sunday because it was a beautiful bright spring day, but the service was scheduled at the home of Ruth and the bishop. Whenever the service was at the bishop's home, Ruth pulled out all the stops for the Sunday meal for the congregation that follows every one of our services, so she can be—or see herself as—the best homemaker in the district. Don't get me wrong, Ruth is a great wife, mother, and homemaker. It would serve her better if she didn't spend so much time trying to prove that to everyone else, over and over again. It must be exhausting to show off so much.

Oh, but there I go, taking notice, and perhaps passing judgment in some way. I didn't resent Ruth for her efforts or even Joelle or Raellen for their propensity for gossip. We each had our quirks—the Amish were no different than the *Englisch* in this way. We were all people, with an assortment of personalities and quirky ways. Come to think of it, my matchmaking was surely a topic of talk in the district. Not all the plain people approved of it.

It felt strange to be leaving for church that morning with no goats to see me off. I missed those two rascals more than I cared to admit. Perhaps later that day, I would stop by the greenhouse and check their progress on clearing the land. They certainly were part of my reason to visit the greenhouse, but I couldn't get the conversation I had had with Iris and the members of Double Stitch out of my mind. How could the greenhouse be in trouble? Edith had never had difficulty managing it in the past. And then there was the point that my nephew Enoch was back. When I had heard the news, my heart flipped. I had been waiting a very long time to make things right with him, and it seemed to me that I would finally get that chance.

As I walked to my buggy and Bessie, I had a Bundt cake in my hand, my contribution to the Sunday meal. I had promised Ruth that I would bring the cake. She'd said that she was short on desserts, which I found surprising. Any Amish woman worth her salt was able to bake at least a simple cake. I didn't claim to be as good a baker as Ruth, or as good a baker as I was a quilter or a matchmaker, but my Bundt cake always seemed to please. I had already put a plate of cookies in the buggy too, for good measure.

I'd tossed and turned all night, worrying about Enoch's return. I couldn't understand why Edith hadn't told me when she was here yesterday morning, and I wondered if her twin brother's return to the village was the real reason she wanted to break her engagement. Was Enoch coming back to take his place in the greenhouse? It was hard to say. My nephew ran away from the Amish faith when he was a young man. It wasn't long after his sister became engaged to Moses Hochstetler that he left.

He not only rejected the Amish way, he rejected *Gott*. As the woman who took on the role of his mother in his life, I felt that I had failed him. Of course, I wanted him to be Amish, but beyond that I wanted him to be faithful to his beliefs in the way he saw fit. Rejecting all belief was the worst possible result, but after what had happened, his reaction didn't surprise me.

I feared that it was too much to hope that Enoch planned to come back to the Amish way, but even if he just came back to the county as an *Englischer*, I would be happy. I needed to see him, and when I saw him, I needed to ask his forgiveness.

I set the cake on the buggy seat, unhitched Bessie from the tree where I had tethered her and the buggy that morning, and set off. If I had traveled to the Yoders' farm by car, I would have been there in fifteen minutes, but by buggy it took me almost an hour to arrive, and the whole time I worried about Enoch's return to Harvest. I made up my mind that I would ask Edith about her brother just as soon as I saw her.

As I turned into the Yoders' long driveway, I scanned the buggies for my niece's vehicle or for the wagon that she would sometimes drive to church on nice days, but I didn't see either.

The Yoders' yard was filled with buggies and plain-dressed children playing tag in the side yard while a handful of mothers looked on. I expected to find Edith and her children in that group. Normally they would be there, but they were missing this Sunday. Her boys were balls of energy and Edith liked them to run as much of it out as possible before services began so they didn't fidget during the sermon.

Edith's home and greenhouse were just half a mile away from the Yoders' farm, so she should have beaten me to the services even if the family decided to walk. I had a bad feeling about her absence. I noted too that I didn't see Zeke Miller standing with the other young men chatting to the right of the wide front porch as he would usually have been doing.

Ruth and Bishop Yoder stood next to the front door of their very large farmhouse. It was a light blue, wood-framed home that was oddly shaped because as the family grew, more and more rooms were added onto it in every direction, and when her husband was chosen to be bishop, Ruth felt it was a necessity that she add a large sitting room on the very front of the house along with a giant front porch to accommodate the entire congregation. If Ruth had her way, church would be at her home every time the congregation met, but that was not the Amish way. The community grew closer by visiting each other's homes, which was one reason that Sunday services moved around the district.

Ruth waved to me from the porch. I waved back, but I was still scanning the grounds for any sign of Edith, her children, or Zeke. I didn't find it comforting in the least that they were all missing the service. Perhaps if one or the other was gone, I wouldn't have found it so alarming. I walked around the giant house, thinking that

Edith might be in the back where Ruth kept her kitchen garden. There wasn't a garden on the planet that Edith could resist inspecting. If she was there, the children would likely be with her. I told myself that it wasn't odd in the least that Zeke Miller wasn't at church that day. In fact, I would have been surprised if he had been there with all the talk that must be floating around the village over his and Edith's broken engagement.

I came around the side of the church and found several young women with babies in their laps sitting under the big walnut tree near the kitchen garden, but no one else.

Despite the ominous worries churning inside me, I told myself it was nothing to be concerned about. Just as it made sense that Zeke wouldn't want to be at services, it was also likely that Edith wouldn't want to be there. She was a sensitive girl. Maybe she didn't feel she could face the gossip. I hadn't been in Holmes County when her first husband, Moses, died, but I completely understood why she wouldn't want to face that level of chatter about her personal life again.

Even so . . .

I decided that I would never be able to sit through the service without checking on her. I scurried back around the side of the blue house and made a beeline for my horse and buggy. All the while, I felt like a bad student who was making a dash away from a one-room schoolhouse before the teacher spotted me.

"Millie Fisher, where on earth are you going?" Ruth called.

The teacher had caught me!

I waved my hand. "I'll be back as quick as I can," I called over my shoulder. "I just need to tend to something quite urgent."

I was climbing into my buggy when a hand appeared at my elbow and helped me up into the seat. I picked up the reins and looked down at the kind face of Tucker Leham, a broad shouldered, beardless Amish man with dozens of freckles on his face.

"I need to talk to you." Tucker adjusted his round glasses on his nose.

"What about?"

The young man bit his lip, and I knew immediately that it had something to do with my niece. Tucker worked at the greenhouse. "Have you seen Edith this morning?"

He shook his head. "I—I—" He pulled on the collar of his shirt as if it was choking him.

"Is something wrong with Edith?" My voice was sharper than I intended it to be, but worry had begun to claw at my heart.

"*Nee*," Tucker said. "I—I heard that she and Zeke are not to wed. Is that true?"

I looked down my nose at him and felt that I was acting like Ruth Yoder. If this young man knew something about my Edith, I wanted to hear about it and quick. "Why do you want to know?"

His face turned the color of a cherry tomato on a hot summer's day, so red in fact that his freckles all but disappeared. A light dawned in the back of my mind. Tucker was sweet on Edith. It was no surprise to me, really. He was over thirty and still unmarried. He worked at Edith's greenhouse as a gardener and had since he was a young teenager. He was almost as skilled with plants as Edith. I'm sure over time he had developed a growing affection for her sweet ways and manners. What a struggle it must have been for him when she again fell for the wrong man just as she had for Moses all those years ago. He had seen her fall and be hurt by Moses Hochstetler too. All this time, he'd waited to the side and loved her from afar.

Why hadn't I seen Tucker's feelings for Edith before? I thought that it only could have been because I had been away in Michigan for all those years. I hadn't had the opportunity to witness his growing feelings.

"*Nee*, Tucker. She is not marrying Zeke Miller," I said in a low voice.

"I . . . I didn't expect that. This is surprising news." He shook his head. "I will not trouble her then."

I cocked my head. "Trouble her with what?"

He shook his head and stepped back from my buggy. He turned and walked toward the group of young men chatting beside the large oak tree in front of the Yoder home. If I called out to him, asking what he was talking about, it would cause a scene.

I flicked the buggy reins, and Bessie backed up and started for the long drive. Church members headed to services in the opposite direction, gave me strange looks. I didn't stop to explain. I needed to reach Edith and reassure myself that she was all right.

On the road, we Amish have to obey the traffic laws just as the *Englischers* do in their automobiles. It's not unheard of for an Amish person to be pulled over for speeding or reckless driving of a buggy. Even drunk driving a buggy is a problem in the county, although usually only with young men on *rumspringa.*

I drove as recklessly and quickly as I dared to Edy's Greenhouse. I knew in my heart that something was amiss. Bessie sensed my urgency and stepped double time. I wished that I had an *Englisch* driver with me, because I would get there so much more quickly in a car. It was at times like this when I could see why the *Englisch* adopted so much technology. It certainly made their lives much easier in emergencies. I shook my head. I was jumping to conclusions, imagining there was some sort of emergency at the greenhouse. Everything might be fine. Everything would be fine.

Ruth would admonish me if she could hear

my thoughts. She would tell me that life wasn't meant to be easy. We were on this earth to toil and do good works, and then find salvation. I couldn't agree with her on that. I thought that *Gott* also wants us to have joy and delight in the lives we are given. Ruth would have argued with that.

Bessie shook her bridle. She felt my anxiety. Bessie was an old team horse whose longtime partner had died. Afterward, she refused to work with any other animal at my brother's quarry. I could understand that. I felt the same way when I lost my Kip.

"We need to hurry, Bessie," I said aloud. "I think something is very wrong at the greenhouse."

As if she could understand me, she increased her pace without my even touching the reins. I knew I should have had more faith that *Gott* would make all things right, but there in my buggy, I couldn't find it. The old proverb said, "Worry ends where faith begins." As much as I knew that to be true, I could not keep the worry at bay.

Chapter Six

A s I pulled into the long driveway that led up to the greenhouse, I marveled at the lovely piece of land that Edith had cultivated in so many ways. Her actual house was small, only bigger than mine because there was a second floor with three tiny bedrooms. The footprint of the house was the same as my own. However, beyond the house was where her real pride and joy lay: Edy's Greenhouse. It was a long building with Plexiglas sides to let the light and warmth of the sun inside. It was as large as a horse barn, and its reputation was far greater now with Edith at the helm than it ever had been under her father's care.

Of a younger generation, Edith could see the greenhouse's potential and knew *Englischers* found charm in buying things that were labeled "Amish," so she'd tailored the business to accommodate both Amish and *Englisch*. In truth, she was a clever businesswoman and advertised her business in *Englisch* newspapers and even on the radio. I have been interested during my lifetime to see how our lifestyle has seemed to grow more fascinating to the *Englisch* as they advance farther and farther away from the plain lives we Amish lead. Perhaps it is the simplicity of our ways that keeps the *Englischers* captivated.

At the road there was a hand-painted sign that pointed down the long gravel driveway. It read, EDY'S GREENHOUSE, CLOSED SUNDAYS.

At least it was a Sunday, and I knew there wouldn't be any customers about the property. There might be no one about at all. All the workers, who were Amish, were most likely at our district service or at services of their own if they were members of a different community.

There were many kinds of Amish in Holmes County. It most definitely wasn't "one size fits all," an *Englisch* phrase that I learned during my time in Michigan.

Edith's front yard wasn't empty though. Her three young children were there sitting in the grass tossing a ball to each other. Well, the older boys were tossing the ball. Little Ginny was plucking blades of grass from the lawn and making a bouquet out of them in her tiny hand, as if they were the most precious flowers she had ever seen. All three children were clean, with combed hair and wearing their Sunday best. That at least told me Edith had every intention of going to church this morning. What could have kept her from leaving for the Yoders' farm? I gripped the reins so tightly, my knuckles turned bright white.

There was no sign of the goats.

The children jumped to their feet just as soon as they heard me come up the driveway. They waited patiently until I parked the buggy and climbed out of it before they rushed me for a four-way hug. I squeezed them tightly, more relieved than I cared to admit to find them well and happy.

"Where's your *maam*?" I asked, pulling upright to look at the oldest child, Jacob.

"She told us to stay here." Jacob was ten years old, and had carried the weight of being the man of the house for the last three years. He was a serious child who always did what he was told, and I worried about him at times. Childhood was fleeting, and I wished that he could enjoy more of it than he had. His father had died when Jacob was only seven. It was his job to protect the property and the family; it was the way of our culture to make the oldest male child responsible, whether he wanted that calling or not. That was a lot of responsibility to be placed on shoulders so slight.

Micah was nine, but not nearly as responsible or mature. Even though he was only a year Jacob's junior, he was still the second born and didn't have the pressure Jacob did.

Micah gave me another hug and was quickly followed by three-year-old Ginny, who was born after her father died. Smiling up at me, the little girl with the long blond braids was the spitting image of her mother at that age. "*Aenti*, our cat had kittens! Tiny kittens. They are in the house in a box, sleeping. *Maam* said to leave them be for a bit. They are so cute. I want to carry them everywhere. They love me."

Jacob looked down at his sister. "You have to let the mother cat have some peace. If you keep picking up the babies, she will tire of them, and they could die."

Ginny's eyes grew to the size of dinner plates and tears gathered in her eyes. "They could die?"

I squeezed her tight. "*Nee, nee,* shhhh." I gave Jacob a look over her head. "The kittens will be fine, but your *maam* is right that they need sleep and rest. I'm sure they will want to play with you soon. Kittens love to play. Speaking of animals that love to play, where are my goats?"

Micah laughed. "*Maam* penned them up after they chased the bishop's wife across the front yard yesterday. I never laughed so hard in my life."

I could very well imagine. "I heard about that. I saw Ruth later that afternoon, and she was none too pleased."

"She can actually run very fast for a bishop's wife. I didn't expect a lady that old to run so fast," Micah said with just a dash of respect.

I put my hands on my hips. "She is the same age as me. You don't think I could run away from a pair of goats if I were chased?"

"That would never happen, *Aenti*, because they are your goats. They would never be silly enough to chase you!"

I nodded. "That's a *gut* point."

Ginny's face cleared as we spoke about the goats, but I could see the hint of worry that remained. Even at such a tender age, Ginny's temperament was so much like her mother's it was startling at times.

"Are you going to stay for Sunday supper?" Micah asked eagerly.

I stepped back. "Do you want me to stay for supper because you want my company or because you want me to make some of my famous biscuits?"

Micah looked serious. "We always want to spend time with you, *Aenti* Millie, but if you wanted to make your famous biscuits too, we would not mind."

Ginny shook her head and sucked on her lower lip.

"I see," I said, trying to keep a straight face, which had never been my strong suit when it came to children.

"*Onkel* Enoch would like them too. He said he misses Amish cooking." He lowered his voice. "*Onkel* Enoch is an *Englischer.*"

My pulse quickened. "Have you seen him?"

"He's been here for a few days."

Days? Why hadn't Edith told me? This might finally be my chance to set things right with my nephew.

"He's not here now," Jacob said. "He left this

morning right after breakfast. He said he had business in the village."

I frowned. "Business on a Sunday in Harvest? Almost every place is closed."

"*Maam* was disappointed because she wanted him to come to church with us," Micah said. "But we have been waiting here for so long, I don't think any of us are going to church now."

I suspected that he was right.

"*Aenti* Millie," Jacob said. "Is everything all right with *Maam*?" He looked as if he might cry. I knew that the stress of being a man at such a tender age weighed on him. I wished that wasn't what was expected of him in our district, but there was no help for it until his mother chose to remarry, if that day ever came. I knew that she wouldn't be marrying Zeke.

"Why do you ask that, my boy?" I asked.

He glanced at his younger brother and sister.

"Micah, why don't you and Ginny check inside my buggy? There might be a plate of cookies under the bench seat." It never hurt to have a spare plate of cookies at the ready for any and all situations, but it came in especially handy when one was trying to distract children.

Micah pumped his fist in the air. "Yay!" He then took off in the direction of the buggy.

Ginny clapped her hands, seemingly recovered from her worries over the kittens, and followed Micah as fast as her much shorter legs could carry her. Jacob watched them go with a tired expression on his face. I wished I could take all the strain and worry off of his thin frame.

"What is wrong with your *maam*?" I asked.

He looked down at the tops of his plain black sneakers. "She was crying last night, and it was different from when she cried before."

"Cried before?" I asked.

"Like the times that she cried over *Daed* dying. Those tears were different from these tears. The tears that she cried last night were . . ." He trailed off.

"What were they?" I asked, my voice barely louder than a whisper.

"They were angry." He looked up at me with bright green eyes that brimmed with tears of his own. Tears that he did not let fall because he was conditioned to be brave. "She was angry, and I didn't know what to do about it."

There was nothing more I could ask him because then the younger children ran back to us with the plate of cookies in their hands and chocolate smeared on their cheeks. It seemed to me that they had not waited before sampling my famous chocolate chip cookies. I couldn't say that I blamed them. I did make the very best chocolate chip cookies that I had ever had. Perhaps that's boastful, which is a shameful trait, but that doesn't make it any less true.

"Where's your *maam* now?" I asked.

"In the greenhouse," Jacob said. "She told us to play in the front yard. She was upset. She said she didn't want us back there until she knew what to do."

"What to do about what?" I asked.

He shrugged. "I don't know."

I frowned. That didn't sound like my Edith at all. She always wanted her children around her. Some in our district believed she clung to the children too much after the death of her husband and felt that she was smothering them. I knew I had been away for many years, but I never saw that behavior in my sweet niece in the months since I had been home.

I had a sinking feeling in the pit of my stomach that something was very wrong with Edith. She must be taking her broken engagement with Zeke much harder than I thought she would. The day before, when she'd told me that she planned to break it off, she sounded so sure and calm about her decision. Her voice let me know that she wasn't looking forward to talking to Zeke, but there was nothing to indicate that she was distraught. However, bravery before an act didn't mean there wouldn't be emotion and repercussions afterward. Perhaps she was just experiencing the emotional letdown and relief from what she had done.

"You children stay here like your *maam* asked you to do, and I will go check on her."

Jacob grabbed my hand. *"Aenti* Millie, tell *Maam* I want to give her a hug. She says our hugs help anytime that she's sad." He stared up at me with such earnestness in his eyes that my heart broke a little. What was Jacob sensing for him to be this concerned? He was a serious child but rarely was so fearful. In fact, I couldn't remember a time I thought he was afraid.

I headed to the greenhouse. Just outside the building, Phillip and Peter bleated from a small pen. I walked over to them. "I heard the two of you were troublemakers and got penned up because of it. I'll take you home just as quick as I can. Let me check on Edith first."

Ruth would chastise me for talking to the goats as if they could understand what I was saying. It was a *gut* thing she wasn't at my house most of the time. Living alone, I'd had some very long conversations with the goats. I knew they listened even if they didn't know what I was telling them.

I patted both of their heads and walked to the greenhouse's main door. It was unlocked, which was what I expected. When I stepped into the greenhouse, the early morning light came through the corrugated plastic over my head. It was spring, and the building was bursting with flowers and color. Everywhere I looked there was another beautiful blossom. I wanted to stop and inhale the sweet fragrance of every last one of them. I loved flowers almost as much as Edith did, but I wasn't nearly as talented in caring for them as she was. She got her green thumb from her father, Ira, and he would be proud to see her keeping the greenhouse going without Enoch's help. Sometimes I wondered if Enoch had no interest in the greenhouse because it was named after his sister and not him or not both of them. Ira only had the two children. It was as if when he'd named the greenhouse after his daughter, he'd declared his favorite between the twins. There was jealousy in a family when it was so clear who the favored child was.

I went through the cooler section of the greenhouse to the hothouse plants. There was no sign of Edith in either place. The last room she could be in would be the small area where desert plants were kept. Edith called this the "cactus room" because of the sheer number of spiny and thorny succulents inside it. These sorts of plants didn't do well outdoors in Ohio's humid summers and died in the winters from the freezing cold, but they were popular houseplants with the *Englischers*, which was why Edith kept them.

Finally, I reached the cactus room. There was a prickly pear cactus on the table with its pot turned on the side. Soil spilled out onto the tabletop. Edith stood beside the fallen cactus and was staring at something on the floor on the other side of the workbench. She didn't hear my footsteps as I entered the room.

"Edith?" I asked in a low voice. She was concentrating so hard on whatever she was looking at, it felt wrong to interrupt her.

She didn't so much as twitch when I spoke. Instead she stared at her feet.

"Edith?" I repeated.

Again, there was no answer. I took another step forward, peeking around the side of the potting table, and stopped in my tracks. I couldn't be seeing what I was seeing. It was a foot attached to a leg that was attached to the body of Zeke Miller, who was lying on his stomach on the concrete floor. His left cheek was pressed on the floor so that I could see his face. Blood pooled on the concrete around his head. Thankfully his eyes were closed. I would remember the scene for the rest of my days.

"Edith?" I asked, my voice sharp now.

She finally looked at me. "Oh, *Aenti* Millie. What have I done?"

CHAPTER SEVEN

I stared at her and blinked my eyes several times. *What had she done?*

This couldn't be possible. There was no way that this nightmare unfolding before me could be true. "Edith?" I whispered. My voice sounded strange and foreign to my own ears. I didn't even recognize it as my own. "Did you . . . ?" I couldn't finish the question. My mouth ran completely dry.

Tears ran down her face. "I told him I wouldn't marry him, and look what he has gone and done to himself. It is my fault!"

I blinked as the fog in front of my eyes began to clear. "You think he killed himself because you broke off the engagement?"

"*Ya,* why else would he be dead? He was a healthy young man." She wrapped her arms around her waist and bent slightly forward, as if holding herself upright was far too much of a burden.

"Step back. You look as if you will be ill." I touched her arm.

"I feel like I will be ill. I feel like my heart has been punctured through. Oh, *Aenti,* how will I ever go on, knowing what I made him do?"

I was relieved when she shuffled backward a few steps and allowed me to take a closer look at the body. Despite my distaste for the scene, I examined Zeke. "My girl, a man cannot bash the back of his own head in like this. It seems that there has been some sort of accident. Maybe he fell and hit his head in just the right spot. It's terrible but not your fault. He didn't kill himself." I looked at the potting table for any sign as to where Zeke's head might have come into contact with the wood. I saw nothing. Nor could the overturned cactus have made the wound on the back of his head. "He must have hit his head on something. It's the only explanation." I searched the room for something else he might have knocked his head on.

While I did that, Edith picked up a large decorative stone that was encrusted with blood and hair. "Like this?"

"Put that down," I shouted at her.

She let it fall to the ground from her hand, and it bounced off the concrete and rolled under the potting table.

"What have I done wrong?" she moaned. "Should I get it?"

I didn't want to tell her that the biggest mistake she'd made was picking up the stone that had killed Zeke. The police would find traces of her on it now. I knew this from the many times I'd been in the hospital with my ailing sister. It seemed to me that the televisions in the waiting rooms in those places were set to crime shows or news. Both I found depressing, and even though I did my best not to watch them and concentrate on my quilting while I waited, it was impossible not to hear them. "*Nee*, leave it there for the police."

"The police? *Aenti*, you think we should call the police and not the bishop?"

"We should call both." I winced at the very thought of what Ruth Yoder would say about this. I hoped that as my friend and a fellow member of Double Stitch, she would take mercy on my niece and not spread the rumors that were sure to fly in all directions, not just in Holmes County, but across the country throughout the Amish community. "There is no other choice. This is beyond what the district can handle. We will call the bishop, of course, but the police must be consulted as well."

She began to shiver. "Oh, *Aenti*, it grows worse and worse."

I removed the shawl from my shoulders and wrapped it around her. "My child, you have seen too much of this. Call the police and the bishop and then go into the house. Take the children with you. The bishop is home as church is at his house today. Someone will answer his shed phone. They will know that it would only ring on the Lord's Day in the case of a dire emergency, which is exactly where we find ourselves this morning. I will stay here with . . ." I trailed off.

"You shouldn't stay here with him," she said.

"That is something I should do since I am responsible."

I placed my hands on either side of her face. "Look at me, child. Do not, do *not* say that when the police arrive. Answer their questions openly and honestly, but do not interject what you *think* might have happened. You may cause yourself and your family much grief if you do."

She stared at me with confusion etched on her lovely face, and then the confusion cleared. "I won't say anything more than what I know for sure."

I patted her cheek. "That's a good girl. Now, hurry and make those calls on the phone in the greenhouse office. When you have done that, I would like you to gather up the children and take them into the house. It is best if they see as little of the police as possible."

Edith's determination wavered. "I don't want them to see any of this."

I glanced down at Zeke. "Neither do I, but we might not be able to shelter them completely from what has happened. *Gott* will show you the way to tell them what has occurred when the time is right. Look to Him for guidance."

Edith left the cactus room to make the call. I was grateful that she had a phone in the greenhouse, a luxury that she was allowed in our district because it was her place of business. The closest phone to my home was the shed phone

75

that I shared with Raellen's family. It was a half mile from my house on their sheep farm.

When Edith was gone, I took a tentative step forward and peered at Zeke's face. He lay on his stomach and his left cheek was pressed into the cold concrete floor. His chin was clean shaven, of course, because he was never married, and he would never marry now. He would never marry Edith or anyone else.

I crouched beside the table and looked at the rock that Edith had dropped to the floor. I could see it just under the potting table. It was about the size of a large man's fist. Edith had a number of decorative stones in various sizes for sale in the greenhouse. Her uncle, my brother, who owned a quarry a few miles away, had a hobby of polishing and etching stones to be sold. He was quite a talented sculptor and the *Englischers* seemed to like to buy them for their gardens. Not all stones had Bible verses on them, but this one did. I could just make out the words etched into the stone: "IF WE CONFESS OUR SINS, HE IS FAITHFUL AND JUST AND WILL FORGIVE US OUR SINS AND PURIFY US FROM ALL UNRIGHTEOUSNESS."

Had Zeke died because of some sin? And who had killed him? Because now that I had seen the stone, I was certain that the man had been murdered.

I pressed my lips together, knowing this was the stone that had killed him. There was blood encrusted in one of the Bible verses. For the briefest moment, I wanted to hide the rock because I knew that Edith had touched it. Because she'd made this mistake, the police might come to the wrong conclusion. They might believe that she was capable of this terrible act, and I knew she wasn't.

It would not be the first time a member of the family had been blamed for a crime that he or she didn't commit. The first time had been my fault and had driven Edith's brother, Enoch, away. I wasn't going to let that happen to his sister.

I squatted next to the table. My knees cracked as I moved. The agility that I'd had in youth was no longer there, and I couldn't be in this position for long without my body protesting loudly. I ignored the protests. I wanted to get a better look at the rock. I lifted my skirt so that it wouldn't touch the floor. I was only inches away from the bottom of Zeke's boots. Had Edith dropped it by his head, I might not have had the strength for a closer look. Being near his boot wasn't nearly as unnerving as that would have been.

I saw the stone, but there was something else there. Something small and metallic. It was likely a gardening tool of some sort; we were in a greenhouse after all. The piece of metal was closer to the other side of the table. That was just fine with me. When I got up, it took a moment for my spine to align again. Perhaps I needed to start stretching in the morning right after my coffee. Not that I had known when I awoke that morning that I would be crouching by a potting table and putting my old muscles and bones to the test.

After moving to the other side of the table, I crouched again. This time I was relieved that my knees didn't crack. The item under the table was a wrench about five inches long. There was black grease on the head of it. There could be many reasons why a tool such as this was on the floor of the cactus room of the greenhouse, but the black grease seemed out of place. I couldn't help but think the presence of the wrench had something to do with the dead man on the other side of the table.

There was a scraping sound behind me in the second room. I jumped to my feet and spun around. "Edith? I told you not to come back. You should be with the children."

There was no response and a chill ran the entire length of my spine. "Who is there?" I cried.

There was no answer, and that's when I knew that it couldn't have been Edith. She would have answered me. She knew the state I was in and wouldn't want me to worry, and worry I did. I wasn't alone in the greenhouse with Zeke Miller's body.

"Hello!" I inched to the door of the cactus room, which opened into the main showroom of the greenhouse where the rows and rows of annuals stood on tables as long as my house from end to end. "You need to show yourself. Who's there?"

There was a crash as a pot fell to the floor. The crash spurred me ahead and quenched my fear. As I reached the middle of the room, the back door of the greenhouse banged closed so hard that I thought it would crack the glass.

I slipped on wet concrete as I ran to the door but was able to regain my footing by grabbing onto a nearby table corner. My stumble took just long enough for the culprit to slip away.

I righted myself and threw the back door open in time to see a dark figure dash across the pasture and disappear over the hill.

Out of nowhere Phillip and Peter raced across the open pasture toward the man. The man yelped and the goats chased him. Clearly, they thought the man was playing some kind of game with them.

"Phillip! Peter!" I cried.

The goats ignored me and kept running after the man. With a shock, I realized he wore Amish clothing.

CHAPTER EIGHT

If I had only been younger or quicker on my feet, I could have caught the man running away from the greenhouse, but it would be of no use for me to go dashing over the pasture and down the hill in search of the intruder. I was more likely to turn an ankle than catch the intruder or whoever he was, possibly even the man who'd killed Zeke.

I heard sirens coming closer to the greenhouse. I put two fingers in my mouth and whistled just the way Kip had taught me all those years ago. Nothing happened. I whistled again, louder this time, and I saw both Phillip and Peter crest the hill. When I whistled that it was time to come home, they knew I meant business.

Behind me in the greenhouse I heard new voices echoing in the large space. I let the back door close as voices sounded in the main flower room.

"She said the body would be in here," the first male voice said.

"I don't know how we're going to find anything in here. All these plants." That statement was followed by a sneeze. "I'm choking on CO_2."

"Little, the plants are giving off oxygen and absorbing CO_2. Don't you remember that from your elementary school science class?" another voice said in reply. "You should be able to breathe easier, not worse."

"Not with my allergies," Little replied and sneezed for good measure.

"You will be fine, Little. Take some anti-histamine and keep it together."

I moved away from the door.

Two young men in sheriff's department uniforms stepped into the main room of the greenhouse. "Millie, are you all right?" Deputy Aiden Brody asked me the moment he saw me there standing by the back door.

He was a tall young man with wavy blond hair and kind, dark eyes. I was relieved to see him. Of all the deputies the sheriff's department could have sent to Edy's Greenhouse, he was the very best. He had the most experience dealing with our Amish ways and certainly had the most compassion for our culture. I thought that had a lot to do with the fact he was dating and in love with Bailey King, a candy maker in the village who came from an Amish family, though she wasn't Amish herself. The moment I'd seen Deputy Aiden and Bailey together, I knew they were a perfect match.

"I am," I said. "I'm so glad you have come."

"Are you sure you're all right?" Deputy Aiden asked.

I could feel him studying my face. "I believe so," I said, but even to my own ears I didn't sound that convincing. "A man just ran away from the greenhouse. He gave me quite a scare."

"A man?" Deputy Aiden's voice turned from concerned to focused. He wanted the details and he wanted them quickly.

"*Ya*," I said, then described what I had seen. "He was wearing Amish clothes."

There was a loud bang on the back door of the greenhouse as if something had rammed against it. Both Deputy Aiden and Deputy Little drew their guns.

"Don't shoot. It's just my goats," I said and hurried to the door. I flung it open, and Phillip and Peter stood outside with shining eyes. They'd had great fun chasing the man down the hill. A piece of dark cloth hung from Phillip's mouth. I held out my hand. "Give."

The black and white goat dropped the piece of fabric in my hand.

"What is that?" Deputy Aiden asked as he holstered his gun.

I handed the scrap of black cloth to him. "I think it's a piece of trouser."

"Your goat attacked the intruder?"

"The boys thought it was a game. They are exuberant at times."

Deputy Aiden's brows drew together. "Little," Deputy Aiden said to the other young man, who was thin with a very short haircut and seemed to watch Aiden—a man just a handful of years older than he—with great attention. "Go check it out. The perp might have gotten away by now, but you can see if he is still out there and if there is any evidence as to where he might have gone. Look for boot prints or whatever you can find."

"Yes, sir," Little said and hurried out the back door of the greenhouse. Through the window, I could see the goats hopping around him as he went down the hill.

"If there is any trail left behind by the man you saw, Little will find it." He paused. "And maybe your goats will lead him in the right direction."

"I'm not sure about that. They can be forgetful and have trouble with obedience."

He sighed. "Deputy Little will do what he can. He's come a long way and is turning into a very fine officer. I don't know if he will be able to catch the intruder, but he is a good cop, and he will do his very best to find any clues that might tell us where the man you saw may have gone."

"You are being very careful not to say that the man I saw was doing something wrong," I noted.

He smiled. "I always knew you were a keen observer, Millie. I'm not saying that because I don't know, and as a police officer, I never say anything I don't know for sure. There is nothing worse than being blamed for something you didn't do." He said this as if the knowledge came from his own experiences.

I nodded, thinking of what I had done to Enoch

years ago. It was a terrible thing to blame the wrong person. I swallowed hard and stared at the screen door the deputy had just gone through. I could no longer see Deputy Little or the goats.

"Dispatch got a call that a body was found in the greenhouse. Were you the one who phoned?" Deputy Aiden's question interrupted my dark thoughts.

I turned back to him and didn't say anything at first. Another Amish saying came into my mind. "Swallowing words before you say them is so much better than having to eat them afterward."

"Millie, did you find the body?" the deputy asked. "Whoever called dispatch didn't stay on the line long enough to answer any questions."

"Who told you to come to the greenhouse then?" I asked, stalling before I gave him my answer. Fear over my niece's part in all this held me back.

"Dispatch said that the woman who called in said there was someone dead in the greenhouse on Briar Road. This is the only greenhouse on Briar Road."

So the police didn't know that Edith was involved. I knew it was only a matter of time before they found out. Should I tell them now or delay it? Was it worth delaying? This was Edith's land, her greenhouse, her home—who else would have been here on a Sunday morning when the rest of the community was at church? Deputy

Aiden knew enough about the Amish to know that.

I couldn't lie. The Good Lord would never ask me to lie. As tempting as it was, I told the truth. "I didn't find the body. My niece Edith did, and she was the one who called the police. I told her to do that while I stayed here and waited for you. She's in the house with her children now. I told her to stay there."

He nodded. "Can you show me where the body was found?"

I swallowed and walked back to the cactus room. There was no door between the main room of the greenhouse and the cactus room. I pointed inside and Deputy Aiden went in. I was a few steps behind him. By the time I entered the room, which was just a second or two later, he was already on his cell phone. "I need two crime scene techs, and call the coroner too. Edy's Greenhouse. They should all know where that is." He ended the call and clipped his phone back onto his utility belt, which also held handcuffs and his gun.

Seeing the gun there made me uncomfortable. Of course, we Amish are not opposed to guns for hunting, but a gun like Deputy Aiden's was strictly to enforce the law, which didn't sit well with my Amish sensibilities. I knew Deputy Aiden was a *gut* man and would only use it if absolutely necessary to save another life. I hoped that I would never be in the position where I had to save one person's life by taking another's. I didn't feel qualified to make such a harsh judgment. Or to carry through with such an action.

Deputy Aiden crouched beside the body as I had, but he was unafraid and positioned himself close to Zeke's head.

I couldn't bring myself to look at Zeke's face again. I didn't need to see it to know exactly what it looked like. It was impossible to forget. I swallowed. "Will we be able to catch who did this?"

He looked up at me. "We?"

I smoothed a wrinkle from my skirt with my hand. "I mean you."

He frowned as if he found my response suspicious. "Yes. It's my job and what I intend to do. First my team and I need to determine whether it was an accident or foul play."

"You think he died in an accident?" I said with too much hope in my voice. I was certain Zeke had been murdered, but if Deputy Aiden didn't think so, I'd take his accident theory.

"This doesn't look like an accident to me," he said, dashing my hopes. "There is no evidence that his head connected with anything that would explain the wound. In fact—" He cut himself off as he stared intently under the potting table.

He had seen the decorative rock; I knew it. Deputy Aiden stood up and stepped around the table away from Zeke, then squatted next to the table. I noted that I didn't hear his knees crack on the way down like mine did. "This was no accident," he said, staring at the rock. "And the very pointed Bible verse makes me wonder if this was planned."

I pressed my lips together and folded my hands in prayer. I had wondered the same thing when I read the words on the stone.

"And the body is Zeke Miller," Deputy Aiden said.

"Do you know Zeke?"

A cloud fell over the young deputy's face. He knew Zeke. I sensed that, but he was reluctant to say how he knew the young Amish man.

"Do you know him?" I repeated.

The wary expression on Aiden's face disappeared, and he returned to his impassive cop face, a look that would give away nothing to me. I wasn't sure I even wanted to hear what he knew about Zeke. As far as I knew, the only way for the police to know an Amish man well was if that Amish person had done something wrong. Although I'd never cared for Zeke and thought he had wanted to marry my niece only for her greenhouse, I never once thought he was in trouble with the law. Deputy Aiden's initial reaction to seeing the body told me I was wrong.

CHAPTER NINE

"Holmes County is a small place," Deputy Aiden said vaguely.

That's when my suspicions were confirmed. I was right that Zeke had been tangled up in something sinister. I wondered if I should bring the wrench under the table to the deputy's attention, but I knew that he would find it, or one of his crime scene techs—I believed that's what he had called them—would.

Poor Edith. However, I realized this could be good news for my Edith too, as far as the police were concerned. If Zeke was mixed up with the wrong crowd, there would be other people besides my Edith who would want him permanently out of their lives. If he was mixed up with criminals, these people would be more likely to turn to murder as a solution.

I shivered at my train of thought. I didn't want someone else to be falsely accused even if it freed Edith of blame.

Deputy Aiden stood up. "Wasn't Edith to marry Zeke Miller soon?"

My eyebrows went up. It seemed to me that Deputy Aiden Brody knew even more about our community than I expected. He must have seen the expression on my face and his cheeks flushed.

"I only know because Bailey mentioned that she and Charlotte were making a wedding cake for Edith and the two of them couldn't agree on the flavor. Bailey wanted it to be Black Forest, but Charlotte wanted it to be lemon poppy seed."

The cake. I had forgotten. It was a surprise that I had planned for Edith. Of course, he would have heard about the wedding from his fiancée, Bailey, and Charlotte, Bailey's cousin, an Amish girl who worked at Swissmen Sweets with Bailey and Bailey's grandmother Clara. I would have to notify Swissmen Sweets that there would be no cake and no wedding. "Do you know if they've started the cake yet?" I asked.

Deputy Aiden shook his head. "I don't know."

"Edith was set to marry him, and I asked Swissmen Sweets to make the cake. It was to be a special surprise for Edith." I said nothing of the broken engagement and hoped that Edith wouldn't say anything about it either when Deputy Aiden questioned her.

I was kicking myself because I'd confirmed to the ladies in my quilting circle that Edith was going to break her engagement. Probably everyone in the Sunbeam Café yesterday also heard. It wasn't as if we had been keeping our voices down. Then I remembered that didn't really matter because Zeke's mother knew and was telling everyone in the community. She even hinted that Edith might have another beau. The police would learn of the broken engagement one way or another.

Remembering Carolina Miller telling everyone in the district brought another person to my mind: Tucker Leham. Tucker knew something about Zeke and had wanted to tell Edith, but when he'd heard that she wasn't to marry Zeke, he'd decided to keep the information to himself. Could what he knew have led to Zeke's death? I would have to have a conversation with the young man and find out what he knew. Even more important, I needed to speak to Edith, alone and soon. What did she know about Zeke that she wasn't sharing?

There was a commotion in the larger room of the greenhouse as male voices filled the place. Deputy Aiden held up a finger. "Hold that thought. I still would like to talk to you about this. I'll be right back." He stepped out of the cactus room, leaving me alone with the body. I stared at the decorative rock, which Deputy Aiden had left in place on the concrete floor, and I thought of the wrench he had yet to see or mention to me. I wasn't sure why, but that wrench felt important. It was something else I would have to speak to Edith about.

"The crime scene is in here," Deputy Aiden said in a clear, strong voice just outside the archway leading into the cactus room.

A moment later Deputy Aiden, along with a woman and man in black coveralls, stepped into the room. They both carried large black bags. The woman pulled up short. "What is she doing here?" She narrowed her eyes. "What are you doing in here?"

"She was one of the witnesses who first dis-covered the body," Deputy Aiden said. "She is a member of the family."

The woman arched her brow. "You left a suspect alone with the body?"

Suspect? I felt sick. I knew Edith would be under suspicion, but I never viewed myself as a suspect until now.

"Mrs. Fisher was alone with the body before we arrived here," Deputy Aiden said. "I want this entire room cataloged and searched. You find anything that strikes you as the least bit odd, I want to hear about it right away."

"We got it, Deputy," the male crime scene tech said.

"What about the murder weapon, sir?" the woman asked, pointing at the rock peeking out from under the potting table. "Because that is surely it."

I felt a little queasy when I looked again at the rock with the blood crusted on it.

"Yes, I assume that is the murder weapon too. We won't know for sure until the coroner gets here and makes an official pronouncement. However, the rock and the injury on the back of the victim's head do appear to match."

I placed a hand on my head and felt a bit dizzy. Perhaps the gravity of the situation had finally hit me. Someone had killed Zeke Miller in my niece's greenhouse. There was no way to sugarcoat it and no way to keep this news from the Amish rumor mill, which might already be grinding, depending upon how much Edith had said when she'd called the bishop's house.

Deputy Aiden must have noticed the green cast to my skin. "I'm going to speak to Mrs. Fisher outside in the main room."

The techs nodded and set their large bags in the corner of the room as far away from Zeke's body as possible.

"Will you follow me, Millie?" Deputy Aiden asked and stepped through the doorway that led into the main part of the greenhouse.

Before I left the space, I looked at Zeke's face one last time. I didn't want to. It was some kind of compulsion that forced me to do it. I prayed for him and hoped that it wasn't too late for my prayer to reach *Gott*'s ears.

CHAPTER TEN

In the larger room, Deputy Aiden studied me. "How well did you know Zeke Miller?"

That was easy enough to answer. "He's been a member of our district since birth, but for the last ten years, I've lived in Michigan caring for my sister. When I left Harvest, I don't believe that he had yet made a commitment to be baptized into the church, so I didn't see him often at church functions. That can be the way with young people, you see, when they are in *rumspringa*. They might spend some time away from the faith to see how the *Englisch* live. There are no rules on how far they may go during their running-around time, or how long they may explore, but most families hope their children will choose to stay close to the faith during that time."

He arched his brow. "So Zeke was wild during his running-around years?"

I flushed. "I don't know that. As I said, I was away at the time, and I only assumed as much because I didn't see him often at church as a teenager. Of course, that could mean a great many things, and I shouldn't jump to any conclusions."

Deputy Aiden nodded and removed a small notepad from the breast pocket of his uniform. He flipped through the pad, and from where I was standing, I could see that the pages were heavily written upon with clean block letters. Deputy Aiden paid attention and took good notes. I could only assume that he had been a very *gut* student in school.

"When did you move back to Holmes County?" he asked.

"At the beginning of this year. My sister passed away in December, and I was no longer needed in Michigan. I knew it was time to come home." I took a breath as I remembered those last difficult days in Michigan. As much as I loved my sister, I never felt at home there. I wished that I could have moved her to Ohio instead of me going there, but she had lived in Michigan for the last fifty-some years since marrying her late husband. I spent the long decade in Michigan out of duty to her. Oh, that might sound negative, but caring for our loved ones, supporting them in sickness and in health, that is a gift. And I cherished every moment I spent with my sister.

"Have you interacted with Zeke since you have been back in Harvest?"

"My interactions with Zeke have been limited. I see him at church now and again; we only meet every other week, and a young man like Zeke isn't the type to spend Sundays chatting with an old widow like me."

"Even though he's marrying your niece, a niece that you raised like a daughter?"

I blinked. Deputy Aiden was very well-informed about my family. "How did you know that?"

He blushed. "Clara mentioned it when Bailey and Charlotte were debating over the wedding cake. She said that Edith's mother died when she was a child and you stepped in and helped your brother Ira raise his twins, Edith and Enoch."

I nodded and wondered what other information he had gleaned from his close relationship to the King family. I would have to be careful what I said in front of Clara King, not that I thought she would say something on purpose to hurt anyone in our community. Even so, it was worrisome.

The truth was I had spoken to Zeke several times since Edith announced their wedding date. I'd wanted to gauge how much he cared for my niece, and I found his interest wanting. Instead of speaking about how much he loved her and the children, he spoke about expanding the greenhouse and maybe getting some animals besides the barn cats on the property. He said that he would do a great job managing the family and the business. There was no mention of respect, love, or affection. It felt more like a pending business transaction than a marriage.

When I didn't respond, Deputy Aiden said, "I will need to question Edith. Should I go to the house and talk to her?"

I swallowed. "Would it be all right if I speak to her first? The children are with her, and I'm sure that she will want them to leave the room or even the house while you speak with her. Or you could question her outside while I stay inside with the children."

He frowned. "It's not standard procedure to let a witness speak to another witness before questioning."

"I'm sure it's not, but I only ask this because of the children." That was mostly true, I thought.

He sighed and compassion relaxed his young face. "I need to check in with my team. I'll come to the house to speak to Edith in five minutes. That should be enough time for you to decide where the children should go."

I thanked him and hurried through the greenhouse into the yard. When the soles of my black sneakers hit the grass, I broke into a run. Just because I was of a more advanced age than my niece or most of the other members of my quilting circle, it didn't mean that I couldn't run when I absolutely had to. Nonetheless, I was panting by the time I reached the house.

I threw open the back door that led into the kitchen. The door was unlocked. Edith and the children were alone in the house and a man had been murdered just a few yards away. Why hadn't my niece thought to lock all the doors and windows?

"Edith?" I called, trying to keep my tone even because I knew the children would be anxious and curious about all the activity outside.

Micah came into the kitchen. "*Maam* is upstairs."

I pressed my lips together as I followed my great nephew into the living room, where I found his brother and sister sitting on the couch like a set of Amish dolls with blank expressions on their sweet faces. Ginny cradled three tiny kittens in her lap. The mother cat, a large white princess of a cat with an impressive plume of a tail, lay in a cardboard box in front of the cool potbellied stove in the corner. She had two other kittens curved next to her body. All the kittens were white like their mother or marmalade orange.

One of the kittens in Ginny's lap caught my eye. It had very, very light colored orange, almost peach, fur with a bright pink nose and paw pads. The little creature looked up at me and meowed for all he was worth.

"Hello there," I said and scratched his tiny head. The kitten couldn't have been more than a week old.

"Why are the police here?" Micah asked, ignoring the kittens altogether. "I wanted to go outside and talk to them but *Maam* forbid it. The policemen looked like they were very nice. Why can't I speak with them?" He cocked his head.

"Your *maam* doesn't want you to speak with them because they are here to work," I said. "They can't be distracted right now."

"Work? Why?" Micah asked, not giving up.

"Did someone steal something from the greenhouse? Is that why she's crying? If they did, I will find out whoever it is and make them give it back. No one should ever make my *maam* cry. She's the best *maam* there is, and I won't let anyone treat her poorly."

"Micah, please," Jacob said. He had his arm around Ginny's slight shoulders. Even though he was only ten, he treated her more like he would a daughter than a younger sister.

"I don't know why she's crying," I said. "Nothing was stolen from the greenhouse as far as I know. Let me go upstairs and talk to her. You wait here."

"I'll go with you," Micah offered. "To make sure she's all right."

I shook my head. "Stay here like your *maam* asked you to."

With a thump, Micah reluctantly joined his brother and sister on the couch, but I could tell that he wasn't done asking questions. It was something that I admired in children. I liked ones with spunk, adults too.

I went up the narrow set of stairs to the second floor. The door to Edith's bedroom was open and when I peeked inside, I noted the stack of library books on her dresser and the neatly made bed, with a quilt in a Texas Star pattern that I had made for her while I was in Michigan. It did my heart good to know that she still liked the quilt well enough to have it on her bed, not to mention the two matching throw pillows that I had also made. There were two more rooms on this floor, Ginny's bedroom and the boys' room.

I found her in Ginny's room. Edith was holding a large woven basket on her hip and staring out the window at the greenhouse below.

When I stepped into the room, she started to move. She walked around the room, picking up toys as she went. There were wooden animals, blocks, toy buggies, and dolls. "It's amazing what a mess one small child can make. I almost forgot what it was like, since the boys were already six and seven when Ginny came along. It's like starting over again and with a girl to boot." Her voice cracked. "On my own. A little girl needs a father, and that will never happen now. She and her brothers might not even have a mother soon if the police arrest me and send me to some *Englisch* prison. *Aenti* Millie, what am I to do?" Tears were in her eyes.

"Child, sit down."

"An Amish woman is always supposed to keep up the house. It's a good task to keep my hands busy while I wait for the police to pass their judgment." She dropped another toy in the basket.

"No one is passing any judgment on you." Well, not just yet. "Now, please sit."

She picked up a faceless Amish doll and tossed it in the basket.

I walked over to her. "Edith." I took the basket from her hands, and she didn't fight me. "Sit down, please." I set the basket on the floor.

This time she did as I asked and settled into the rocking chair by the window. The window overlooked the greenhouse. From this vantage point, we could see a number of police officers and other personnel coming and going from the greenhouse. Before I could make Edith look away, the two crime scene techs I'd met at the green-house came out of the building, pushing a stretcher with a black bag on top of it. By the length and shape of the bundle on the stretcher, it wasn't hard to imagine what or who was in the bag.

Edith looked away and I squeezed her hand. "I'm so sorry. I know that even if you and Zeke were not to marry, he was still an important person in your life."

She sat up a little straighter. "I will be all right. The children need me to be strong, and I will be, for them. It is not the first time, is it?" She picked up the doll from the top of the toy basket beside her chair. "This is Ginny's favorite doll. It was a gift from her father, a man she never met. But she knows it's from him because I told her it was. Moses had his faults, but I never wanted the children to think poorly of their father. Despite the bad choices he made, he will always be their father, and I want them to remember him in the best way. It's too hard for them to recall the difficult things about Moses and his death. And now, another man that they were starting to think of as a father is dead. I don't know what to tell them. I suppose that's why I came up here and hid from my own children. You know that Micah is relentless when he has a question, and I didn't know what to say."

I smiled. "I do know how inquisitive he can be. He asked me a number of questions when I first came into the house. He is by far your most curious child."

She smiled. "He is indeed." She set the doll back into the basket.

"Edith, I saw something in the greenhouse I need to ask you about."

She nodded and seemed to brace herself.

"I saw a small wrench about five inches long under the potting table in the cactus room. There was some sort of black grease on the end of it. Do you know where it came from?"

"It doesn't belong to the greenhouse. We have many tools but none like you have described. I don't know where it came from. It could have been Zeke's or maybe Tucker's. No one else would be working in there. I don't know why either one of them would need a wrench like that or why it would have black grease on it."

I frowned. "Don't you have more employees? I thought you had five or six people working for you."

She pressed her lips together.

Jacob came into Ginny's room. "*Maam*, I'm sorry to come up and bother you like this when you told us to leave you alone, but there is a policeman downstairs and he wants to talk to you. He told me to fetch you." Jacob said all this with worry etched on his face. Knowing the eldest of Edith's children, I guessed his fear stemmed more from concern about disappointing his mother for disobeying her than from the police.

I stood up from where I kneeled by Edith's rocking chair. I had been expecting this summons and was surprised it hadn't come sooner. Deputy Aiden had said that he wanted to speak to Edith in five minutes and that was well over ten minutes ago.

"I'm sorry, *Maam*. I know that you asked us to leave you alone." His voice quavered.

Edith stood up, and I gave a sigh of relief. She needed to be focused and strong when speaking with the police. I knew Deputy Aiden Brody would have compassion for her and her situation, but he was still an officer of the *Englisch* law and had to speak to her in a direct way that she wouldn't be used to hearing from an *Englisch* man. "It is fine, Jacob. You did the right thing by finding me. I need to talk to the police."

An expression passed over the boy's face as if he wanted to ask something more, but he didn't.

He didn't because he was quiet and serious Jacob. Had it been Micah with the question sitting on his tongue, he would have asked.

Edith walked out of the room without saying another word, and I couldn't have been more proud of her in that moment. People who don't know our culture tend to think that Amish women are weak and submissive. They are wrong. We are as tough as any other women, or any other people, and my niece was about to prove that.

CHAPTER ELEVEN

Deputy Aiden Brody stood in the middle of my niece's living room with his hands behind his back. Deputy Little stood a few feet away with a small notebook and a pencil in his hand.

"Would it be all right if I pulled up a chair, Edith?" Deputy Aiden asked in a kind voice. "Why don't we all have a seat?"

"That's a fine idea," I said, taking a spot on the sofa. The children, kittens, and mother cat had been banished to the front yard.

Edith sat beside me on the edge of the sofa and smoothed her skirt over her legs.

Deputy Aiden raised his eyebrows at me. "I thought you planned to be with the children, Millie?"

"I think Edith would be more comfortable if I stay while you ask her your questions. I plan not to interfere." I smoothed my skirt over my knees and settled back in my seat. I wasn't going to move a muscle.

Deputy Aiden nodded. After asking Edith permission a second time, he grabbed a ladder-back chair from the long dining table beside the kitchen door and set it in front of the sofa where we sat.

Little did the same, but he kept his chair about four feet behind Deputy Aiden. If he moved it back any more, he was at risk of being outside the small house.

I heard the shouts of the children through the open window as they played with the kittens outside.

I was relieved Zeke Miller's body had already been removed from the property. There were a few crime scene techs still in the greenhouse, but they were out of the children's sight.

Micah and Jacob, at least, knew that something very strange was happening inside the greenhouse. They would have questions later, I was sure, and they were old enough that Edith could not shelter the truth from them forever. Zeke's death surely was already the talk of the district.

"Edith, can you tell me how you discovered Zeke's body?" Deputy Aiden asked.

A tremor went through Edith's frame when he said "Zeke's body," but then she pressed her hands together as if to steady herself. "I went out to the greenhouse this morning to water as I do every morning. However, I went later than I normally would because it is a church day, and I had to get the children ready for services. It takes time to dress three children for church. When I went inside the greenhouse, I watered the plants the way I always do, starting with the annuals, and working my way back to the cactus room.

The cacti don't need to be watered every day, but I do check the room several times a day just to make sure the plants are happy and healthy. It's very important that they get enough light. It's what they crave most."

"So you watered everything except the cacti before you found the body?" he asked.

Without a moment of hesitation, she said, "*Ya.*"

I thought back to what I remembered of walking through the greenhouse, and I recalled that the plants didn't appear to be watered. Usually when Edith watered the greenhouse or when one of her workers did it, the concrete was soaking wet with a number of slowly drying puddles throughout. I saw nothing like that. I remembered looking at my feet and noting that the floor was dry, and when I ran after that man who went out the back door of the greenhouse, the floor was dry too. Had she watered so early that the floor was already dry? I could not see how the concrete would dry that quickly. It was still spring, long before the dry summer season, not that it was ever that dry in Ohio. Late July and August could have long stretches of bright sun and rainless weeks, but nothing was hot enough to dry up the water in the greenhouse that quickly. Was she lying to the sheriff's deputy?

I said nothing of my suspicions when Deputy Aiden asked, "What did you do when you saw the body?"

Edith looked down at her folded hands. "Nothing."

"What do you mean, nothing?" Deputy Aiden asked.

She looked up. "Nothing. I did nothing. I was frozen in place until my *aenti* walked into the room and snapped me out of it. I just couldn't believe what I was seeing. It reminded me . . ." She trailed off.

I knew what she was going to say. It reminded her of when she'd found her husband, Moses, dead behind their home, presumably from a drug overdose. Drug culture hadn't spared the Amish community. It wasn't spoken about often, but it was well-known that Moses Hochstetler had had a problem with drugs for a long time, to the point that he stole from his own family to feed his habit. Ultimately, it had cost him his life.

I squeezed my niece's hand. I wished I could have been with her at the time. I wasn't then, but I could be at her side now.

Edith swallowed. "My *aenti* told me to call the police and bishop, and then take the children into the house. That's what I did and that's where I have been until now."

"You were with the children the entire time?" Deputy Aiden asked.

"The children were here in the living room, but I went up to my bedroom because I was quite upset and didn't want them to see it." She glanced at me. "My brother was here earlier this morning too."

I started at the mention of Enoch.

"Your brother Enoch."

She nodded. "He's my twin. He's visiting Harvest for a few days."

"When does he plan to leave?" Deputy Aiden asked.

"He hasn't said."

"And when did he arrive?"

"A few days ago," she said.

"Where is he now?" the deputy asked.

"I don't know. He left very early while I was getting the children dressed. He said he had business to attend to."

"On Sunday?" Deputy Aiden arched his brow.

"That's what he said."

Deputy Aiden nodded, and Deputy Little scribbled notes in his book.

"Where were you upstairs just now?"

"In my daughter's room."

"And where is that?" Deputy Aiden asked.

She frowned but answered the question. "It's in the back of the house."

Across the room, Little made a note in his little book.

"Does it have a window that overlooks the greenhouse?" Deputy Aiden said.

She nodded.

I squeezed Edith's hand.

"Your aunt saw someone in the greenhouse after you left. Did you see anyone on your land?"

Edith's head snapped in my direction. "Who did you see? Who was there?"

"I don't know," I said. "I heard a noise outside the cactus room. When I went out to investigate, the man ran away. The goats chased him."

"The goats? How did they get out?"

That was a good question, one I hadn't thought of. It reminded me that the goats were undoubtedly still running free at the moment on my niece's property. That was probably not the best place for them to be. There were too many plants that they might view as snacks. Before I could comment, she asked, "Do you think he was there when I was in the greenhouse alone? Was he the man who did this?"

"I don't know," I said. It was the best answer I could give her.

"Did you see anyone around your property who shouldn't have been there at this time of day on a Sunday?" Deputy Aiden asked.

"None of us should be here," she told Deputy Aiden. "We should all have been at church."

Deputy Aiden nodded. "But did you see anyone run away from the greenhouse?"

She licked her lips. "*Nee*," she said barely above a whisper, and her hand twitched.

"It seemed to me if you were in your daughter's bedroom at the back of the house," Deputy Aiden said, "you would have the best view of what was going on down below."

She stared at her hands.

Deputy Aiden leaned forward and propped his elbows on his knees. "What did you see out that window, then?"

"Nothing. I was cleaning my daughter's room. I wasn't watching what was happening outside. The last place I wanted to look was the greenhouse after what I found there."

My heart fell just a little. I knew that my niece was lying now. I had seen her at the bedroom window with my own eyes. Why would she lie about this unless she had seen something and wanted to protect someone? Did she want to protect the Amish man who had run away from me? I had so many questions, and I couldn't ask any of them with Deputy Aiden and Deputy Little in the room. These were questions that I would have to ask my niece when we were alone. I had to get to the bottom of what was going on.

Deputy Aiden sat up straight again as if he'd come to a decision about something. Whatever that decision was . . . he wasn't letting on. "We will need you to come to the station tomorrow," Deputy Aiden said.

"What?" Edith asked. "Why? I have told you all that I know."

He nodded. "But we need to collect your finger-prints. We'll also need the fingerprints of everyone who works in the greenhouse, so we can compare them to the ones found in the cactus room. Also, there is a statement that I will need you to sign." He glanced at me. "You will need to sign a statement too, Millie."

"How can you hope to find the fingerprints you need? You don't understand the number of people, workers and visitors alike, who visit Edy's Greenhouse during the season." I sat up a little straighter. "Dozens of people, both Amish and *Englisch*, go in and out of the greenhouse every day, especially now at the height of planting season. I don't know how you will ever find fingerprints that will help you discover who did this."

"Usually, yes, fingerprinting would be a waste of time in a public place like this, but we do have what we believe was the murder weapon. We will be testing that for prints, and we need Edith's prints and her staff's prints for that."

My niece bristled, and I knew she was remembering that she'd picked up the decorative rock.

I sat there wondering if I should tell Deputy Aiden this. They would surely find her fingerprints on the rock. Would it be better to tell him now, so that he wouldn't think we were trying to hide that fact from him? Before I could make up my mind, Edith said, "If you mean that rock that was on the floor of the cactus room, I touched it."

Deputy Aiden's eyebrows disappeared into his hairline.

"I wasn't thinking and saw it on the floor. I picked it up. I didn't know what it had been used for."

"I thought you froze when you saw the body," he said as if he'd caught her in a lie.

"I did." She lifted her chin. "This was after my *aenti* was there with me in the cactus room."

"I saw her pick it up," I said, supporting her story. "I told her to put it back on the floor, which she did. However, you will find her fingerprints on the rock. I don't know how fingerprinting her will help when you already know they are there."

"I still need them," Deputy Aiden said.

"I didn't do anything wrong." Edith squeezed my hand so tightly, I thought my bones would break. I didn't pull away though. She needed my comfort right then even if her need left a sizable bruise on my hand.

"But you might have killed him and waited to pick up the rock again when a witness was present," Deputy Little said. "That way you'd be able to explain away why your prints were on the murder weapon. We have seen it happen before. It's a clever trick to confuse the investigation."

Deputy Aiden shot his deputy a harsh look, and Deputy Little stared down at his notepad again. I bet he was sorry for speaking up. I glanced at my niece. Now that I knew she wasn't being completely truthful with the police, a tiny part of me wondered if maybe the younger deputy was right.

Edith let go of my hand. "I didn't do anything wrong. I'm sorry Zeke is dead. I may have decided not to marry him, but I did care for him. I wish—I wish that his life could have been different. He made things harder for himself than they had to be."

Deputy Aiden's eyes narrowed. "You weren't going to marry him?"

And I felt my heart sink.

CHAPTER TWELVE

Edith looked at me. "I thought my *aenti* would have told you that I broke off my engagement to Zeke."

Deputy Aiden glanced at me again before looking back at Edith. "She did not. When did you do this?"

Edit shot a panicked look at me, but I nodded to her to keep talking. She couldn't take it back now. "Saturday afternoon."

"Yesterday afternoon? The day before you found him dead in your greenhouse?"

"*Ya.*" She clasped her hands together in her lap.

Deputy Aiden looked as if he were going to ask her more about that when the front door of Edith's house banged open and Ruth Yoder filled the doorway with her hands on her hips. "What's going on in here?"

I jumped to my feet. "Ruth, shouldn't you be at church?"

She narrowed her green eyes. "I was at church, church in my very own home when the bishop and I received word that Zeke Miller was dead at Edy's Greenhouse. What's going on, Millie Fisher? You had better tell me quick."

Deputy Aiden stood up. "Ruth, please calm down. There has been an incident. Millie and

Edith did the right thing and called the police."

"Called the police? Called the police before you told the bishop what is happening in his own district? With his own people? Millie, I thought you knew better than to do anything without telling the bishop first. What kind of district did you live in in Michigan that they were so lax about this sort of thing? The bishop and the church elders should be the first to know if something bad is happening in the district. I would think that a church member's death certainly qualifies." She placed her hands on her hips as if for emphasis.

"Ruth, don't get your bonnet strings in a knot." I put my own hands on my hips, matching her stance pose for pose.

Ruth opened and closed her mouth as if shocked that anyone would snap at her as I had. But she didn't leave me much choice. I knew Ruth, and if I didn't jump in, she would just keep going.

"Edith called your shed phone. I told her to do that at the same time she called the police. It's not our fault if no one answered the phone. Furthermore, we had to call the police. We couldn't leave poor Zeke Miller lying on the floor of the greenhouse forever. I know that your husband would have told us to do the same thing. This is beyond what the district can handle alone."

"We didn't get any call to the shed phone. I would have known about it by now."

I glanced back at Edith, and her gaze didn't meet my eyes. Ruth was telling the truth. Edith had never called the Yoders' shed phone.

"Why didn't someone come to our farm and tell us in person?" Ruth asked. "This is important news for the district."

I turned back to Ruth with an ache in my chest. Something was going on with Edith, and I didn't know what it was. "Only Edith and I were here, and frankly, I wasn't going to leave my niece and her children alone under the circumstances." I sat back down next to Edith and put my arm around her shoulders. "If you didn't hear about it by phone, how did you hear about Zeke's death?"

"Everyone at church knows about it," Ruth said, more than a little frustrated that she hadn't been the first to hear. "It is the talk of the district. The bishop had to stop the services because of the whispers running through the congregation like wildfire."

"Oh dear." Edith covered her mouth. "Was his mother, Carolina, there?"

"*Ya*, she was, and she is beside herself." Her face fell and for the briefest moment Ruth allowed us to see the compassionate woman beneath the tough exterior. "She wanted to come herself to see if the rumors were true, but I insisted she stay back under the care of the other church members. I don't look forward to telling her the rumors are true."

Edith shook her head. "The poor woman. I know she was already upset . . ."

Ruth folded her arms and looked as large and as fierce as ever. "She was already upset because she knew you had no intention of marrying her son. She felt that she lost you, as her future daughter and your children as her future grandchildren, and her son on the same day. The woman is a complete wreck. I hope you are pleased with yourself."

"Ruth!" I shouted. She'd gone too far. Oh, the woman had a good heart and her penchant for drama was usually more amusing than antagonistic. But she'd gone too far. "That is not fair," I said. "We're sorry for Carolina's loss— of course, we are—but don't bring my niece's decision on her future into this. Who started the rumor about Zeke's death?" I asked.

Ruth scowled at me. "We don't know. That's why I came here. You know it's hard for the bishop to get around, and he had to tend to his flock. It made the most sense for me to come and see what was going on, especially since you and I are friends."

I guessed that Ruth had told her husband it made the most sense for her to go, and rather than argue with her in front of the entire district, he'd agreed.

I stood up and smoothed my apron over my skirts. It worried me that a faceless and nameless person knew about the murder and had already informed the entire district about it even before the police had left the greenhouse. How would anyone have learned about it?

Tucker Leham knew that I was leaving the services before they even started that morning, but he hadn't known where I was going. Ruth saw me leave as well. Could it have been the man I saw running away from the greenhouse? I had thought he was Amish. He was at least dressed as if he was Amish. But if he was guilty, why would he run right to the church meeting and start the gossip mill? If he was the one who'd killed Zeke, wouldn't he have wanted the murder to go unsuspected for as long as possible, so that he could get away?

I felt Deputy Aiden watching me. His face was blank, but I knew there were many questions in his mind. I didn't want to answer any of them.

"Deputy Brody." A crime scene tech poked his head into the room over Ruth's left shoulder.

Ruth jumped. "What are you doing, young man? You shouldn't sneak up on people like that. It is extremely rude. Didn't your mother raise you better?"

The tech took a step back, and I think I would have too if I didn't know Ruth. She could be scary when she wanted to be.

"I'm so sorry, ma'am. I only—"

"You only nothing. You can't come barging

into someone's house uninvited. It is very ill-mannered."

I noted that everyone in the room was far too polite to point out that Ruth had done just that only a few minutes ago.

The tech looked as if he might cry.

"Watterson, what is it?" Deputy Aiden asked.

Watterson inched into the room, staying as far away from Ruth as possible. "We're done with the scene and thought you would like to do one final walk-through before we rope it off."

"Rope it off? Do you mean we won't be allowed in the greenhouse?" Edith asked, jumping to her feet. "How will I take care of the plants?"

"You'll still have access to most of the green-house," the tech said. "We're only going to close off the cactus room where the body was found."

Ruth's hand fluttered to her chest. "He died on a cactus?" She made a face.

I shook my head. "*Nee*, Ruth, that's just where he was found."

"But there are plants in the cactus room as well," Edith protested. "They need to be cared for. This is my livelihood and I need to do all I can to save—" She stopped herself from saying more.

What did she need to save? I had a feeling Deputy Aiden was about to ask just that. I wasn't sure I wanted him to hear the answer before I did, so I jumped in and asked, "How long will the room be off limits?"

"At least for a couple of days," Deputy Aiden said, watching Edith.

I glanced back at my niece. "When was the last time you watered the plants in that room?" I knew the cacti and succulents in the cactus room didn't need to be watered every day.

"Yesterday," Edith said. "Tucker did it." A strange look crossed her face.

Why would Edith feel strangely about Tucker? I wanted more and more to speak with the green-house worker.

"Who's Tucker?" Deputy Aiden asked.

Edith looked at him. "Tucker Leham started working at the greenhouse years ago when my father was alive. He did most of the watering and maintenance around here."

Ruth straightened her back. "Tucker is a very fine young man, one of the kindest and hardest working in the district. He constantly lends an extra hand to my husband for whatever might be needed in the community." She narrowed her eyes at Edith. "It would serve us all well if his contributions to the community were more appreciated."

I looked from Ruth to Edith and back again. What was I missing here between the two of them?

"So they won't need to be watered for some time?" I asked, hoping Deputy Aiden would put Tucker in the back of his mind. I wanted to speak with Edith's employee first.

"When was Tucker here yesterday?" Deputy Aiden asked.

I realized I'd been guilty of wishful thinking; of course Deputy Aiden would want to know more about Tucker.

"In the morning," Edith said. She looked at me. "The cactus won't need to be watered for another four days."

"The police should be out of there by then and even if they are not, they will let you in to water." I looked at Deputy Aiden for agreement.

"We can do that," he said. "If we still need the scene to be secure, then one of my officers will go in with you to water the plants." There was a pause. "Where is Tucker? When will he be coming in?"

I pressed my hands together.

"He won't be coming in today. It's Sunday," Edith said.

"Tomorrow?" Deputy Aiden raised his eyebrows and waited.

She looked at her feet. "He won't be coming in tomorrow either."

"Why's that?" Deputy Aiden asked.

She glanced at me.

I nodded to encourage her to go on. She was the one who'd brought up Tucker. There wasn't anything we could do to stop Deputy Aiden from wanting to know about him now.

"He did a lot of the maintenance around the

greenhouse until Zeke started to help me out. We didn't need two men to do the same work."

"So what happened?" the deputy asked.

"Zeke told him that he would be doing the work around the greenhouse from now on, and we didn't need Tucker any longer."

"What?" Ruth asked. "I didn't know that. No one had mentioned this to me."

It must be a great disappointment for Ruth to know she wasn't the best-informed person in the district. However, the truth was I didn't know that Tucker had been let go either.

"When was this?" Deputy Aiden asked.

Edith looked at the floor. "Two weeks ago."

"But you said he was here yesterday morning to water."

She swallowed. "Sometimes he still comes by and helps us without pay."

Deputy Aiden cocked his head. "That seems likes a very generous thing to do for a business that just fired you."

"Tucker is a kind man," Edith said.

"This is awful," Ruth interjected. "I can't believe you have treated Tucker so poorly. He's too humble to make a fuss about it too. That's just like Tucker."

"How did he take being let go?" Deputy Aiden asked, ignoring Ruth's outburst.

She shrugged. "I don't know. I wasn't there when Zeke told him. He's worked for my family for a very long time. I missed working with him, but Zeke thought it was best to let him go to save money. Zeke said he could do the work that Tucker did. Tucker is so kind—he has a way of noticing what a person or plant might need. He stopped by to visit Saturday morning and noticed the plants needed to be watered. I was busy with other things and he just stepped in and did the job. He expects nothing in return."

"Who was supposed to water the cactus room yesterday?" Deputy Aiden asked.

She looked down. "Zeke."

I guessed that Deputy Aiden and I had just added Tucker Leham to our separate lists of murder suspects.

CHAPTER THIRTEEN

It's my fault that Zeke forgot to water the cactus room," Edith said quickly. "Zeke had been so busy these last few weeks working extra construction jobs because of the fair weather. You have to take work like his when you can get it because you never know when or how the weather will change. I should have handled the watering myself. It was careless of me not to. But I was too distracted with other parts of the business and with the children."

I pressed my lips together. Even on his busiest work day, a loving and caring man would have found time to water the cactus room. I would like to think that it was just an accident that Zeke hadn't. However, I knew better. Zeke wanted the money from my niece's greenhouse, but he did not want any of the work. If that was the case, why had he let Tucker go? Tucker would have continued to do the greenhouse work for minimal pay. There must have been another reason Zeke had wanted him gone. Could he have suspected that Tucker had feelings for Edith too?

Deputy Aiden glanced at me. "Before Zeke died, when was the last time that you were in the greenhouse?" Deputy Aiden asked Edith.

"I—I don't know. It was just before dark yesterday. I usually walk around the greenhouse before locking it up at night to double-check on the plants."

"You do that, not Zeke?"

She frowned. "Zeke doesn't live here. Just the children and I do, so yes, it's up to me to check the greenhouse and the rest of the property at night. Even my oldest son is not yet old enough to do it."

Deputy Aiden nodded and glanced at me again. His looks in my direction were beginning to make me nervous.

"Deputy?" Watterson asked, again shifting nervously from foot to foot.

"Yes?" Deputy Aiden asked.

"What do you want to do about the scene?"

"Secure it. I'll be there in a little while. I'd like to speak to Mrs. Hochstetler alone." Watterson and Deputy Little shared a look. "I would like you all to go outside. I won't be long."

The two men went out the door, scuttling by Ruth as they went. I couldn't say that I blamed them for doing that. Her scowl at them was so fierce it would have scared a charging bull away. Ruth and I didn't move a muscle.

Deputy Aiden's face softened. "Ruth, Millie. I need you to leave too."

"We are not leaving a young woman from our community alone with an *Englisch* man," Ruth said. "That just isn't right."

"I think Deputy Aiden is trustworthy," I said.

125

The deputy's face turned bright red. "I am. I just need to ask Edith a few questions in private. If I can't do that here, I will have to ask her to come to the station."

"Well, I never," Ruth began.

"Please," Edith said, looking at us imploringly. "Please, just let him ask his questions, so that this nightmare can be over and the police will leave."

"I don't think—" Ruth began.

"All right, Edith," I said, interrupting the bishop's wife. "If that's what you want, that's what we will do."

"It is," she said with tears welling in her eyes.

There was so much I wanted to say to her, to ask her, but I couldn't in present company. I couldn't in any company.

I ushered Ruth out the door. When I went out, I left it cracked just a hair. A moment later, I heard the door click shut. So much for my plan to overhear their conversation. I stared at the closed door, wondering if I had done the right thing. I had no concern that Deputy Aiden would be unkind or treat my niece poorly, but I was afraid Edith would say something that would dig her even deeper into trouble.

Behind me, the bishop's wife was in the middle of a rant. "This has been most upsetting! Mark my words, this will bring trouble down on the district again. We can't seem to steer clear of it. Bishop Yoder will be so upset, and the other

Amish communities in the county will surely wag their tongues over our misfortunes," Ruth said. "I don't—ahhhh—!"

Her sentence broke out into a cry for help.

I spun around on the front porch to see Ruth Yoder being chased across my niece's front yard by two Boer goats that I knew very well. The goats had silly grins on their faces and their ears flapped in the wind.

"Ahhh!" Ruth cried. "Millie Fisher, do something!"

I ran down the porch steps. "Phillip! Peter!"

The goats didn't even bother to look over their shoulders at me as they chased Ruth in a zigzag pattern around the yard. They were having a ball of a time. Out of the corner of my eye, I saw Edith's children each holding a kitten or two while they tried to cover their mouths to stop laughing. Ginny held the little peach kitten that I had admired. The little animal was jostled with every giggle that escaped from the girl's lips. He didn't seem to mind it all that much. Maybe he thought he was being rocked to sleep in some strange way.

I felt my face crack at the reaction of the children, and I was just as tickled by Ruth's predicament.

"Miiiilllllleeeee!" Ruth cried.

The crime scene techs and some of Deputy Aiden's officers came around the house from the greenhouse. It was officially a spectacle.

"Phillip! Peter!"

This time the goats had the *gut* sense to look at me. They could tell that I meant business from my tone, but they still didn't come to me when I called them. The goats' abrupt pause gave Ruth enough time to dash to her buggy. She grabbed the reins and untied them faster than I had ever seen a barrel racer do at the county fair. It was impressive.

"Millie Fisher, you need to do something about those goats!" She hopped into her buggy and kicked at the goats with her feet. Thankfully, they had the *gut* sense to stay clear of her shoes. "I'll have a word with you later, Millie!" She flicked the buggy reins and her horse was spurred into action.

I knew that she would be going straight home to tell the bishop and everyone else who would listen what had happened at Edy's Greenhouse.

I whistled again and the goats ran back to me like well-behaved Labs. I knew that I could have whistled for them when Ruth was running around the yard, but I'd conveniently forgotten at that time. Maybe I'd enjoyed the show just as much as the children. I would never be so bold as to tell Ruth that. I still had to quilt beside her in Double Stitch, and I knew in her mind that would be grounds for being kicked out of the group entirely.

The children ran over to the goats and me after Ruth left, and all the workers there for the investigation went back to their tasks.

Micah set the kittens he was holding in the grass and clutched his sides, he was laughing so hard. "Oh, oh, *Aenti* Millie. That was the funniest thing I ever saw. Did you know the bishop's wife could run so fast?"

"Actually, I didn't," I said with a smile. "The last time I saw her run like that she was just a few years older than you when we were in school."

Ginny covered her mouth, and then she held the peach-colored kitten out to me as a small child's gift. I accepted the kitten and tucked him in close to my chest. Immediately, he began to purr.

"*Aenti* Millie," Jacob said, "it looks to me like that kitten has picked you."

Both of the goats' ears perked up, and they inched toward me. I held the kitten out of their reach. Not that I thought the goats would hurt him on purpose, but they were clumsy and silly. That was how accidents happened.

As I snuggled the kitten close, I felt a match being made. There could be matches between people and creatures. That's what I believed anyhow, and this little cat was my match. "I think you might be right. What should I name my new little companion?"

"Peaches!" Ginny cried.

I looked at the peach-colored kitten. "That's just perfect, Ginny. Peaches it is."

The kitten snuggled even closer, burying its downy head into my neck.

"I think he likes the name," I said.

The front door of the house opened, and Deputy Aiden and Edith came out.

"*Maam*," Micah said excitedly, "*Aenti*'s goats chased the bishop's wife away!"

Deputy Aiden raised his eyebrows at me, so I explained. "The goats and Ruth have a strained relationship, mostly because they want to play with her and she wants nothing to do with them."

"I see," Aiden said.

Edith's face was drawn. "Children, please take the kittens into the house and wait there for me."

"But," Micah whined, "we didn't even get to speak to the policeman."

"You have nothing to say to the policeman," his mother replied firmly. "Now, do as I say and go into the house."

Jacob gathered up four of the kittens, giving them to his brother to carry. "Come on, Micah. *Maam* said."

Micah looked as if he wanted to argue some more, but one more stern look from his mother was all it took to keep his lips sealed.

Ginny reached up to me and I set Peaches in her arms. I was sad to see the little cat go, but I promised myself that I would take him home just as soon as he was weaned.

Deputy Aiden watched the children and kittens disappear into the house. "You have sweet children, Edith. I know this will be a difficult time for you, but please remember that I can only help you if you trust me. I want to keep you with your children just as much as you want to stay with them."

"What are you saying?" I asked. "What's going on?"

Deputy Aiden pressed his lips into a thin line, and Edith said nothing to make the deputy's ambiguous words any clearer.

"I will see you at the station tomorrow, Edith," Deputy Aiden said.

She nodded.

"Station?" I asked.

"We need to get a sample of her fingerprints. It will be easier to do that at the main office." He rested his hand on his duty belt in a practiced way. "Now, I should go check on the crime scene one last time so that we can get out of your hair." He nodded to Edith. "Please try to trust me. I have many friends who are Amish. I won't do you wrong."

She wouldn't look him in the eye.

The deputy's face fell just a little, and he walked away.

"What was that all about, asking you to trust him?"

She wouldn't look at me either. "He's a police officer. They want everyone in their community to trust them, don't they?"

"I suppose . . ."

She turned to go back toward the house.

I followed, stopping her before she went inside. "Maybe you shouldn't stay here alone. Why don't you and the children come and stay with me? It might be a tight squeeze in my little house, but there is plenty of sleeping space in the living room. The children will enjoy it. It will be like a campout. We can make a game of it. They can bring the mother cat and kittens if they don't want to leave them here alone. You know I love to have animals around."

Edith frowned. "This is my home and my livelihood. I'm not going to leave. Whoever did this had a problem with Zeke. It has nothing to do with me. I see no reason for me to leave my home for his mistakes. The truth is, *Aenti*, I think you are the one who should leave."

I stared at her. "You want me to leave."

She wouldn't meet my gaze. "Enoch will be back soon, and I think it's best if you aren't here when he arrives."

I felt a stab of pain in my chest. I knew why she was saying this. Everyone, including myself, believed that I was the one who drove Enoch from the Amish way because I made a mistake that I couldn't seem to make right.

CHAPTER FOURTEEN

Ten years ago when Enoch was in *rumspringa*, he was reckless. He smoked, got his driver's license and a car. I heard rumors that he had gone to the wild parties that some of the young Amish threw. These were parties that no parent, *Englisch* or Amish, would want their child to be at. He was testing the absolute boundaries of his *rumspringa*, and I prayed for him every day.

By this time my Kip at been gone for ten years, and I'd spent the last few years living at Edy's Greenhouse with my brother Ira and his twins. After my sister-in-law passed, they needed a woman to keep house for them while my brother ran his business. I was the widowed older sister. It made sense for me to give up my little home in the village and fulfill the family obligation. However, I had never had any children of my own, and even though I grew up in a family of many children, I didn't know how to raise a child who was determined to be disobedient at every turn.

That's the way Enoch behaved the moment he got out of school when he was fourteen and started *rumspringa*. He was defiant and sullen and made no attempt to help his father with the greenhouse. Edith was the one who was the perfect twin. She took interest in the greenhouse and learned all she could about plants. Enoch squandered away his time.

Enoch still lived at home when he started to dress like an *Englischer*. He cut his hair and bought expensive tennis shoes. I never knew where he got the money for those shoes. Instead of plants, he was interested in cars and motorcycles, and I found magazines about both in the barn, where he spent most of his time when he was home, which wasn't often.

Ira would not do anything about the boy. He believed that Enoch was acting in such a way because he'd lost his mother when he was young. I felt sympathy for Enoch's loss, but I didn't believe that was his only reason for acting up. I did believe it was his excuse. I tried to speak to him many times and asked him to behave for his father's sake, but my words fell on deaf ears. I was his *aenti* not his *maam*, so, as he told me many times, I really didn't have any authority over him.

Then a motorcycle went missing. An expensive motorcycle was taken from an *Englisch* neighbor's garage. The police came to the greenhouse to see if any of us knew about it. I was the only one home at the time. They said that the neighbor suspected Enoch had taken the motorcycle and they were looking for him. The neighbor told them that Enoch made no secret of how much he wanted that motorcycle. They only had a few questions to ask Enoch about it.

Despite everything that Enoch had done since beginning *rumspringa* years before, I told the police that I didn't believe he would steal. It would go against his very nature as an Amish man.

Even so, they asked me where they could find my nephew, insisting they only wanted to speak to him about the motorcycle, and I told them. That was my worst mistake.

I never said he took it. Those words never came out of my mouth. But that small fact didn't matter to the arresting deputy at the time, who was Marshall Jackson—Deputy Jackson, who was now Sheriff Jackson, a man who hated the Amish, and wanted to blame my culture for everything that went wrong in Holmes County.

When he came to the greenhouse asking after Enoch, I had been intimidated by his size and his hostile demeanor. And as soon as he learned Enoch's whereabouts, he tracked him down. I don't think he even spoke to Enoch before he arrested him and charged him with the crime. Enoch sat for weeks in jail, and there was nothing anyone from our district could do to free him. I even went to the sheriff's department myself to explain that I didn't think my nephew had done anything wrong. I was ignored at every turn.

After days of trying, I finally found the only

person who would listen to me: Deputy Aiden. He believed me, and he promised he would do all he could to get Enoch out.

In the end, he did by continuing to follow leads until he found the missing motorcycle over fifty miles away. It had been stolen by an *Englischer* from another county.

It took some doing on Deputy Aiden's part, but Enoch was eventually released from jail. Unfortunately, the damage was done. Enoch blamed me and the rest of the Amish community for his arrest, and he left the village.

After Enoch left, life at the greenhouse was fractured. My brother made it no secret that he partially blamed me for Enoch's leaving. When I heard that my oldest sister was ill in Michigan and needed twenty-four-hour care, it only made sense to go to her. Edith was old enough at that point to help her father and to keep house for him and work in the greenhouse. She had recently married Moses Hochstetler, who would live at the greenhouse as well. I wasn't needed or wanted any longer. I knew that I had to start over and as the saying goes, "Begin a journey by first deciding on a destination." That's what I did.

I was lucky in some ways that Edith never blamed me for her brother's leaving as her father had. That would have truly crushed me. However, now she was telling me to leave the greenhouse before Enoch returned, and I had to wonder if she had held me responsible all these years. If that were true, I wasn't sure I could recover from it. I was wondering if I had made a terrible mistake coming back to Ohio.

"Is that what you want me to do?" I asked.

"*Ya*," she said. "It's for the best, *Aenti*. I know that Enoch would like to see you eventually."

"Has he said that?"

"*Nee*, not in so many words, but I don't think now is a *gut* time with what has happened. And if you could ask members of the community to stay away too, that would be helpful."

I frowned. "The community will want to gather around you during this difficult time. That is the Amish way." I couldn't understand that part of her request. I knew why she didn't want me there, but why not the rest of the district? Whether someone dies, is hurt, or is just upset, we all come out to show that person compassion and love. Edith knew this. To ask district members to stay away could lead to a misunderstanding, and I wasn't sure how her request would be received by the community. More assumptions would be made.

"Enoch is not ready to see them, and I would prefer not to be overwhelmed by visitors. It took me months to convince Enoch to come stay with me. Too many people might drive him away." She looked at me with tears in her eyes. "After what has happened with Zeke, I so much want my brother to stay and rejoin our family, rejoin

137

our faith. We can't rush it if we're going to have any hope of success. I need him to come back. I'm not sure I can do this alone any longer."

She had a point. Even with the best intentions, the community's enthusiasm for his return might scare Enoch off. People would have many questions about where he had been and what he had been doing over the last ten years. I had those questions too. I'd never expected to see my nephew again and wanted to know how Enoch was. There would be questions too about why he didn't come back when his father died. The community would be caring, but some, like Ruth Yoder, would want answers. I could see now why Edith would like to ease Enoch back into our culture.

"All right." I nodded. "I will do as you ask on both counts."

"*Danki, Aenti*. I know that you must have many questions for Enoch, but please try to hold them back." Tears came to her eyes. "I have missed him so much, especially now that our parents are gone. I'm hoping he will work with me at the greenhouse."

"Would you turn the greenhouse over to him?"

A strange look passed over her face. "I would have to do that if he rejoined the church, wouldn't I? That's the Amish way—the man in the family inherits the property. If I had married before Enoch returned, it wouldn't have been an issue because the business would have gone to my husband. He would have missed his opportunity to reclaim the greenhouse."

I wondered if she realized that she'd just given her brother a motive to murder Zeke. He was in the village when Zeke died. More specifically, he was at the greenhouse. That was opportunity.

Edith shook her head. "I don't think ownership of the business will really be an issue. I doubt that Enoch will want the greenhouse or anything to do with our way of life. I have asked my brother so many times to come back into the fold of the church, but he has no interest in it."

"Does the bishop know that Enoch is back?" I asked. I assumed that Ruth had told her husband, the bishop, the moment she got home from the quilting circle yesterday, but I wanted to know whether Edith knew the word was out that Enoch had returned.

"*Nee*, I don't know for sure, but I think Ruth Yoder would have mentioned it if she had known, don't you?"

Ruth knew Enoch was back, but she had likely been so kerfuffled by the murder and then by my goats, she'd forgotten to question Edith about it. I knew she would soon. Ruth wasn't going to let something like the return of the district's most famous prodigal son go by unnoticed.

"Please go, *Aenti*. Enoch will be here any moment."

I started to open my mouth to argue but stopped myself. For a very long time, I'd wanted to make things right with Enoch but had no way to reach him. Now was my chance—if not today, soon, because I owed my nephew the apology that had been weighing on my heart these last ten years.

Maybe if I could clear Edith's name and find out who'd murdered Zeke, then I would be able to right the wrong I'd done the family. More importantly, I would help Edith. I was the best person to do this. The man who'd run away from the greenhouse was Amish. Deputy Aiden would have a very difficult time finding a faceless Amish man in Holmes County, but I could go places he couldn't, with very little notice. No one would suspect a sweet, older lady like me was poking her nose in where it didn't belong, which was exactly what I intended to do.

CHAPTER FIFTEEN

In an Amish church, services go all day long and sometimes into the early evening. I knew that everyone in the district would still be at the Yoder farm, which meant that Tucker Leham would most likely be there too. I was willing to risk the gossipmongers in order to find out what Tucker knew about Zeke.

I flicked the reins. "Bessie, back to church."

She looked over her broad shoulder at me, as if to ask whether I was serious.

I flicked the reins again. "Come on now. We have a murderer to find. There is no time to waste."

Phillip and Peter ran with me to the end of the driveway and stopped at the road as I had trained them. People said that you can't train goats. You can with lots of patience and sugar cubes, their favorite snack. I would come back later to fetch them. It would give me an excuse to return and hopefully speak with my nephew.

Bessie turned straight ahead and clip-clopped down the county road with renewed vigor.

The congregation was pouring out of the Yoders' farmhouse when my buggy turned up the long driveway. The women from the district began setting out the food for the Sunday meal on long tables in the middle of the front yard. Raellen was the first to notice my buggy. She hurried over to me. Four of her nine children followed in her wake.

I pulled the buggy to a halt and climbed down, tethering Bessie to a free hitching post.

"Millie Fisher, oh my word, I have heard the news, and I can hardly believe it. It's just terrible. A murderer in our district!"

I glanced down at the four little faces behind her skirts and raised my eyebrows. I wasn't going to talk about this in front of the children, and Raellen wanted very much to talk.

"Children, go play," their mother said.

They didn't move.

"Go play! Off with you. Shoo." She waved them away with her hands.

Finally, they turned and ran off, shouting as they went.

Raellen grabbed my hand. "Oh, Millie. This is horrible. The worst thing that could have happened." She made a clicking sound with her tongue. "Have the police arrested Edith yet? What will happen to the children? Perhaps I can talk to my husband about taking them in for a time. What's three more children when you have nine?"

"Raellen, do you think Edith killed Zeke Miller?"

"That's what everyone is saying."

I blinked at her. "Edith didn't kill Zeke."

She dropped my hand. "She didn't?"

I pressed my lips together and an old proverb came to mind. "He who talks to you about others will talk to others about you." As much as I loved Raellen, I knew that was true of my friend and many others in the district.

"Just because everyone is saying it doesn't make it true. How many times do I have to tell you that, Raellen?"

She ran the back of her hand across her forehead. "*Gut.* I am glad to be corrected in this case. Very glad. I like Edith very much and was afraid that I was friends with a killer. My husband would not like that in the least. You know how he can be."

"I would think that most Amish husbands would disapprove of their wives being friends with killers," I said mildly.

She nodded vigorously, completely missing my sarcasm. "So true, Millie, so true."

"I do have a favor to ask you, Raellen."

Her eyes went wide, and she adjusted her glasses on the bridge of her nose. "Anything. You know I always want to help."

"Can you please spread the word that Edith had nothing to do with this murder? She is heartbroken over Zeke's death. It's true that she decided not to marry him, but she cared about him."

Raellen grabbed my hand and squeezed it. "Oh, I know, I know. She must be completely torn up over this, and for it to happen at her greenhouse too. What a horror. I will make sure that everyone knows the truth. You can count on me, Millie." She spun around. "I'll start right now."

I watched her make a beeline for the ladies setting the food out on the tables. Sometimes it worked to a person's advantage to be friends with the biggest gossip in the district. I just had to feed Raellen the right information, and she would take care of the rest.

I scanned the members of the district, taking time to examine each of the young men. Was one of them the man I'd seen running away from the greenhouse? I examined their manners and movements to see if they reminded me of the figure chased down by the goats. I couldn't make the identification by their clothing. All the young men wore plain trousers and shirts. Some wore suspenders and some went without, and most wore broad-brimmed black felt hats. There wasn't enough variety in the attire to tell the difference between them at a distance, and surely not at the distance I had seen the young man at the greenhouse. I didn't see any of them with a missing piece of their trousers that might have been ripped away by my rascally goats.

Ruth was standing at the long serving table when she spotted me. I gave her a smile and was more than a little relieved when a church member stopped her before she could come my way. I had come to find Tucker Leham and find out what he knew. I couldn't do that with Ruth following me around the farm.

Tucker wasn't with the main group of young men who were lollygagging around the barn. They laughed and clapped each other on the shoulder while the womenfolk got the meal ready. Nor did I see him with the older men who sat on the front porch or with the handful of thoughtful men who were helping the ladies set the table. My Kip would have been with that last group. He never saw much use in loitering when there was work to be done, even work that most in the district would have said was more suited for a woman.

Even from yards away, I felt the women at the table staring at me. Some dabbed at their eyes with handkerchiefs. Even the men, young and old, looked my way and whispered. I felt as nervous as I had been as a young woman when I stepped in front of the church to be baptized into the faith.

Maybe Tucker had left. I felt my heart sink. I could go to his home, but I wasn't certain where he lived. If I started asking around, soon he and others in the district would know that I was looking for him.

I didn't know what I was thinking when I decided I was going to find out who'd killed Zeke Miller. I was an Amish matchmaker and quilter, not a detective.

I had turned to walk through the back door of the kitchen when a young man came rushing out and nearly knocked me onto my backside. Even more shocking, it was the person I had been looking for all this time, Tucker Leham.

"I'm so sorry," Tucker said quickly. "I didn't . . ." Whatever else he was planning to say died on his lips as he saw that it was me he'd run into. "Millie!"

"Just the person I was looking for." I patted my prayer cap to make sure it hadn't been knocked out of place.

His eyes went wide. "You were looking for me? Why?" He looked back and forth with a panicked expression on his face.

"Because I need to talk to you."

"I—I don't know why."

I put my hands on my hips, hoping that I sounded as stern as Ruth Yoder when she was riled up. "I think you do know why. It's about Zeke Miller."

His eyes rolled around in their sockets as he looked for a means of escape. He wouldn't just walk away from me. He'd been brought up to be respectful of his elders, for which I was grateful.

I put him out of his misery. "What do you know about Zeke?" I asked.

"I don't know anything about him."

"Lying is not something that becomes you, Tucker, and I have never known you to lie. What do you know about Zeke? This morning you stopped me when I was leaving to ask if Edith was going to marry him. When I said that she wasn't, you said that was *gut*. It seems to me that you have information about Zeke that you were going to tell Edith had she still planned to marry him."

Tucker stopped looking around the grounds. Behind him, I could see the cluster of young men at the barn. They noticed Tucker and me standing there together and whispered to each other. I guessed that they were wondering what a young gardener and an old matchmaker could be talking about, or perhaps, knowing what had happened to Zeke, they knew exactly what we were discussing.

"What do you know, Tucker? Tell me that, and I will leave you be."

He shifted back and forth on his feet. His work boots were scuffed and stained from countless hours working in the greenhouse, doing a job that he no longer had. I knew that I would have asked him about losing his job as well, but I didn't think that was the information he'd wanted to share with Edith. She already knew.

He cleared his throat. "I'm glad that Edith is not going to marry Zeke. I'm sorry he is dead, but I was happy about that."

"There must be a reason why you feel that way . . ." I trailed off. "Did you know Zeke well?"

"Well enough to know that he wasn't right

for Edith." His lip curled in disgust. "He was completely the wrong person for her. She's too kind and sweet to be with a man like that. He would have squashed her spirit. He was just . . ." He trailed off.

"He was just what?" I prompted.

He started to walk away from me. "It doesn't matter."

I stepped in front of him. "It does matter; it matters a lot."

He wouldn't look at me.

I lowered my voice. "I don't think you want me to make a scene, especially with that group of young men from the district watching us, but I need your help. If you know something, you have to tell me."

"*Nee*, I don't." He stepped around me.

"Don't you care about Edith?" I threw out.

He stopped in his tracks and turned to face me. "*Ya*, of course I do. I care more for her than . . ." He stopped himself and glanced over his shoulder at the young men.

Now they were making no secret of openly watching us. I knew I had to make this quick before one of them walked over and asked what was going on. "I know you care about Edith," I said quietly, turning my body away from the group of men. "I can see it on your face anytime her name is mentioned."

He clenched and unclenched his fists, but I

wasn't afraid. I knew he wouldn't hurt me when so many people were watching us. Truthfully, even if we'd been alone, I still wouldn't be worried that Tucker would resort to violence. He was a *gut* young man. But regardless of his demeanor, at one cry from me, the entire district would come running. I realized with the nosy group of young men looking on, this was the perfect place to talk to someone who might just have a motive for murder.

"Zeke shouldn't have tried to marry her," Tucker said. "He had no right to ask such a *gut* woman to marry him. He wasn't a man worthy of a woman like Edith Hochstetler. He never even tried to prove that he was. He continued with his corrupt life even after she was betrothed to him."

"Corrupt life?" I asked with a shiver. "What do you mean by that?"

He curled his hands.

My brow went up at Tucker's emotions. "Tucker, is there something you know about Zeke? Something that could have gotten him into enough trouble to get him killed? You have to understand that I am asking you this because I care for Edith too. She's in a lot of trouble."

His brows went up. "What do you mean?"

"What do you think I mean? The police think she killed Zeke in order to escape marrying him."

"She would never do that!" he shouted. I winced and could not resist looking at the group of young men. They had inched closer to us. They were about halfway between where we stood behind the house and the barn. I thought they were still too far away to hear what we were saying as long as we kept our voices down, which meant no more shouts from Tucker.

"Give me a reason that someone else would then," I said in a measured voice.

"There is only one reason that makes any sense."

"And what's that?" I asked.

"He had another woman on the side." Tucker's face turned bright red as he said this.

"On the side? What does that mean?"

"He had another girlfriend who wasn't Edith." His face grew even redder. "He always had a woman or two waiting in the wings for him. He was handsome and a charming man. He couldn't have been more different from me," he said quietly.

I ignored his comment about himself. "And who was this other woman? Is she a member of this district or another nearby district?"

"Neither."

"Then what?" I asked, growing more frustrated by the second.

"She's *Englisch*."

CHAPTER SIXTEEN

I stared at Tucker for a long moment. He could have told me that the woman had two heads, and I wouldn't have been more surprised. For all his faults and mistakes, the one thing I knew about Zeke Miller was he was committed to being Amish. He was baptized in the faith and active in the district. As such, he couldn't have a romantic relationship with an *Englischer* even if he weren't already engaged to my niece.

"Who is she?" I wanted to know.

Tucker looked away. "I don't know." By the way he said it, I knew he was lying. He knew exactly who Zeke's *Englisch* girlfriend was, and he knew where to find her too. This was information I needed because *I* very much wanted to find her. She could be the reason that Zeke was dead. He'd been killed with a stone to the head. Either a woman or man could have done it. If she'd caught Zeke off guard, she could have killed him before he even knew what was happening.

I shivered to think what Ruth would say about the thoughts going through my head. She'd believe they weren't becoming of an Amish woman, and she would be right. The truth was they weren't becoming of anyone, man or woman. *Englisch* or Amish. They were dark ideas that I wished circumstances hadn't forced me to have.

"Don't you want to help Edith?"

He frowned. "I do. I would do anything for her if she would let me. She doesn't even know how much I care, or she pretends that she doesn't."

Oh, that was a whole other "can of worms," as the *Englisch* said. I'd not even acknowledge his comment about Edith pretending not to know of his affection. That was a conversation for a different day—a day when Edith wasn't a suspect in a murder. I took a deep breath and kept my voice calm. "So who is the *Englisch* girl?"

"I don't know her name."

I sensed he was waffling and was ready to tell me, so I waited.

"I've only seen her in the village. She works downtown, near the square."

"Where?" I asked. It was clear to me that Tucker was going to make me pry the information from him. He certainly wasn't proving to be very forthcoming on his own.

He didn't say anything.

"Where, Tucker?" My voice become more forceful.

"The Sunbeam Café in Harvest," he said finally.

I felt a gasp rise in my throat, but I tamped it down. "The Sunbeam Café?" I asked as if I'd never heard of it, but of course I knew it. It was the place where I had seen my childhood friend Lois Henry.

"It just opened last month, right after Easter. The girl I have seen with Zeke works there. I have noticed her behind the counter when I walked by."

"What does she look like?" I wanted to make sure that I had the right girl. And, yes, I had strong suspicions about who the woman was. The tray she dropped on the floor when the quilting circle was talking about Edith and Zeke was telling. But I didn't want to walk in and accuse the wrong person of having a love affair with an Amish man, and truth be told, I very much wanted to be wrong.

"She's not Amish, I can tell you that. She has curly blond hair and big blue eyes. She wears *Englischer* clothes. I don't know much beyond that. Her hair is very, very curly, so if you go there, you will know who she is right away. I've never seen hair like it."

As I feared, he'd described Lois's granddaughter Darcy to a T. I tried to hide the disappointment on my face.

He shifted his stance. "If you talk to her, leave me out of it. I've told you everything I know."

I wasn't certain I believed that he'd told me everything he knew, but I nodded.

He swallowed and his Adam's apple bobbed up and down. "You have to understand, I would do anything for Edith. Anything. I've told her that so many times, but she doesn't listen. She has always been distracted by other men. She never notices the one who is right in front of her."

I knew this was true about my niece as well, but I said nothing because I wondered if Tucker really meant that he would do anything for Edith. If that were true, did it include killing for her? I prayed I was wrong. I thanked him for the information and walked away, not looking at the whispering young men as I went.

As I was leaving the Yoder farm, Ruth stopped me. Even though the potluck was in full swing, I suppose it was too much to hope that I would make a clean getaway.

"Millie Fisher, you can't go skulking around my farm and not say hello to me. It's childish and rude."

"I wasn't skulking, Ruth. I'm sorry if you were offended, but I saw you were busy trying to get the potluck under control, and I didn't want to interrupt you. The spread looks delectable, by the way. I hope everyone enjoys my Bundt cake. It's lemon poppy seed."

She put her hands on her hips the way she normally did when she was perturbed. "Don't you go changing the subject! I know you tend to do that when you don't like what is being discussed."

I didn't argue with her on that point but realized that I would have to change my tactics when arguing with Ruth if she was on to some of my tricks. I couldn't have that. I needed to keep my strategies fresh. She was a worthy competitor when it came to wit.

"What did you want to talk to Tucker Leham about?" she asked.

"What do you think?" I asked. "I was asking him if he might have seen Zeke yesterday before he passed on. Tucker did work at the greenhouse."

She harrumphed. "And did he?"

"He didn't say," I said.

Because I didn't ask the question, but I thought I'd keep that tidbit to myself. I wanted to kick myself for being so distracted by Tucker's revelation that Darcy was Zeke's *Englisch* girl-friend that it had completely slipped my mind.

"Well, this is just terrible. We need to take care of this as soon as possible."

"Who's *we?*" I asked. "And what's *this?*" I asked with more than a little trepidation. I had a feeling I wasn't going to like what I was about to hear.

"*We* is Double Stitch, and *this* is the murder."

I blinked at her. "The quilting circle?"

"*Ya.*" She nodded as if it made perfect sense. "Double Stitch is a group of women from all over the district. We are all different ages. We all see different things. If we put our heads together, we might be able to figure out what happened to Zeke Miller."

Actually, I realized, it wasn't a terrible idea. She was right about the fact that we all came from different corners of the district, and I couldn't shake the feeling that this was a very Amish murder. Even so, I could see from a mile away the problems Ruth's plan would cause. Raellen was a terrible gossip. Whatever anyone said at the circle would be repeated. Ruth was terribly judgmental, and I wasn't sure I was up for her criticism of Edith.

However, Ruth didn't give me a chance to voice my opinion; instead, she went on to say, "Of course, today is Sunday, so nothing more can be done now. However, I have told the other ladies that we will be having an emergency meeting of Double Stitch at your house. I will let you know when it will be."

"Nice of you to call a meeting in my home without asking me," I muttered.

"It's for your own *gut*, Millie Fisher, and the *gut* of your family. You should be thanking me. I'll talk to Iris in particular."

I raised my brow.

"Her husband, Carter, worked with Zeke at the same construction company. He might have some information that we can use."

I had forgotten that. "Thank you, Ruth," I said ironically. "Was there anything else?"

Her brow shot up in surprise.

"*Gut*, if not, I'm going to go home. I hate to miss fellowship, but this has been a very trying day and I need to lie down."

She stepped back and let me go. Ruth was never one to argue with a need for a nap. She took one every day. "We'll see you soon then."

I nodded.

CHAPTER SEVENTEEN

The next day, I couldn't concentrate on my chores or quilting. I was too preoccupied with the previous day's events, and the goats weren't home to distract me either. I knew that I couldn't sit idly by. I had to go to the Sunbeam Café and speak to Darcy myself.

By horse and buggy it took me almost an hour to travel from my farm on the outskirts of the village to the village center. It was afternoon and the shops and square were bubbling with activity as people went in and out of the businesses. Tourists bustled about carrying shopping bags, and it seemed to me that Swissmen Sweets, the cheese shop, and the pretzel shop were getting the most business. Across the square from where I stood, I saw redheaded Charlotte Weaver standing outside of Swissmen Sweets passing out free samples of fudge. Seeing her reminded me that I needed to tell the candy makers that Edith's wedding was off, and we would no longer be in need of a wedding cake. I was sure that they would already have heard that news, but out of respect, I needed to tell them myself. But first, I wanted to talk to Darcy. I couldn't get what I had learned about the girl off my mind.

I tied up my buggy in the parking lot between

the church and the village playground. The café was only a few yards away.

I patted the star on Bessie's forehead. "You will be my escape horse if this goes terribly wrong."

She fluttered her long eyelashes at me, and I walked out of the parking lot.

The big white church was the largest building in Harvest, so the *Englisch* pastor, Reverend Brook, allowed it to be used for a community meeting place as well, and any time there was any kind of special event on the square, the crown jewel of the village, the church was where things were stored and planned.

Outside the church, I saw Juliet Brody, Deputy Aiden's mother, working in the garden. Her black and white polka-dotted potbellied pig Jethro was snoozing next to her in the grass. She waved at me. "Hello, Millie! What brings you to the village on this beautiful day?" She tucked a marigold plant into the ground and piled topsoil around it.

I walked over to her. As soon as I was within three feet, Jethro got up and started to snuffle my shoes. I wondered if he smelled the goats. "Good afternoon, Juliet. I was just out for a drive on this lovely spring day."

Juliet looked up at the sky. "It is lovely, isn't it? The perfect day to plant—that's what I told Reverend Brook. I know it's a bit early, but I could not resist putting a few flowers in. I bought these from Edy's Greenhouse. I only purchased a few flats but will most certainly be going back." She stood and removed her gloves, and I saw the large diamond ring on her left hand from her fiancé Reverend Brook.

"When's the wedding?" I asked.

"July Fourth weekend. Doesn't that sound lovely? We'll celebrate our marriage with fireworks!" She clasped her hands against her chest as if the very idea stopped her heart.

"That's less than two months away," I mused.

She nodded. "It doesn't give me much time to plan, but my maid of honor, Bailey, has been such a dear. She's done so much of the work to keep me organized. I keep telling her when she and Aiden get married, it will be a piece of cake, and, seeing how good she is with sweets, it will be even easier for her. I almost look forward to that day as much as my own wedding. I can't wait until we are all a real family. It will be positively perfect."

Jethro lay by the flat of marigolds. He sniffed them.

"Ummm, I think the pig might eat your plants," I warned.

She laughed. "Don't be silly. Jethro would never do that. He knows what is food and what is not. He is a wonderfully well-mannered pig."

I wasn't as sure that was the case when Jethro buried his nose in one of the blossoms.

"Is everything at the greenhouse all right?" Juliet asked.

I turned my attention away from the pig and back to her. "What do you mean?"

She waved at me with her purple polka-dotted garden gloves, which matched her long-sleeved dress. "I'm sure it was nothing, but Edith seemed so distracted and worried when I was there."

"When were you there?" I asked.

"Friday morning."

Well before the murder, I thought.

"I had some questions to ask her about taking care of the shrubs we bought from her for the church last year," Juliet said. "And I got the distinct feeling that she was trying to get rid of me. She kept looking over my shoulder as if she was searching for someone else."

"Was anyone else there?" I asked. "Was she worried about another customer?"

She shrugged. "Not that I could see. I was the only customer, and it was during the school day, so the only child there was her little girl and she was quietly playing with some blocks in the front yard."

I pressed my lips together. This was bother-some. It wasn't like Edith to ignore a customer. She was lucky that Juliet was such an easygoing one and had been buying plants from Edy's Greenhouse for years. I wasn't afraid that Edith would lose Juliet as a customer, but I was concerned she'd been so distracted by some-thing and someone else that she'd ignored Juliet's questions. This was before Zeke's death, so was she worried about breaking up her engagement or something else, something that would lead to Zeke's death?

"I also found it strange that I was the only customer there. Usually this time of year the greenhouse is bustling with shoppers. Doesn't everyone have to buy flowers for spring planting? It can't just be me, can it? I distinctly remember going there last year and seeing many more people shopping, and now that I think about it, I saw many more people working there too. However, the day I went, it was just Edith and me, and the little girl too, I suppose."

I bit the inside of my lip. What had been going on at my niece's greenhouse that would cause such a drop in business? I had to think Zeke was behind it. Why, when I could only assume he wanted to marry Edith for control of the greenhouse, would he do anything that might threaten the business? It didn't make any sense to me at all.

Juliet squeezed her gloves in her hands as if she was saying a prayer. "Oh, I can tell that I have upset you. I'm certain it's nothing to worry about. She's such a sweet girl, and her children are darling. I would hate for anything bad to happen. She's been so brave and strong since her husband died." She shook her head. "Terrible tragedy. I hate to see drugs in any community, but to know that they have even reached the Amish, that is somehow more heartbreaking. I just don't think your community has the resources in place to deal with such a problem."

I made no comment on this. But I didn't want Juliet to think my niece had been acting oddly. It was clear to me that she hadn't heard about Zeke's murder yet. If she had, she would have said something about it. Gossip about his death was running through the Amish community like wildfire, and I was relieved to know it hadn't gotten so widespread as to cross over to the *Englischers* just yet.

I smiled. "I'm sure it was just the pressure of the growing season that was distracting her. This is the busiest season for the greenhouse. I would guess that she was waiting for a delivery of more flowers when you arrived. That's the most likely reason she was looking over her shoulder. Also," I went on, "there are lulls throughout the day at any business. You must have just hit the greenhouse at a slow time. That would explain why no one else was around."

She loosened the stranglehold on her garden gloves. "Yes, that must be it. I'm sure you are right. That's such a relief to hear."

It was time to change the subject, I thought. "Have you been to the new café in the village?"

"Oh, you must mean the Sunbeam Café. Yes, it opened right after Easter. It is adorable. Jethro and I love the quiche they make here."

"You take Jethro into the café?" I asked.

"Of course. He comes with me everywhere." She smiled. "The café is really darling. You should visit while you're here."

"I might just do that," I said, and then I looked down. Jethro had his head buried in the flat of marigolds and was chomping away. "Oh dear!"

"What?" Juliet asked and then she yelped. "Jethro!"

The pig froze.

Juliet put her hands on her hips. "Oh, Jethro! How could you?"

The pig looked up at her with big brown eyes, and marigold petals hanging from his lips.

Juliet laughed. "How can I stay mad at that face?"

I had no idea.

CHAPTER EIGHTEEN

I said my good-byes to Juliet and her pig and walked beyond the church, past the newly renovated playground to the Sunbeam Café. The bright yellow sun painted on the side of the building was cheerful, as was the yellow awning, but I wasn't feeling cheerful. Just days ago, I had been reunited with my childhood friend for the first time in nearly twenty years, and now I considered her granddaughter a murder suspect? That was no way to rekindle a friendship.

I straightened my shoulders and went into the café. A bell jingled when I entered. Today, the only guest in the café was the man that I had seen previously, clicking away on his laptop. I had arrived between the breakfast and lunch rush.

"You drink up that coffee. Seems to me you have a lot of writing to do," Lois said to the man sitting by the window.

I had noticed him the day before, but I hadn't looked at him carefully. He had close-cropped hair, wore jeans, and was very tall. I could see that by the way he had to tilt his legs so that they would fit under the table. He had a plain face and utterly forgettable features. This was probably why I didn't remember the details of his appearance from the day before.

"Millie Fisher, I didn't expect to see you again so soon!" Lois said and set her coffeepot on an empty table nearby. "I was kicking myself that I didn't get your phone number—I assume you have access to a shed phone somehow—or your address before you left, and here you are in the flesh."

I smiled. "It's good to see you again."

"I am so glad to see you. I wasn't sure if Ruth would let you all come back here to host another quilting circle. I was going to reach out to ask you to visit whenever you might be free."

"Oh, I'm sure that we will be back with the quilting circle," I said with a smile. "Ruth doesn't have veto power over the rest of us, even though she might think she does."

"When we were children and Ruth agreed to play with us, she thought she had veto power over our games too."

"She was wrong then too," I said with a grin.

She laughed. "Darn right."

She pointed at the man with the laptop. "Bryan, you good?" She held up her thumb at him.

"I'm fine, Lois. I'm just grappling with these characters that don't want to listen to me."

I must have had an inquisitive look on my face because Lois said, "Bryan Shell is a writer and is currently at work on the great American novel— right, Bryan?"

The writer held up his thumb at her this time

but never looked up from his computer screen.

"He's been here almost every day since we opened last month," Lois said to me. "He's a nice young man." She ushered me forward. "Enough about that. Take a seat, take a seat. I'm tickled that you came back and left Ruth Yoder behind this time." She shook her head. "That woman! Is she just as judgmental as she was when we were younger?"

"More now, I would think. She's older and she happens to be the bishop's wife."

Lois laughed. "The bishop's wife? There will be no stopping her now."

Lois didn't know the half of it.

"Do you still like your coffee black with no sugar, cream, or flavor?" she asked.

I nodded.

"Well, you're not getting it today." She shook her glittery pink-tipped finger at me. "You are going to have one of Darcy's mochas. She taught me how to make it. Don't you worry—it's delicious!"

I opened my mouth to protest. From what I remembered Lois was as terrible a cook as her mother had been. She grew up on TV dinners or ate at my house when we were children.

"No, I'm not taking no for an answer. There is nothing un-Amish about a mocha." She paused. "You're not diabetic, are you?"

I shook my head and sat down at the table closest to the counter.

"Good. You look fit as ever, must be that clean Amish living. You haven't rounded out like I have, but seeing that I'm a grandmother, I don't mind having a little extra weight on my hips. It gives me grandma cred. You look like you could use something to eat. My granddaughter makes the best vegetable soup you've ever tasted. I'd challenge any Amish cook to claim that she makes a better one. You need a large bowl of that and some crusty bread. You look like you have the weight of the world on your shoulders." Her face broke into a smile. "We didn't have a chance to catch up! And our reunion is twenty years in the making—I've missed you, Millie!"

I felt something catch me in the throat. I had missed her too. I'd thought of her often over the years.

She clapped her hands. "But we need to feed you before we get down to business."

Business? What business could we be getting down to? As happy as I was to see her again, she didn't know why I was really there, to talk to her granddaughter about Zeke Miller. Before I could ask, she disappeared around the counter and through the door into what I guessed was the kitchen. I sat there for a moment, trying to process all that had happened in the last three minutes.

Lois, that's what happened. I never thought for a moment when moving back to Ohio that I would see Lois again. The last I heard she'd moved to Cleveland. The last time I had seen her had been at my husband's funeral twenty years ago. After Kip died, my family circled around me, pushing everyone else away. I had been in too much shock to argue with them. By the time I came out of my fog, Lois had moved away, and no one could tell me where she had gone. I had been devastated because I thought I'd lost my friend forever, but here she was again many years later.

I smoothed the swirl-covered tablecloth on the table. There had been many times in the last few years that I'd wondered what had happened to my childhood friend. I regretted not having tried harder to find her in all these years.

I glanced around the café. Bryan was hunched over his laptop computer as if his very life depended on whatever he was doing. Seeing his dependence on electronics, I was happy that wasn't a concern in my own life. There were many perks to being Amish, and no computers, in my opinion, was one of them.

"This will fix you right up," Lois said as she came through the door from the kitchen, carrying a tray with a huge bowl of soup and two of the largest coffee mugs I'd ever seen. They were dripping whipped cream from the sides.

I squinted at the concoction. "That looks more like a dessert than a beverage."

"That's the idea!" Lois said with a smile and

set the tray in the middle of the table. "Also, Darcy was back there and made the mocha for you." She wagged her finger at me again. "I saw the look on your face when I said I was going to make it. You panicked. Truth be told, my cooking hasn't improved a whit. I help Darcy out in the café, but mostly stick to taking the orders and cleaning. I leave the culinary arts to her. Who knew I would have a granddaughter who was a good enough cook to open up her own café? It boggles the mind."

"Do you have other grandchildren?" I asked.

"Darcy is the only one I have. After my disastrous marriage to Rocksino-man, I decided to come back to my roots and help Darcy open this café." She moved the items from the tray onto the table. "Not that she needed much help. My Darcy has a good head on her shoulders when it comes to business."

"I am so happy to see you," I said. "It's been twenty years. I'm surprised you recognized me after all this time."

She laughed. "Oh, Millie, you are funny. We might be a wee bit older, but I would recognize you anywhere. It's not like your style of dress has changed." She laughed at her own joke.

I felt myself relax. "It hasn't. Neither has yours."

She patted the top of her aggressively lacquered hair, and it barely moved. "When you find something that works for you, why change? That's what I always say." She settled back in her seat. "I am happy to see you too, my friend. I have thought of you often over the years. Mostly wondered what you would think I made of my life. When I came back to the village, I asked after you but heard you'd moved away."

I nodded. "I moved back to Harvest this winter. I was in Michigan caring for a dear sister. She passed on," I said sadly.

"I'm sorry to hear that. Which sister?"

"Harriet."

"How sad. She was my favorite of your sisters."

"Mine too." I shook my head, not wanting to dwell on sad things.

Lois removed the glasses from the top of her head and perched them on her nose. "Now you tuck into the food. The chocolate in the mocha is from the candy shop on the other side of the square, so you know it's good."

"Swissmen Sweets?"

"You know it?" she asked.

"Everyone in Holmes County knows it."

"It's just delightful, and it's a quick walk from the café. I can walk around the square, burn calories and earn them back with a bit of fudge. As long as I break even, I'm doing just fine."

I chuckled. "I don't think one quick walk around the square is going to cancel out a piece of fudge from Swissmen Sweets."

She sniffed, but she was still smiling. "Don't you mess with my delusion, Millie Fisher."

I grinned. "That's not the first time you've said that to me." When we were girls, I always was the one who brought Lois's fantasies back to reality. She dreamed about being a movie star or traveling to faraway places like Egypt. I always asked her how she would do those things. In return, she always said, "Don't you mess with my delusions, Millie Lapp." It had been a running joke between us ever since.

Oh, how good it felt to share jokes with an old friend again.

"I have no doubt that you will succeed in all you want, Lois, by sheer force of will."

She blew on her mocha, and a light spray of whipped cream dusted the top of the table. She grabbed a napkin and cleaned it up. "I need to keep everything as neat as a pin around here. Darcy is a ball of nerves. Margot Rawlings from the town council is supposed to drop by the café any day to take a look at things. You know how nitpicky that woman can be. She hasn't changed in forty years. She's much like Ruth Yoder in that way."

Ruth complained about Margot's vision for the village often. Margot wanted to make it more of a tourist destination, and Ruth didn't want to lose the true Amish essence that Harvest had. They were constantly at odds.

"Go on, go on and try the mocha before it gets cold. The soup too. You shouldn't be sitting there waiting for an invitation." She picked up her own mug.

I took a sip of the mocha. It tasted just as I imagined it would. Chocolate and sugar to the nth degree. It was delicious, but I felt I would need a nap right after drinking it.

The vegetable soup was soothing and warm, and Lois was right—it was just what I needed with the state I was in. The beef and vegetables plus the crusty bread warmed me all the way through. I had come to the café to find Zeke's *Englisch* girlfriend and instead I was having a delicious meal while chatting with my childhood friend and possibly getting a sugar overdose from her killer mocha.

"I'm sorry we lost touch all those years ago," I said between bites.

"Me too. I thought about you often, but life has a way of getting away from us. And it's not like you can watch my updates on Facebook."

"Facebook?" I wrinkled my nose.

"It's on the Internet."

I knew that there was such a thing as the Internet, but I had no interest in it.

"I'm so glad that Raellen suggested our café for your quilting circle. I guess we were destined to see each other again," Lois said.

The soup and mocha mingled in my stomach

and I felt ill. It pained me that Lois was so excited to see me and catch up when I was there to confront Darcy about her relationship with Zeke. I felt I was betraying her in some way. I didn't know how to start the conversation either. How did I ask my dear friend such a thing about her only grandchild?

I took a deep breath. "Lois," I began just as Darcy stepped into the main room from the kitchen. She was tall with wide-set green eyes. She had a wide mouth that I guessed would turn into a beautiful smile, though she wasn't smiling at that moment. The feature I noticed most, though, was her hair. It was shoulder length, blond, and incredibly curly, just as Tucker had described and just as I remembered it.

"Grandma," Darcy said, "I hate to ask this, but can you run to the store for cheese? The grilled cheese sandwiches have been our most popular item, and I'm not sure I can wait until morning to restock. What if Margot Rawlings wants a grilled cheese sandwich? That could just be the thing that ruins me." Darcy of the beautiful blond curls smiled at me. "I'm sorry to interrupt. My grandmother said that an old friend was here. I never expected for her friend to be Amish."

I turned to face her head on, and she grew pale. "You!" She pointed at me and then burst into tears.

CHAPTER NINETEEN

L ois stared at me. "What have you done to my granddaughter?"

"Nothing, I just saw her for the first time at Saturday's Double Stitch meeting."

Through her tears, Darcy said, "I've seen you with her! I thought I recognized you the other day, but I wasn't sure. Then when you all started talking about Zeke, I had to leave, but now that I see you today, I'm sure. I know who you are!"

"What on earth are you talking about, Darcy?" Lois jumped out of her seat, and then before Darcy could answer, she added, "Millie Fisher was my neighbor growing up. We were friends as children. How can you know her?"

"She—She—" Darcy couldn't get the words out.

"I'm sure this is some kind of mistake." Lois smiled at me. "You know how the Amish can all look the same to *Englischers* like us. I remember us joking about that when we were kids, don't you?"

I didn't think it was a mistake at all. I thought Darcy knew exactly who I was even though I had never met her before, and it had something to do with Edith.

"Darcy!" Lois yelled. "Snap out of it!"

Darcy's mouth shaped an O.

Lois smiled at me. "It was the same tactic I had to use with husband number two, who was Darcy's grandfather and also a crier. Tough love comes in handy from time to time."

Darcy sniffled.

"Now," Lois said in a much more soothing voice, "please tell us why you think you know Millie."

Darcy looked as if she might start crying again, but Lois was having none of it. "I promise you can cry all you want when we are done with the conversation, but first you have to let us know what is going on."

Darcy took a ragged breath. "I saw her with that woman who Zeke promised he wouldn't marry because he loved me more. I was such a fool. How could I believe that a man would leave his whole world, his whole life behind for me? I have never been worth so much to any man before. I was kidding myself to think it was like that for Zeke."

There was a scraping sound over the hardwood floor. I glanced behind me and saw Bryan adjusting his seat but still staring at his laptop.

Lois shook her finger at her granddaughter. "Don't you go and speak like that about yourself. You're an amazing woman and are worth all the love in the world. Just because some man doesn't see that, you shouldn't think less of yourself. He probably has all sorts of issues. In fact, I wouldn't be surprised if his—"

"Can you tell us who you saw me with, Darcy?" I asked her, cutting off Lois. I had a feeling that she wanted to say something about Zeke that an Amish woman in good standing shouldn't hear. Lois, even when we were younger, had been prone to be very descriptive when she didn't like a person, and of course, she wouldn't like the man who'd broken her only grandchild's heart.

"I—I saw you," Darcy managed to say. "Outside of the greenhouse. You were with her, the woman he was going to marry. Edith."

Lois gasped and then covered her mouth as if stifling her reaction in loyalty to her grand-daughter. I could understand her feelings, but my face fell as I wondered whether Darcy had known all along that Zeke was engaged to another woman. What could he have said to make her believe that being with him was the right thing to do, or had she known it wasn't, but had done it anyway? Either scenario made me impossibly sad for Edith and for Darcy. My sympathy for Zeke was far less, at least in this regard.

When I'd entered the café I had wondered how I was going to bring up Zeke to Lois. It seemed that I had worried for nothing.

"When was this?" I asked.

"Last Wednesday or Thursday." She sat at the table. "I can't remember when. I have been in a fog ever since and thrown myself into my work and into the café. To make matters worse, Margot Rawlings said that she is going to come to the café any day to try the food, and yet she never comes. The suspense is killing me." She looked at her grandmother. "That's why I need the cheese, Grandma. What if Margot orders a grilled cheese because she has heard how great they are and I don't have any cheese? I will be ruined. I can't come back from that. If Margot likes the café, I stand to do a lot of business here on the village square because she handpicks the vendors for all the events. If she doesn't like what I have to offer, she will never hire Sunbeam Café. My business will go down the drain before it even starts, and after losing Zeke, I will have nothing left!"

"You're starting to spiral, girl. Keep it together," Lois said.

Darcy sniffled.

Lois held up her finger. "Fight it. Fight it. No crying until we are able to get the whole story, and I will get your cheese, dear. Don't you worry about that."

"What did you mean when you said that you lost Zeke?" I asked. My fingers had grown very cold. Did she already know he was dead? Was this pretty yet high-strung young *Englisch* woman sitting across from me actually a killer? I prayed it wasn't true, for Lois's sake. I might not have seen my friend in years, but I didn't want her granddaughter to be guilty of such a terrible crime even if it saved my niece from the heartache of going through the police investigation into her relationship with Zeke Miller.

"Well, when I saw you on that day—" she began.

"If I was there, it must have been Wednesday. That was the only day during the week that I was at the greenhouse."

Typically, if I didn't have anything else to do, I would help my niece out on Wednesdays at the greenhouse because the middle of the week was the busiest day for Edith. Lots of bus tours arrived in Holmes County on Wednesdays and many of those buses carried avid gardeners who wanted to know all the Amish secrets for gardening. The truth was, we didn't have any gardening secrets that *Englischers* didn't also know, like using coffee grounds in the soil or pruning in the early fall for better spring growth. The only difference was patience. The Amish were experts on patience. We had to be. We moved through life at a purposely slower pace than the *Englischers*.

I tried to think back to last Wednesday to see if I could remember seeing a curly-haired blond woman. I couldn't, but I wasn't that surprised I didn't remember her. It made sense that Darcy might have seen us without our noticing. Thinking back to the day, I realized how quiet the greenhouse had been. I knew now it was because the business wasn't doing well, and most of the staff was gone. When I'd asked about it, Edith just said it was a lull in the day. At the time, I took her word for it, but it did strike me as odd.

"Who is this Zeke Miller character?" Lois wanted to know.

"He's a member of my district. He and my niece, Edith Hochstetler, were engaged." I didn't say a word about the broken engagement, but it wouldn't be long before Darcy heard about that too. The Amish grapevine was fast, and the biggest news—like the death of a district member—would eventually spill over into gossip in the *Englisch* community. *Nee*, I thought, it wouldn't be long before Darcy knew Zeke was dead.

Darcy gripped my hand. "Were engaged? They aren't anymore?"

I winced. By using the past tense in my sentence, I had made a mistake. I wasn't sure how to answer her question. It was true that Edith had called off the engagement before Zeke died, but should I tell her that? Luckily, I didn't have to think of an answer because Lois refused to be ignored.

Lois wrinkled her brow. "If Zeke is Amish, how did you even meet him?"

"I don't know where to begin," Darcy said. "It was before you moved back to the village, Grandma. I was driving my pickup truck loaded with supplies for the café. I had boards and paint, and the truck was full to the gills. I had spent all my money on the café, every last cent, so I didn't have any money for a good truck. I bought a clunker, but I thought I would be able to get by with it until I had enough money earned back from the café. Then I'd buy something better. I was two miles from the village on an abandoned county road when the truck broke down. To make matters worse, I'd forgotten to charge my phone. I was stranded. Just when I was about to leave the truck and start walking, an Amish buggy pulled up alongside me." Tears sprang to her eyes. "It was Zeke. He offered his help. I told him that I could use a ride to the nearest auto shop, but he said that he could fix my truck."

Lois wrinkled her nose. "An Amish man could fix your truck?"

"A lot of young Amish know things about cars and how to fix them. It doesn't surprise me so much," I said. "It wouldn't be unheard of even if Zeke owned his own car while he was in *rumspringa*. Once he was baptized into the church, he would have needed to give the car up."

"Yes." Darcy nodded. "That's what he said. He offered to try to fix the car himself, and, since I was so low on cash, I didn't think I could argue with a Good Samaritan. So I let him try, but I told him if he couldn't fix the vehicle, then all I needed was a ride into town. He agreed. As he worked on the truck, he asked me about all the supplies in the back. I told him about the café, and he said that he was impressed a woman like me wanted to start her own business. That wasn't very common in his culture. I've lived in Holmes County my whole life, but he was so different from the other Amish I knew. Also, I couldn't help noticing how handsome he was even in plain dress."

"Even in plain dress," Lois snorted. "My girl, you are acting like the Amish are from another planet when they are some of our closest neighbors."

"I know that," she said. "But I'm just trying to show you that Zeke was different. He was different from any man, Amish or English, I'd ever known." She swallowed. "After he fixed the truck, he offered to lend a hand at the café while everything was under construction. He said he worked in construction and could be a great help. I turned down his offer and told him that I couldn't pay him. I had spent my last dime on supplies to do the work. He said he wasn't looking for money and was offering to work for free when he was between construction jobs. Again, I turned him down, saying I couldn't take his charity." She shook her head as if remembering the conversation with Zeke as it happened. "I left not long after that."

Lois frowned. "But I am guessing you met up again."

Darcy nodded. "About a week later, I was trying to hang new shelves in the kitchen of the café. I was doing a terrible job of it. Every time I hung up the shelves, they were lopsided, something that would not do when I set a bunch of breakable dishes on them. To make matters worse, I had drilled so many holes into the wall trying to hang the shelves, it looked like a piece of Swiss cheese."

Lois squeezed her hand. "Darcy, why didn't you call me? You could have asked me for the money to help. I know how to use a power drill with the best of them."

She shook her head. "I couldn't do that, Grandma. I knew you were in the middle of divorcing the Rocksino guy. I didn't want to cause you any extra stress."

"Pish," Lois said. "That? That divorce wasn't anything to get stressed about. I have had much more intense divorces. Rocksino-man and I broke up very quickly. I can barely remember why I married him in the first place."

"Even if that is the case, I couldn't take your money. I couldn't do that." She took a breath. "Just when I was about to throw my drill against the wall in frustration, Zeke was there."

"He showed up in the kitchen?" Lois asked.

Darcy nodded. "He said he was passing by and wanted to see how I was coming along. The front door was unlocked—it must have been unlocked—

otherwise he wouldn't have been able to get in. In any case, he found me in a terrible state. Took the drill from my hand and took over the job. Within a half hour, those shelves were up and the wall where I had made my mistakes was patched. When he asked to come back the next day to help again, I didn't turn his offer down.

"Over the next several weeks he came anytime he wasn't working, and before I knew it, the café was ready to open. We worked nonstop together and talked about everything. He told me how hard it had been for him to grow up Amish." She shot a look in my direction.

I nodded for her to continue.

"Over those few weeks while we worked side by side almost every night, we fell in love. I had never been so comfortable with anyone in all my life. It was like we were meant to be together. I wasn't just his girlfriend. I loved him. We even talked about getting married."

Lois held up her hand. "Wait. Back up. You were going to become Amish?"

Darcy blinked at her grandmother. "No, I would never do that, and Zeke didn't want me to. He wanted to be English. He was going to leave his church to marry me. I didn't ask him to do it. It was his idea. He loved me enough to walk away from everything he knew. By the second week, Zeke was already talking about leaving the Amish so that he could be with me. He saw the potential in the café, he said, and he wanted to be part of the business with me. It wasn't something he could do while remaining Amish. His family would shun him. He was already baptized in the church. If he decided to leave at this point, he would have to leave everything and never go back. I told him that I would never ask him to do that, but there was no doubt in my mind we were meant to be together."

Lois shook her head. "This is my fault. You learned to be a hopeless romantic from me. How many dead-end marriages have I jumped into? Rocksino-guy doesn't even count when compared to the others. They all were horrible, except for my third husband, God rest his soul. With him, I finally had the real thing."

I sat at the table with my mouth hanging open, feeling as if I wanted to both hug the girl to comfort her and smack her on the side of the head. I knew hopeless romantics. I'd met many of them in my life as a matchmaker. However, most love starts, in my experience and observation, under much more mundane circumstances.

Lois pushed what remained of her mocha over to Darcy. "You need this much more than I do, my dear."

Wasn't that the truth? Darcy was too pale. A hot drink was just what she needed. I wasn't sure about all the sugar and caffeine in the mocha though. I thought a calming herbal tea would have been a better choice. That was what my mother always gave me when I was upset as a youngster, and she made it with the herbs and edible flowers from her very own garden.

"How did you end up going to the greenhouse?" I asked.

She didn't sip the mocha but wrapped her hands around the warm ceramic mug. The warmth seemed to steady her, and the lines on her forehead smoothed some. "It was the note."

CHAPTER TWENTY

N ote?" Lois asked.

Darcy nodded. "About a week ago when I came in to the café—this would be about five in the morning because we open at seven for the breakfast crowd—there was a note that had been tucked under the front door. I always come through the back door, so I didn't see it until I was unlocking the front door for the day. I read it and tucked it in my pocket. I couldn't let myself think about it just then. I had customers to serve." She let out a breath.

"What did the note say?" Lois asked.

I was so glad that she asked because I desperately wanted to know the answer to that question too.

"It said that Zeke was engaged to be married to an Amish woman in two weeks, and it would serve me well to stay away from him and the rest of the Amish community." She looked as if she might start to cry again.

"Do you still have the note? Can we see it?" This time I was the one to ask.

Darcy's eyes flitted back and forth. "I burned it."

I knew she was lying, but I didn't want to press her any more because I was afraid that she wouldn't tell me the rest of the story.

"I had to know if it was true. The only clue the note gave me was that the other woman was Amish and had a greenhouse. I thought there couldn't be too many Amish women in Harvest like that. I asked some of the Amish women who supply the produce for my café. I asked them about a greenhouse in the village. Right away they told me about Edith Hochstetler. As soon as I heard her name, I knew she was the one, but it didn't take long to confirm because the women spoke to each other about Edith's upcoming wedding. I asked who the lucky groom was and much to my disappointment, they gave Zeke's name. The next day, I left Grandma at the café alone—"

"I remember," Lois said. "I was surprised that you left me in the café even at a quiet time. We both know I can't cook. What if someone wanted to come in and order something more than a pre-baked dessert?"

Darcy looked at her grandmother. "Did anyone come in?"

"No," Lois said. "But it could have happened."

Darcy shook her head. "I just had to know if what I had learned about Zeke was right, and I knew the only way it would sink in for me was if I saw Edith with my own eyes. I left the café and drove to the greenhouse." She looked me in the eye for the first time since she'd recognized me. "That's when I saw you standing with Edith outside the greenhouse. I knew it was Edith the moment I saw her. I could see why Zeke wanted to marry her. She's beautiful, and I could tell by her mannerisms that she's kind and gentle. She's everything that I am not."

I frowned. Wherever did this girl develop such a low opinion of herself? Not that I was overcome by too much sympathy. But then, she hadn't known Zeke was engaged, had she? In many ways, she was another victim. Or another suspect . . .

"Did you talk to Zeke about what you learned?" I asked.

"Yes, of course. He was so upset when I told him I'd gone to the greenhouse. He was angry. It was the first time I had ever seen him act that way, and by this time we had been talking about our future together for months. I thought I knew him. I felt so betrayed. What a fool I was."

"Oh, honey," Lois said. "We all think that when we make the mistake of trying to rescue a man."

Darcy shook her head. "I knew he was too good to be true. He was too perfect, and he said all the right things. I can't believe I was so stupid. I have always prided myself on being self-sufficient, and the first time a nice-looking man comes along and offers his help, I snap it up. I'm pathetic."

Lois patted her hand. "The most important thing is you realize that now, and you can move on. Next time, you will make a wiser choice." She paused. "Don't look to me for guidance though. Not after

I almost threw my life away on Rocksino-man."

Darcy laughed under her breath, but her eyes were still sad. "I can't believe I was so stupid." She shook her head again.

"You said that Zeke was angry at you when you confronted him. What did he say?" I asked.

I thought she was going to ignore my question, but then she spoke. "He said that I'd endangered his position in the community by going to the greenhouse. I could have ruined everything for him." She squeezed her hands together so tightly, the knuckles turned white.

Lois and I shared a look.

It took everything in me not to point out that a man who vowed to leave everything for a woman would not have said such things. But then, we all knew that Zeke had lied about many things, and Darcy, well, she was discovering the extent of his lies firsthand.

"He said he had no choice in the marriage," she went on. "He had to marry her because it was an arranged marriage his parents had agreed to when he was a baby. There was no way out without being shunned by the community. He said that everything changed for him when he met me on the side of the road. That's when he knew his life could be something more than being trapped in the Amish community. Even so, it was a hard decision to leave because he would be leaving his way of life and his family forever. It wasn't something that I could ask him to do. It's not something I could ask anyone to do."

I frowned. An arranged marriage? That was a lie. Not only were arranged marriages *not* part of Amish culture, I would have known if my niece had been promised to a man when she was an infant. Not to mention Edith's first marriage to Moses. *Nee*, that wasn't what happened. It went against the Amish belief in choice. That's why we Amish believed in *rumspringa*: It was a young person's time to experience the world. And, after experiencing everything, that individual had to *choose* to follow the Amish faith.

The last thing any Amish parent wanted for his or her children was a divorce, which was a sin in our community. They would much rather their children never marry than pick the wrong person. That's where I came in as a matchmaker. I could spot when a man and a woman had potential to be a happy match and when they didn't, but ultimately those two people had to decide if it was the right fit for them.

"That's the most ridiculous thing I ever heard. The Amish don't have arranged marriages," Lois said with a frown on her face. "If you had told me about Zeke, I would have told you that. I would also have told you to be wary of a man who wants to keep you a secret. That's not healthy and never a good idea. There is a reason for his secrecy and many times it's a flaw in his character. I'm sorry to say that I learned this from personal experience." She hugged Darcy. "Tell her that I'm right, Millie, at least about the marriage part," Lois said.

"You are right about all of it." I nodded. "We do not arrange marriages. Parents want their children to fall in love. It's the best indicator that a marriage will pass the test of time."

Darcy let out a long sigh. "I know he lied to me. He lied to me about everything. I shouldn't be the least bit surprised that he lied to me about how marriage works in his community."

"Darcy, when was the last time you saw Zeke?" I asked.

Darcy blew her nose in the napkin and took another one to wipe her eyes. Makeup smeared across the pink paper. "Friday. Friday night. That's when I told him I had learned about his Amish fiancée, and I broke up with him. I can't believe I was so stupid. I was so naïve. He said all the right things and I believed him. I deserve the broken heart I got."

I shook my head. "I would say that Zeke is mostly to blame for your broken heart, and you learned a lesson, one I am certain you won't repeat. It's easy to fall in love with someone when he only shows his best self. It's the hard times that prove love is true."

"I just thought . . . because he was Amish that he was different."

"He was still a man, a flawed human," I said. "There are good men, both Amish and *Englisch*. Maybe they just take more work to find." I reached across the table and squeezed her hand. "But the wait is worth it."

"My Mr. Henry was good," Lois said with a nod. "We were married only three years before he died. It seemed cruel that the man I loved most I would have for the least amount of time." Lois shook her head. "But we did have *some* time, and that's what matters."

I wrapped my hands around my mug. Most of my mocha was still there. It tasted wonderful but seemed a little too decadent for such a serious conversation. A nice cup of black tea would have suited me much better right then because the conversation was about to get a lot more challenging. I couldn't keep Zeke's death a secret from Darcy any longer. I felt guilty that I hadn't said anything earlier, but I had been afraid she wouldn't tell me what she knew.

"Darcy, I have some bad news to tell you," I said. It pained me to have to tell her, but I could no longer keep it to myself.

She grabbed my hand and squeezed it so tight, I thought she would break my bones, but I didn't pull away. "Is it about Zeke? Please tell me that he's okay. Is he all right?"

My heart broke for her. Despite everything, she still loved him. She loved him, and seeing her reaction, I realized that Edith hadn't, not in the same way. Edith had been planning to marry him for the security having a husband would bring her in our community. It wasn't for love, and so it wasn't right. Not that Darcy's love for Zeke was right either. Her love was based on the person he'd pretended to be for her. The question was why had he chosen to lead Darcy on in such a way, and did that relate somehow to his untimely death?

"Darcy," I said, giving her hand a squeeze. "I'm so sorry to tell you this, but Zeke is dead."

All the color drained from her delicate face.

"He was found dead yesterday morning in the greenhouse."

She ripped her hand from mine. "How could you?" she screamed at me.

"I—I—"

"You sat there all this time asking me questions about Zeke, making me think that you cared about what I had gone through in my love for him, and all this time you knew he was dead. How could you do that?"

"I—I'm sorry. It wasn't my intention to upset you any more than you already were, but I had to hear whether you knew anything about his death."

"How would I know anything about it? It happened at the greenhouse. I've only been there the one time that you tricked me into telling you about." She jumped out of her seat, knocking her chair to the floor.

Bryan looked up from his computer, reminding me of a squirrel coming out of its winter nest for the first day of spring; everything was a blur and confusing. Bryan was halfway out of his seat.

"I'm sorry," I said quietly. "You're right. I should have told you the truth right away. It was wrong of me to keep it a secret."

"You Amish think that you're so much better than the rest of us, like you are God's chosen people that can do no wrong, but both Zeke and now you have taught me that you're not." She turned to go. "You're just as awful as everyone else."

"Darcy," I said. "I know it might be hard, but I think you should tell the police about the note."

She spun around. "No, I'm not dealing with the police. I had nothing to do with all this."

"It proves Zeke was a liar to you and to Edith. It shows that he might have been up to other things, which may have gotten him killed."

She froze. "Killed? The police think someone killed him?"

I nodded. "It looks like that's what may have happened."

There was a tapping sound as Bryan settled back into work, but I could tell he was listening in on the conversation. Not that I could blame him; we weren't being quiet about it. And how often do people talk about a local murder?

I glanced at Lois, who had said nothing up to this point. "I think you should go to the police and tell them about your relationship with Zeke. If one member of the district knew about you, it is most likely that others did as well. They will tell the police."

Lois nodded. "She does have a point. I know that was the case with my first husband's many run-ins with the law. The coppers don't like it when they believe they have been lied to. They're testy folks, and we can't forget that terrible man Sheriff Jackson. He will want this to go away as soon as possible. If that means arresting you, he would be happy to do it. You also have to think about your business. Even though you are completely innocent, if you are arrested, it could impact the café."

I nodded. "Your grandmother is right. Now the police think that Edith might have something to do with the murder, and I'm trying to help her. If they think Edith is guilty, then they might think you could also be guilty. You were both wronged by Zeke. You have the same motive."

Darcy glared at me. "I'm not going to the police. Now I have to get back to work." She went around the counter and through the door into the kitchen but not before I heard a muffled sob.

I glanced at my old friend. "Lois, I'm so sorry. I completely muddled that. I never meant to hurt Darcy. I would never hurt your granddaughter or anyone." I sat back down at the table where Lois had remained throughout my entire argument with Darcy.

She nodded. "I know that. I may not have seen you for twenty years, Millie Fisher, but I know your heart. You would never intend to hurt someone on purpose. Me, on the other hand, would love to wring Zeke Miller's neck if his sorry behind still had the good sense to be alive."

I tried not to think about the fact that my old friend Lois was very much a suspect in Zeke's murder too. If she'd known about Darcy's relationship with Zeke Miller, she would have a motive. Had she known? She'd looked shocked when Darcy told us the story, but I hadn't seen Lois in twenty years. How could I really gauge her reaction as true or false?

"What are you going to do about it?" Lois asked, leaning across the table between us.

I blinked at her. "What do you mean?"

"Well, you said you were here because you wanted to help your niece Edith. How are you going to do that?"

I thought about it for a moment, and then I said in a low voice, "I want to give the police other suspects. I know that Edith is innocent." Even as I said this, I remembered thinking that she was holding back information from the police. I swallowed. "I *know* she couldn't have done this, and I want to prove it."

"And I want to help Darcy too," Lois said. "I want to prove she is innocent. It seems to me if we can put our heads together, we could do a better job of it. We were quite a team back in our younger days. There's no reason we can't be that again."

"I don't think—"

"I won't take no for an answer. You aren't going to be running around out there being the Amish Miss Marple without a proper sidekick. It's just not how this is going to happen."

I suppressed a smile despite the tense situation. "I know it's been a very long time since I read those stories, but I don't think Miss Marple had a sidekick."

"Well, she should have." Lois sniffed, setting the dirty dishes from the table back on her tray. "Miss Marple would have solved those tricky cases a lot sooner if she'd had backup."

I shook my head. "Lois, I appreciate your offer, but I can't ask you to become involved. Look how upset Darcy is over all of this. If you help me, she will be constantly reminded of Zeke. That's not what she needs right now."

"She's my granddaughter and I will be the one who decides what she needs right now."

"All right," I said warily.

"Darcy is the very reason I have to be involved. I love my granddaughter. She's all that I have in the world. Don't you think I would be willing to chase down a killer to protect her? I do Pilates. I'm much stronger than I look."

"Pilates?" I asked, confused.

"That's not important. What's important is we have to take care of our girls. Together."

Actually, what Lois was saying made some sense, and I realized I was in over my head. I knew that the moment I told Darcy that Zeke was dead.

"I know you, Mildred Fisher," she went on, "and you are investigating this murder. I want to be a part of it."

I wrinkled my nose. "Don't call me Mildred. I hate my given name."

"As you should. You are so not a Mildred. Mildreds don't solve crimes."

"Please, Lois. I don't think this is a good idea. It could be dangerous."

"So it's okay for you to put yourself in danger but not me?" She pressed her lips together as if she found this distinction particularly offensive. "I have as much business investigating this murder as you do."

"I know you do, but this is an Amish crime. I am almost certain of that. You would . . ." I searched for the right word.

"You don't think I will fit in with the Amish?" she asked, looking down at her multicolored outfit and jewels.

"Umm . . . you might stand out a bit."

"So what? You need me."

I raised my eyebrow at her.

"You do!" she insisted. "I even have my own lock picks. You need someone with lock picks if you're going to be investigating a murder."

"You have your own lock picks?" I squeaked.

"Sure do. Got them for a good price on eBay." She said this like I had any idea what she was talking about. "I thought they would come in handy with my first husband. He had a knack for getting into jams. They're German made, so you know they're good."

"I have no idea what makes lock picks *gut*."

"See, there is plenty I know about crime-solving that you don't."

"I'm sure," I said.

"Okay, so the lock picks don't impress you, but I do have something that you don't have, and it's something you'll need if you are going to be traipsing all over the county searching for a killer."

"What's that?"

"A car."

She had me there.

CHAPTER TWENTY-ONE

I left the Sunbeam Café not long after that. Lois agreed to pick me up at my home at eight the next morning. She wasn't able to leave the café that day because she was Darcy's only help. Darcy's part-time employee would be there the next day, so Lois promised she could slip away.

As I was leaving, *Englisch* tourists were arriving at the café, and business picked up considerably. I wove around them and ran into a man on the sidewalk.

"Take care there!" a man said, holding me lightly by the arm so that I wouldn't fall over. I'd scarcely left the café and already I was bumping into people.

"I am so sorry," I said in a rush. "I should have looked before I came through the door. Are you all right?"

The man dipped and scooped his black felt hat off the sidewalk. "I'm as right as rain, Millie Lapp."

I jerked back. "Have we met?"

He smoothed his white beard and his blue eyes sparkled behind wire-rimmed glasses. He had long tapered fingers and a ready smile. "I should think so."

I gasped. "Uriah Schrock! I—I—"

"I haven't seen you in forty years, not since you threw me over for Kip Fisher. It's all well and *gut*. I didn't stand a chance against him. Everyone loved Kip."

It was true that everyone loved Kip, but it wasn't true that I had thrown Uriah over for him. Uriah and I had been friends in school, nothing more than that. We had gone to the same one-room schoolhouse. At that time there hadn't been many students in the school, so my district combined with several others in order to keep the doors open. Uriah had been from another district. I had thought when we were young that he was sweet on me, but it never entered my mind to look beyond my district for a husband, and it was love at first sight for Kip and me.

These days, Uriah had a beard, a long white beard that was neatly trimmed. So he was married. I was happy to see it. Uriah had been the class clown in our old school, and there were many times when our teacher would tell him that he would never marry because no woman would have the patience for him. I was relieved to see that wasn't the case.

"And how is your wife?" I asked.

He shook his head. "Gone. I lost my wife about three years ago. She was an amazing woman and gave me five wonderful children. Now I have so many grandchildren and even great grandchildren, I can't keep up with them all. Most of them live in

Shipshewana, Indiana. That's where my dear wife was from. I went out there for work as a young man and never came back until now. I need to take care of some old affairs here to do with my family in Harvest, and then I will be on my way back to Indiana.

"How many children do you have?" he inquired.

I felt a slight blush color my cheeks. "None. Kip and I were never blessed with children."

He frowned. "I'm so sorry. I shouldn't be talking to you in such a familiar way. We haven't seen each other in years."

I smiled. "It is quite all right. We are old friends and have been blessed to live long lives; we don't have to skirt around topics. Who has the time for that?"

He laughed. "Something that I like best about you is the way you say just what you think. That's refreshing in an Amish woman."

" 'When you speak, always remember that *Gott* is one of your listeners,' " I quoted.

"Still muttering the old proverbs as well, I see."

"They do have a lot of wisdom."

He nodded. "They do indeed."

For some reason, I found myself blushing, and I looked down at the tote bag in my hands as if I'd just remembered I needed something out of it. When I looked up again, I saw Lois watching through the front window. She flashed me a thumbs-up. It seemed to be her encouraging sign of choice.

In the other window, Bryan was watching Uriah and me. When he caught me looking, he returned his attention to his computer.

"*Ya*, well, I am happy to see you," I said. "Will you be in Harvest very long? Are you heading back to Shipshewana soon?"

He shook his head. "In a few months' time. It depends how long it takes to handle these affairs." His cheerful face clouded over for just a moment. "I miss my family, of course, but it is nice to be back in Harvest. I like the quieter pace here. And I like that there are more groups of Amish. We aren't all put in one category. There is far less variety in the community in Indiana."

"Did a member of your family come with you?"

"*Nee*. They all have busy lives with businesses, farms, and children."

"You came this far to live alone with no family?" I asked, surprised. "That's very brave."

"No braver than you, Millie Fisher, no braver than you."

I found myself frowning. I didn't know how he would know that I was being brave about anything. As he said, we hadn't seen each other in over forty years.

He cleared his throat. "You might be wondering what I'm doing wandering around the village on a lovely afternoon."

I hadn't been wondering that at all, but he went on to say, "Since I've been back, I have taken a temporary job as head groundskeeper of the square. I need something to do while I wait for some news." Again, the clouded expression crossed his face. "It's my job to make sure that not a single blade of grass is bent in the wrong direction. There are so many functions on the square now that it's reached the point that someone has to make sure Harvest always looks its best, and since the square is the most important and central part of the village, the village council created this position. Luck—or more likely providence—would have it that I'd just been back in the village for a few hours when I heard about this opportunity. I snapped it up. No Amish man worth his salt wants to stand idly by. I need something to keep my mind and hands busy, especially during a time of waiting."

"I know that Margot Rawlings always wanted the square to look perfect," I said. "I'm not surprised that she would like someone to maintain it."

He nodded. "And I'm happy to do it. It keeps me out of trouble." The mischievous twinkle he was known for at school was back in his eyes. I could almost hear our old teacher reprimand him for his roguish demeanor. She never could stand for that. Many believed that Uriah Schrock drove the teacher to her very wit's end.

"I'm not idling away my time as I wait for news." His face turned red at the possibility that I might believe so.

"I didn't think that at all," I said.

His face flushed. "Oh, I know you aren't quick to judge, Millie. I should have remembered. It's just with no family nearby anymore, I find myself walking to the square every day to make sure everything is in its place. It passes the time."

"I'm sure Margot appreciates your dedication, and I have noticed that the shrubs around the white gazebo and the other bushes around the square are much more neatly trimmed than usual."

"*Wunderbar*! A true compliment indeed." He laughed. "And you are right—Margot appreciates people agreeing with her and going along with her schemes. I'm not sure of much else—" He rocked back on his heels. "But I do believe she has been good for the village. Harvest has grown much since I've been away, so very much, but it doesn't have the commercial feel that some of the other Amish communities have. I'm glad that it has—either because of Margot or despite her— maintained its Amish essence."

I nodded, feeling the same way about the village. "I should leave you to it then," I said. "If you need to make your rounds of the square, I don't want to interrupt."

"You could never be an interruption, Millie. I have always thought that."

I blinked and gave him a small smile in return. I was unsure what to say. "If you will excuse me," I murmured and hurried down the sidewalk. Before I got too far, I glanced over my shoulder and found Uriah watching me as I left.

He tipped his black felt hat to me and went on his way.

I tamped down the odd feeling that it stirred deep in my heart.

CHAPTER TWENTY-TWO

I crossed Church Street, aptly named for the big white church where Reverend Brook ministered, on one side of the square. An Amish family from another district was picnicking in the gazebo. The plain-dressed children ran around the large white gazebo, playing a vigorous game of tag. Other than the gazebo and a dotting of trees and shrubs, most of the square was open green space. That's just how Margot Rawlings wanted it because if she had her way, every day of the week there would be an event or festival on the green space in the middle of the village. In the short time that I had been back in Harvest, she had all but accomplished that.

However, that day the square was quiet, other than the normal village and tourist traffic that was common on a nice spring day in any Amish town. I waited for a moment as two buggies drove by before I crossed Main Street to reach the candy shop. Charlotte was no longer outside passing out fudge. Even from the sidewalk, I could inhale the enticing smells of warm chocolate and sugar. They mingled with the scent of fresh baked dough from the pretzel shop.

I glanced at Esh Family Pretzels before entering the candy shop. Esther Esh, a young Amish woman of almost thirty, watched me from the window. She had a deep frown on her face. She ran the pretzel shop with her older brother Abel, who was also unmarried. It was well-known in the village that Esther did most of the work for their shop and family. She caught me looking and dropped the white gauzy curtains that covered the window, disappearing from sight.

Shaking my head, I went into Swissmen Sweets. The bell on the door rang to announce my entry. There were three *Englischers* at the counter being helped by the three women in the shop: Bailey, her grandmother Clara, and her cousin Charlotte.

The front of the shop, which was the only portion I had ever seen, had pine floors and polished blond wood shelves that were lined with jars and baskets of the most mouth-watering candies I had ever seen. The glass of the jars sparkled as they were carefully polished each and every day. In the main part of the room there were four small café tables with paddle-back chairs where visitors could sit and enjoy their candies and visit with friends and neighbors. The centerpiece of the shop, though, was the long glass-domed counter that was filled with trays of fudge, truffles, and chocolates of every kind. This was the counter behind which the three women stood, working in perfect sync.

All three women were helpful and patient while the *Englischers*, who were clearly from outside the county, appeared to agonize over their candy choices.

"I just don't know if my husband would like the vanilla fudge or the cherry vanilla fudge more," one woman said.

Bailey smiled at her. "How much were you going to get?" Bailey was a tall *Englisch* woman with long dark hair and sparkling blue eyes that matched Clara's. She was completely at home working in an Amish shop even though Charlotte and Clara were in pale blue plain dresses and sensible black sneakers and she wore jeans, a plaid button-down shirt, and feathered earrings.

"I was thinking half a pound." The woman frowned as if she was unsure of even how much fudge to buy.

"How about this," Bailey said. "Get a quarter of both. The fudge is delicious, but is best enjoyed in small doses."

"All right," the *Englischer* said. "That does sound like a plan."

"I'll throw in some of our white chocolate drops for free, just to be sure that he enjoys it," Bailey said.

"Oh, would you? That would be so kind."

Bailey smiled. "Charlotte will ring you up while I pack your items."

The woman thanked her and went to the cash register, where Charlotte stood waiting.

Clara waved at me in her kind way and wiped her hands on a white muslin towel. "Millie, it is so *gut* to see you." Sadness clouded her face. "I was so sorry to hear the news about Zeke Miller."

I nodded. *"Danki."*

"How is Edith?" she asked. Her face was a mask of concern.

I blinked as tears threatened the corners of my eyes. I hadn't realized just how upset I was over the situation until Clara asked. I looked down for a moment, embarrassed by my tears. The Amish, both men and women, were taught to be strong; crying in public did not show strength.

Clara was looking away out the front window, allowing me time to collect myself. She understood my need to compose myself before I went on. I appreciated that.

I cleared my throat. "Edith is doing well, staying strong for the children."

Clara nodded, accepting my answer as fact.

The last *Englischer* left the shop, and Bailey came out from behind the counter and gave me a hug. "Millie, it's so good to see you. I'm sorry . . ." She trailed off.

"I appreciate it." This time there were no tears. I had a much better handle on my emotions. "I thought I should stop by to tell you that we no longer need that wedding cake I ordered. I'm still happy to pay for it."

"We know," Bailey said. "Aiden told us."

I nodded, thinking not for the first time that I would have to be careful what I said in front of the ladies of Swissmen Sweets because of their close relationship with Deputy Aiden.

The *Englisch* customer walked out the door with her vanilla-flavored sweets.

"And you don't need to pay us for anything," Bailey added. "Charlotte and I never could come to an agreement about the flavor."

"That's true," Charlotte called from behind the counter where she was working tying yellow ribbon around cellophane bags of freshly made lemon drops. "Bailey doesn't know how to compromise."

Bailey rolled her eyes, but she was smiling. It was clear to me that it was something the two of them had joked about many times before.

"But you might have ordered some ingredients to start the cake," I argued, "even if the flavor wasn't completely settled."

"If we did, it does not matter," Clara said. "We can always use the ingredients in something else."

"That's right," Bailey agreed.

"*Danki.*"

"Is there anything we can do to help?" Bailey asked. "If you need me to talk to Aiden, I'm happy to do it." Worry creased her forehead. "I have to leave for New York tomorrow morning. I'm doing some press and interviews for my television show, *Bailey's Amish Sweets*, but I can ask to cancel or move it."

I shook my head. "*Nee*, please don't do that. Deputy Aiden has been very kind through the process. We must just wait and see."

Clara cocked her head. "I haven't known you to be a wait-and-see kind of woman, Millie."

I laughed. "I suppose I'm not. All I would ask is that you pray for Edith and everyone else involved." I caught myself before mentioning Darcy. The girl could also use prayer to deal with her broken heart, but I didn't want to spread the word about her relationship with Zeke any farther.

"Of course," Clara said.

I thanked them again. "Do you have any of that blueberry and lavender fudge?"

Bailey laughed. "I have never met anyone who loves blueberry as much as you do, Millie. Yes, we have plenty. Let me pack up some for you." She went behind the counter.

As I waited for my fudge, the front door to Swissmen Sweets opened again, and Deputy Little strode inside. As soon as he was in the room, Charlotte became very interested in her task of packing lemon drops. She stared at her busy hands.

After greeting us all, Deputy Little walked up to her. "I'd like a pound of chocolate peanut butter fudge."

She looked up. "You bought a pound of choco-late peanut butter fudge two days ago. Did you already eat it?"

Now, his face was red. "I—I gave it away at the station."

"Oh," she said. "That was nice of you."

He smiled.

She shook her head as if shaking herself from a daydream. "I will get that for you."

Beside me, I saw Clara's face crease in worry. She was seeing what I was seeing, I was certain. Bailey held out a little white box to me. "Here's your fudge."

"How much do I owe you?"

"Nothing." Bailey shook her head. "No, it's a gift. Please."

I took the box from her hand. "All right." I thanked all the ladies again and walked out the door.

I stood on the sidewalk for a moment, and a second later Deputy Little came out the door. He held his box of fudge in his hand as if his life depended on it. Then he crossed Main Street without so much as a second glance at me. There would be some very difficult choices in the future for those two, I knew, if things went the way I believed they would.

I shook my head. The romantic entanglements of the young! Then I thought of Uriah, and maybe the not-so-young too . . .

I stopped and admired the square and the apple trees and gas-powered lampposts that marched up Main Street. Harvest was lovely, and despite this latest event, I was happy to be back in the village where I had friends like Lois and happy memories of falling in love with Kip.

I was about to cross Main Street again to return to Bessie and my buggy when the door to the candy shop opened after me. "Millie!" Charlotte Weaver called.

I turned and looked at the young Amish woman. Her cheeks were a lovely shade of pink. I didn't know if that was from the heat of the kitchen or the close proximity to Deputy Little.

I smiled. "Can I help you, Charlotte?"

Her face turned even redder, changing from a pretty blush to the shade of a sun-ripened tomato. "I was wondering if . . ." She blushed even more.

I patted her arm. "You want my matchmaking help?"

She looked at me with her bright green eyes. "*Ya*, I have been confused about so many things, and I thought that if . . ."

"If you were being courted by a nice Amish man, things would be made clearer."

Deputy Little stood across the square, speaking with a tourist. It was clear from the way he was pointing that he was giving directions.

"Charlotte?"

She looked away from the young deputy. She nodded. "That's my hope."

"It may be easier if you first decide whether you want to remain Amish or not. You cannot base your decision about what you believe on someone else."

She hung her head. "I know. I'm so torn. I wish I could be in both worlds, like Bailey."

"Bailey isn't in both worlds," I said. "She has access to both and you will too, no matter what you decide." I paused. "If you make the decision before you are baptized."

She nodded. "I know what will happen if I'm baptized and change my mind." She looked over her shoulder at the candy shop as if to check that the door was firmly closed and no one could hear us. "But can you let me know if you see the right man for me, please?"

I smiled, thinking that I might already have seen him. "I will." I took a step toward the street.

"That's not all though," she said.

I raised my brow. "You have more you want to tell me about finding you a match."

She shook her head. "I heard a rumor that there was something strange going on at the place where Zeke worked, Swartz and Swartz Construction."

"What do you mean?" I asked, leaning in and searching her face for any clue as to what she was trying to tell me.

"I—I don't know, but I heard at a volley-ball match with the youth of the district that it might be something illegal. I thought you should know." With that, she spun around and went back into the candy shop.

CHAPTER TWENTY-THREE

My sleep that night was fitful. Nightmares clouded my mind, nightmares about Zeke's death, Enoch's return, and stumbling into Uriah. In my dreams, they all intertwined like a pattern on a crazy quilt.

If Enoch returned to take his place in the community, he would take control of the greenhouse from his sister as the only son of their father, Ira. Had she married before he returned, it would have gone to her husband. Enoch had the very best motive to get Zeke out of the way, and the timing was telling. At the same time, Edith didn't seem to believe that her twin was here to return to the Amish faith.

I knew I needed to talk with Enoch, but I wasn't sure it was a conversation I wanted to have with Lois trailing around behind me. Some family matters were strictly to be kept in the family. This certainly felt like one of those times. Consequently, I decided to go back to my niece's greenhouse alone, and I had the perfect excuse to return to the greenhouse in the early morning hours. I'd left my goats there, hadn't I? Oh, sure, I'd "lent" them to Edith to help with clearing some of the land, but I'd also promised to come for them. I thought it was a good time to collect them. Besides, I missed their company on my little farm.

It was five in the morning and still dark when I made up my mind to collect my goats. I knew I had plenty of time to get there and back in my buggy before Lois arrived at eight. Also, if I remembered correctly, she had almost always been late.

In the predawn light, I hitched up Bessie and climbed into my buggy. A few minutes later, the buggy creaked and rattled on the quiet county road between my little hobby farm and the greenhouse. As we rolled along, I saw the beginnings of dawn in the east over the rolling Holmes County hills. There was a large beef farm on this stretch of the drive and a dozen cows were silhouetted against the rising sun on the hill.

I let out a breath and prayed that my encounter with Enoch would go well. I had been wanting this moment for such a long time. Since I had been back in Ohio, I seemed to think about Enoch more often, wrestling over how to right the wrong I'd done. I also thought about Kip a lot more. It seemed that I missed him more acutely in this place where we had been so happy together.

I sighed again, and Bessie shook her head.

"I know, old girl, it's hard to reach our age and find we have some regrets about our lives."

Bessie blew a raspberry through her horsey lips. I started to laugh, but the laughter died on my lips when the roar of an engine came up behind us. Bessie shuddered at the noise and I looked over my shoulder through the back window of the buggy. All I could see was a pair of high-beam headlights. For a moment, I was blinded before I turned back around in my seat.

Bessie's stride skipped, causing the buggy to hiccup as a result. I took a firm hold on the reins. "Steady, girl, steady."

Her trot smoothed out again, but the car was still there right behind us. It felt like it was only a yard away from the back of the buggy. "Easy girl," I said to the horse. "He will pass us by."

But the car did not pass us by, and there was no other traffic on the road. There was plenty of space for the driver to move around us, more than enough space actually. A knot tightened in my stomach. Something about this felt very wrong. Why was he back there?

I looked in my buggy's rearview mirror, but the car's headlights were too bright to make out the face of the driver.

I licked my lips and slowed the buggy. The driver slowed his car too, keeping pace with me. It felt intentional. It *was* intentional.

I had no way to call for help. Nothing to do but keep going forward. I knew if I let Bessie stop, it would be a bad idea. My old horse and I were no match for the obviously angry person inside the other vehicle.

The car followed us for a while longer. It could have been ten minutes or it could have been two. I was in such a state, the passing of time seemed to tick by at a crawl. Then with no warning, the driver gunned his engine and flew around us, disappearing around a curve in the road in a matter of seconds. The sun was up high enough now that I could see there was mud covering the license plate. That felt intentional too.

The passing of the car rocked my buggy back and forth, and I held on to the reins so tightly that the old leather dug into my palms. I prayed for calm. It did not come. My heart raced, and I felt like I wanted to both stop the buggy completely and shake the reins hard so that Bessie and I could run away.

I straightened my shoulders, prayed to *Gott* that Bessie and I were both all right, and continued on to the greenhouse at a steady pace. It took us another twenty minutes to reach Edith's place. By the time we turned into the long driveway, the sun was up and my pulse was back to normal.

Phillip and Peter spotted us right away and the two goats galloped in our direction with wide grins on their faces. The front door of Edith's house opened, spilling children and kittens out to greet me as well. A peace fell over me. You really couldn't beat being welcomed by children, cats, and goats.

The front door opened again just as I was pulling

Bessie to a stop, and Edith stepped onto the small porch, followed by a man in *Englisch* clothes. Enoch.

I closed my eyes. The last time I had seen my nephew, he had been furious with me and blamed me for being wrongly sent to jail. The last time I had seen him, he had been a fifteen-year-old boy. Now, he was a man.

I climbed out of the buggy as the children, the kittens, and the goats circled around me.

"*Aenti*, why have you come so early?" Jacob asked.

I finished tying Bessie's lead to the hitching post and scratched Phillip between the ears. "I came by early because I have missed these two knucklehead goats and would like to take them back to my farm. They are *gut* company for me."

"Can we come too?" Micah asked. "We can be *gut* company for you. We can bring Peaches. He is almost weaned. *Maam* said it will be just another few weeks and he can go home to live with you." He held the peach-colored kitten up to me.

I took the downy ball of kitten fluff into my hands.

"We should visit you," Micah argued. "To make sure that you have everything you need to raise a cat. Cats are interesting creatures, as *Maam* says, and you have to take care of them properly."

It sounded to me as if Micah was repeating an argument that his mother had made to her more

222

active son in order to convince him to be gentle with the kittens.

I smiled because I knew the boy was sincere. "How about this? When it is time for me to take Peaches home, you can come to my farm and make all the proper recommendations to be certain that my home is kitten ready."

Micah thought for a moment. "That will work."

"*Gut*," I said with a laugh and handed the kitten back to him, then patted Ginny's plump cheek. I stepped around the children and the animals and walked toward the twins. As I drew closer to them, the similarities between them became evident. Enoch might be *Englisch* now, but he was still Edith's twin brother.

They came down from the porch together, reminding me of when they were young, when they were inseparable.

"*Guder mariye*," I said. "I'm sorry to come so early, but I thought I would collect the goats before it got too late in the day. Have they done the work you needed?"

Edith nodded. "They have. Those two goats can eat a lot of weeds."

I glanced over my shoulder at the children, who were playing with the kittens and goats. "That is very true. They are fine workers even though they are also a great amount of trouble." I turned to my nephew. "*Guder mariye*, Enoch. I am very happy to see you. You look well."

"As do you, Aunt Millie." He walked toward me and, much to my surprise, gave me a hug.

I squeezed him back with all my strength. I closed my eyes. He smelled *Englisch*, of expensive aftershave. Tears pooled in the corners of my eyes. "I am sorry for what happened—"

"Stop apologizing," my nephew said with a kind smile on his face. "All of that is over. I don't blame you for what happened when I was young. I know you tried to make it right. I was too angry to see it then. Let's just start from here."

And like that, ten years of guilt was gone.

CHAPTER TWENTY-FOUR

*D*anki, Enoch. That is very kind," I said. "Enoch has changed so much since he's been gone," his sister said, looking up to him lovingly. "He's like the boy I remember when we were children."

Enoch laughed. "I hope I'm more than that. After I left Holmes County, I will admit things were not easy. I thought when I left the Amish community, all my problems would be solved. I fell in with some wrong people, I made my mistakes, but I realized what I really wanted. Got my GED and went to college."

"I'm so glad to hear it," I said, thinking that it didn't sound to me like he had any intention of coming back to Harvest to live. "And what do you do now?"

"I'm in sales for the most part. I sell things to people who may or may not need them, but they have money and want stuff. It's very different from the way the Amish shop."

I knew this to be true.

"Enoch said that he will stay for a week or two," Edith said, smiling at her brother. "He's offered to help me at the greenhouse."

"I'm between jobs right now and have plenty of money from the job I had. If I can help Edith out for a couple of weeks, I'm happy to do that."

"That's so kind."

"I want to get the greenhouse back on track for her." His cheek twitched ever so slightly. "She told me what Zeke did with the greenhouse. His horrible choices and mismanagement. If there is something that I'm good at now, it's business. We will get her back in the black in no time."

"The black?" Edith asked.

"It's means you will be making a profit again," he said to his sister.

"I know that Edith will welcome the help."

He nodded. "My father and I might not have always seen eye to eye, but I know how much he cared about this greenhouse and about Edith. He named the greenhouse after her for goodness' sake." He paused. "I will repay my debt to him for being a terrible teenager by saving it."

I frowned. There was something about his comments that didn't sit well with me, but I couldn't put my finger on what bothered me.

"Is everything all right?" Enoch asked. "Aunt Millie, you do look a little bit shaken."

"Ummm." I couldn't tell them that Enoch's words bothered me, not right after he had forgiven ten years of hurt. "The strangest thing happened to me while I was driving here . . ." I began, and I went on to tell them about the car with the high-beam headlights.

"It was likely some kids still out joyriding, ones

who haven't even made it home for the night. You were lucky you weren't hurt. They might have been drunk," Enoch said. "I'm sorry to say that was the kind of trick I would have pulled when I was a teen. There are so many young men in this county out on *rumspringa*."

"You think it was an Amish young man?" I asked.

He smiled. "Considering where we are, the probability is very high."

"*Ya*, you are probably right." However, in my heart I didn't think he was right at all. I had a very clear sense that the car behind me was driven by an *Englischer*, but I didn't know why. All I had was a feeling, and the only other possible witness was Bessie. She was a sturdy old horse, but she wouldn't be much help supporting my story.

"*Aenti*, we were just about to sit down for breakfast," Edith said in her sweet way. "Would you like to join us? I made pancakes and bacon. I also have local maple syrup. I know how much you love anything maple."

That was true. I loved maple almost as much as I loved blueberries. Almost.

I pulled my pocket watch out of the pocket of my apron. It was a gift that Kip had given me when we were first married and one that I always kept with me. It was six thirty now. "I can stay for maybe fifteen more minutes. I have an old friend who is visiting me this morning. She

227

should be at my home by eight. This will give me just enough time for one pancake and two pieces of bacon. Oh, and coffee. It's early, and after this morning's scare, a cup of coffee to wake me up would be most welcome."

Enoch laughed.

Edith's eyebrows went up. "Who's your friend, *Aenti*?"

As we walked to the house, I told them about meeting Lois again. I didn't say where I'd met her or mention Darcy and the café. I would need to tell Edith those things, but not yet, not when her brother was here smiling at me with an inquisitive look on his face. It would have to wait until Lois and I started our investigation.

Fifteen minutes later on the dot, I was driving away from the greenhouse with two goats in the back of my buggy and a sense of peace about seeing Enoch again. The old saying came to me, "Forgiveness is better than revenge and in the long run a lot cheaper."

Of all the Amish proverbs there were about forgiveness, I didn't know why that was the one that came most readily to my mind.

I could not shake the uneasy feeling I'd had while speaking with my nephew. I told myself it was only an aftereffect of my early morning encounter with the car on that quiet dark road.

The county road where the incident had occurred was now empty. Everything was clear and brightly lit. No phantom cars would sneak up on Bessie and me now.

As I suspected, I made it back home with plenty of time to spare before Lois arrived. She was over forty minutes late.

Rather than sit in the house and twist my hands, I decided to do some yard work. It felt like much longer, but it'd been only a few days since Edith had helped me shape the new garden, and with all the turmoil that had unfolded in the community since, the garden remained unfinished.

Phillip and Peter, who I thought were happy to be home, circled me as they were inclined to do any time I worked with plants. Suddenly, the two goats lifted their heads and bolted for the front of the house. Lois had arrived.

I walked around the house at a much slower pace and was greeted by the sound of laughter. Lois's laugh took me right back to my childhood. She had the loudest and most authentic laugh I had ever heard, and it made me smile. If nothing else fruitful came from these difficult times, finding my old friend again would be a gift.

Lois chortled. "Oh my word! Where did the two of you come from?"

I couldn't help but smile at my old friend's cheerful reaction to my two rambunctious goats.

"Millie, will you call off your attack goats?" she shouted in the midst of her laughter.

"Phillip! Peter!"

The goats looked at me and fell to all eight hooves.

Lois held her sides. "I haven't laughed that hard since I pushed husband number four into the pool and told him I wanted a divorce. That was a red-letter day." She dusted off her hands. "Are you ready to do some sleuthing, Amish Marple?"

I sighed. "Is that my new name?"

"It is while we are on the case. I thought it would be good if we had code names. That way people will know we're serious."

"I don't think that code names for two women in their sixties will make anyone think we're serious. They will think we're ridiculous."

She thought about this. "That might be even better. Let them underestimate us. My second husband did that to me, and I was the one who ended up with his fishing boat in the divorce."

"Do you fish?"

"Of course not, but I sure wanted that boat." Her lips curled into a smile.

I shook my head. Lois's world and logic could not be farther from mine. "We had better get going." I made no comment about her being late. "I think it would be best to start at the place where Zeke worked. He spent the majority of his time with those men. They will know the most about him."

She scratched Peter, who had sidled up next to her, on the top of the head. "So we are going to just walk into the place where he worked and ask questions?"

"That's what I was thinking, unless you have a better plan."

"Nope. That's a good start, and remember I have those lock picks for backup."

"It's impossible for me to forget." I paused. "Just keep them in your purse until we need them. I hope it won't come to that."

She patted the enormous pocketbook on her hip. "I hope it will. I'd like to brush up on my skills."

I tried not to think about what other crime-solving equipment might be in her purse. I knew there was something else though. "Let me close up the house and we can leave."

"What about the goats? Don't you put them in the barn while you're gone?" she asked.

I shook my head. "They just run loose. They are *gut* about staying on the property, and I always keep the barn door open for them if the weather turns bad. Also, I have found that they keep unwanted guests off my farm. Most people don't react with the same amount of glee as you did when two Boer goats start running at them full speed."

"Wow, they could give some straying advice to my first husband. He could have really used it. Now that I think about it, the second and fourth could have used the lesson as well."

She petted Peter and then Phillip on the head. "Maybe I should get a pair of goats, but I don't think my landlord would like it. I have a little house in the village that I'm renting."

After closing up the house, I climbed into Lois's massive car and felt like a doll sitting on the long front bench seat. My feet didn't touch the floor if I sat all the way back. Hanging from the rearview mirror was a pink stuffed poodle that was as big as my fist. "Can you see to drive with that thing dangling in your line of vision?"

She started the engine. It made a grinding sound, and then caught. "Of course I can. And it completes the 1950s vibe I was going for, paying homage to the decade in which we were born. Sadly, we're far too young to really appreciate poodle skirts, but my mother had one, and it was amazing. I used to put it on when she was out of the house and twirl around like I was in a big dance number with Mickey Rooney."

I remembered Lois's mother. She was a colorful, outspoken farm wife who wasn't that different from Lois herself, but she had been married to the same man for over fifty years. There was the difference. She'd passed on while I was in Michigan. I had heard that much about Lois while I was away.

"I am sorry about your mother. I'm sorry that I couldn't come back for the funeral."

She nodded, and for a moment her sparkling

232

demeanor cracked, and I could see the true and tender Lois there. However, as quickly as it came it was gone. "I appreciated the card you sent. It was a good thing you sent it to my son's house. I was between husbands then, which meant I was between homes. Life is funny that way."

I wouldn't know. I'd not known Lois's whereabouts at the time and had wondered if my card would reach her at all. I'd sent the card to her son's home with the hope that he would know how to contact his mother.

"Where are we headed?" she asked as we rolled down my driveway.

I gave her the address of the construction warehouse that was on the outskirts of the county near the town of Holmesville. It was located on a county road that had no street signs or lines painted on the road; few rural roads in Holmes County did. When you got out of the 39 and 62 crossroads, it was a lot of open fields, big farms, and unmarked turns. It was common for *Englischers* who had been led astray by GPS to wander up to the front door of my farmhouse asking for directions back to one of those two main roads in the county. It was also common for the goats to chase folks away before I had a chance to give them proper directions.

Having grown up in the county and having been born before the advent of GPS, Lois knew where we were. All I had to do was tell her the road name, and she knew exactly where we were going. There was something to be said for a strong memory.

As we drove to the construction company's headquarters, Lois told me about her life over the last twenty years in the most concise way she knew how, which truthfully wasn't that concise because Lois was doing the storytelling.

She had just gotten to the part about being on a vacation with husband number two, or was it number three—I can't remember—when we came upon a modest hand-painted sign along the road that read SWARTZ AND SWARTZ CONSTRUCTION.

You wouldn't know from the sign that it was one of the most sought-after and biggest Amish businesses in the county. As far as I knew, every Amish family in Holmes County had one son, brother, or father working at the construction company at one time or another. It was the place where many of the young men from my district worked, including Zeke; both Enoch and Edith's first husband, Moses, had worked there too. In fact, now that I was allowing myself to think about that time again, I thought the three of them must have worked together. Zeke was the last one of the group who had still been working for Swartz and Swartz. Of course, he wasn't any longer, and Enoch was the last one alive. I shivered at the thought.

Lois shifted the car into park. "Okay, what's the plan?"

"The plan is to find out what Zeke did here and if anyone he worked with had any reason to want to kill him."

"Then we track that person down and make a citizen's arrest." She thrust her fist into the air.

I grabbed her arm. "*Nee*, we take the information to Deputy Aiden and let him handle it."

She crossed her arms. "You're no fun at all."

CHAPTER TWENTY-FIVE

Lois sighed more deeply, as if I had really hurt her feelings in some way. "Here I am thinking we are going to bring in a perp, and all you want to do is tell the police about it."

I glanced at her, knowing she was just being dramatic for effect. "Do you really think we can bring anyone in at all?"

She held up her enormous pocketbook. "I might not be able to take someone down without risking pulling a muscle, but let me tell you . . . *this* really packs a wallop when I need it to."

"Please try not to hit anyone with it. I can only guess what else you might have in there other than your lock picks."

"I have a small brick for one," she said as if she was telling me she'd brought a pen.

"A *brick*? Why on earth would you have a brick in your purse?"

"In case the lock picks are taking too long," she said as if it made perfect sense.

I was afraid in Lois's mind that it did.

She sighed. "Okay, I'm fine with telling the police if that's how you want to play it."

"It is," I said mildly.

"But I still have a problem."

"What can that possibly be?" I was starting to really regret my decision to allow Lois to be my driver for this investigation.

"I don't have a code name. What about code names? Yours is great. I think Amish Marple is some of my best work, but what is mine? How can I be on a case even in this amazing outfit if I don't have a proper name to support it? You don't think Wonder Woman could be called 'Sue' when she was wearing her red boots, do you?"

"I'm not sure who Wonder Woman is."

She groaned. "So much important cultural history is lost on the Amish."

I must have made a face because she said, "I don't mean that as an insult. Only you have missed a lot."

"Intentionally," I said. "We have chosen to separate ourselves from the rest of society." Since I didn't want to get into a philosophical debate with her about Amish culture, I said, "I'm sure you'll think of an excellent code name for yourself. Just let me know what you come up with."

"I'm not sure that you should give me free rein on my code name, Millie, but if that's what you want to do, I won't fight you. You might be alarmed at the results."

More alarmed than I already was over the fact she had a brick in her pocketbook? "We can't sit in this car forever. The men inside are going to start to wonder who we are and what we are doing here. Let's make this visit short and sweet, as you *Englischers* say."

"You bring the sweet," she said. "I'll bring the hammer."

"Please don't tell me that you have a hammer in your pocketbook too."

"Oh-kay," she said slowly. "I won't tell you that."

I got out of the car. I was too nervous over what I was about to say to the men in the warehouse to argue with Lois over her code name or about the hammer that I now knew was also in her purse. However, I had to admit that Amish Marple was starting to grow on me a bit, not that I would ever tell Lois that.

Lois got out of the car too and hiked her massive purse onto her shoulder before locking the car. I hoped that we wouldn't go anywhere that we had to be searched because I guessed there was a lot more in that bag I didn't want to know about.

I examined the warehouse in front me. It was the height of a two-story building, but I knew it was only one floor inside. The building had a steep shed roof made of aluminum, and the siding was gray vinyl. One of the three black garage doors was opened wide. The other two were closed. The open door made the building look like a monster with a wide, angry mouth because of where the windows were on either side of it. The windows looked a little too much like eyes watching me, for my taste.

At this late hour of the morning, I knew that most of the men had already been at work for hours. Most would have arrived around six a.m. for work, and that was after doing a number of chores at their own farms and homes when they awoke.

"Ready?" I asked.

She nodded, looking as serious as I ever saw her. "Ready. Let's find this killer."

Her comment about finding the killer didn't make me feel any more confident we'd actually be able to do that, but I was willing to try. I was here for Edith, and Lois had come for Darcy. They were more than enough reason to go inside that warehouse.

I walked toward the building, with Lois just a step or two behind me. I glanced over my shoulder. "What are you doing back there?" I asked.

"Don't worry. I have an idea. It will be part of our cover."

"Our what?"

She didn't get a chance to answer because a man came up to me. "Millie Fisher?"

Carter Young, Iris's husband and a handsome blond man with a reddish complexion, walked toward me with a broad smile on his face. He wiped his hands on a kerchief from the back pocket of his denim trousers. His shirt and workpants were clean; remnants of black roofing tar scuffed his work boots.

Iris had confessed to me once that it had been Carter's smile that had caught her attention before they started courting. His smile was so wide and genuine that it threatened to split his face in two from sheer happiness. I had known the moment I had seen Carter and Iris together that they were a match and told them both so. They were one of the couples I was most proud of putting together before I moved to Michigan.

He shoved the cloth back into his pocket. The vigorous cleaning hadn't made a great deal of difference on his grease-stained fingers. "You will have to excuse my appearance. I was trying to fix one of our forklifts. As of yet, the engine has gotten the better of me." He smiled. "Iris said that you might be stopping by for a chat, but I didn't think you would actually come. I'm happy to see you but . . ." His speech trailed off when he saw Lois standing behind me.

Lois smiled, clutched her purse to her middle and made no comment.

I frowned and wondered how Iris would know that I would stop by when I'd said nothing to her about it. Then I remembered Ruth had said she would talk to Iris.

I looked back at Lois. When she didn't say anything, I said, "This is Lois. She's my—"

"Driver," Lois interjected. "I'm just her driver.

You know how you Amish need someone to take you about."

Carter's smile wavered just a bit. "*Ya*, that is true." Then the smile returned at full force. "I'm happy that you have a driver to take you about, Millie. You have to be careful on these roads as tourist season picks up. Holmes County is a much busier place than it used to be before you moved away. More buggy accidents are reported than I care to think about."

I wrinkled my nose. "I know how to drive a buggy, Carter Young."

He waved his hands. "I wasn't saying that you don't. It's just when you get older, you . . ."

"I think you should stop right there, young man," I said, teasingly.

He laughed. "All right. That's fair."

"Iris told you that I was coming?"

He nodded. "She thought you would want to talk to someone about Zeke. She wanted me to keep an eye out for you in case you stopped by."

That sounded like Ruth had told the quilting circle members I was investigating. As frustrating as Ruth's meddling might be, I was happy that Iris had given her husband a warning to be on the lookout for me. It would make it easier if I had a person on the inside of the construction company to talk to about Zeke. I wasn't sure that many of these men were going to be very forthcoming with a woman old enough to be their *maami*.

Having an *Englischer* at my side wasn't going to help either.

"Everyone here is shocked over what happened to Zeke. He was a strong, healthy man. If someone attacked him, his reaction would be to fight back," Carter said.

I blinked at him when he said that. "Why do you say that? Usually nonviolence is the way of our people."

"He was Amish, but he wasn't a very *gut* pacifist. I have seen him come to blows with some of the Mennonite men who work here, and he's even tried to spur some of the Amish into fights."

I shivered. This was new upsetting information about Zeke. I hated to think how close he'd come to marrying Edith. If he was so openly violent at work, what was he like at home? I didn't even want to think about it.

Lois and I followed Carter to the open garage door; just inside was an Amish man not much older than Carter. I hadn't known he was there. It wasn't a stretch to think he had heard every word Carter and I had said outside the warehouse. He gnawed on a large piece of chewing tobacco. I tried to keep my expression neutral even though I hated the ugly habit.

The dark-haired, beardless man spat chewing tobacco onto the dirt floor of the warehouse, and I averted my eyes. Chewing was a common vice among Amish men. It was even more common than smoking. I wasn't fond of it. It had cost me my husband. The few times that I had seen my Kip partake—he tried not to chew in front of me—I had asked him to stop. I should have insisted on it because he died from throat cancer. The *Englisch* doctors told me it was because of his tobacco habit. I didn't bother to tell any of this to the young man who spat on the ground. It was easy to tell if a person was receptive to advice or not. This young man was most certainly not.

The inside of the warehouse smelled like freshly cut wood, motor oil, and vinegar. It was my first time in such a building. It wasn't the sort of place an Amish woman went, but I straightened my back and held my chin up as if I had every reason to be there.

It was something my Kip had taught me. He told me, "Millie, when you feel unsure of yourself, straighten your back and hold up your chin; then you will change your own mind."

Every time I followed his advice, I found that he was right, and this time was no different. I stood inside of the warehouse as straight as a board and began to feel far more confident than when I had entered. Lois was right next to me, holding her massive bag at the ready. I prayed we wouldn't need to call on its contents.

Men, mostly Amish men, moved around the warehouse with purpose in their stride. It seemed to me that every last one of them knew where he was going and was in a hurry to get there. The only man who didn't seem to be in much of a rush was the one chewing tobacco at the door.

Carter noticed him too, and for the first time since we'd arrived his winning smile faltered. "Reuben, I believe your break was over a good ten minutes ago."

Reuben stood up slowly as if he was made of folded paper and had to unbend every limb to work out the creases. After what seemed like an unnecessarily long delay, he replied, "I must have lost track of time, Carter."

Carter's wide mouth pressed into a line. "You keep losing track of time, Reuben, and we will have to part ways. I think it's clear that you might not be a *gut* fit working here."

"Because I'm not like the rest of your Amish robots who follow every command you issue. I suppose I think too much for myself."

"*Nee*, Reuben, the truth of it is you are too lazy. Jeremy will be here later to talk to you."

Reuben paled just a bit. "He can't touch me."

Carter shook his head. "That's between you and him. Please get back to work." He walked away without waiting to see if Reuben did as he was told. We followed. When we crossed the warehouse, Carter smiled at Lois and me again. "I'm sorry you had to see that. Even though we're Amish, we still have some bothersome employees." He said this last part for Lois's benefit, I knew.

I nodded.

He glanced at Lois. "Are you coming with us?"

Lois's drawn-on eyebrows went up. "Well, do you expect me to go wait in the car like a servant?"

Carter's face turned bright red.

"I thought it would be nice to learn a little bit about the construction business while I'm here," she added. "I am ever curious."

I suppressed a grimace. "It's fine with me if Lois comes along. She's not just my driver. She's my friend."

Carter seemed to relax when I told him that. I gave Lois a look.

She whispered to me, "I thought that saying I was just the driver was a good angle. It would give me a good reason for being here."

"You are driving me around," I whispered back. "But being my friend is another *gut* reason for you to be with me."

"Oh, I didn't think of that."

CHAPTER TWENTY-SIX

Carter led us through the warehouse. There were Amish men scattered about measuring cut wood, shooting nails into boards with nail guns, and sawing planks. As we went, Carter told us what each man was doing. "I'm the foreman of the onsite operations. Basically, that means I stay back at the warehouse and make sure all the pieces are made properly before they're assembled out on the build site. It's much easier to correct any problems that might come up here than do it at the build."

I took a few steps forward, so that I was walking next to him. "What did Zeke usually do on the job? Edith mentioned roofing work."

He glanced at me. "Zeke was one of the guys we could stick in anywhere. He was great with just about everything. He could build anything and fast. He was also the best at fixing the mechanical equipment. Anything with a motor, he could take apart and put back together again with little trouble. I could have used him today with that forklift, to be honest. He didn't have the best attitude, but he will be difficult to replace. He was a jack of all trades. I can't think of anyone we have working for us now who has the same skills he did."

Carter's talk about Zeke being *gut* with motors reminded me of Darcy's story, how Zeke saved her after her truck broke down on the side of the road, and how he was able to fix the truck. A lot of Amish men were good with motors and mechanics. Really, that was out of necessity. At times, Amish men measured their personal worth in things they could fix themselves without the help of someone else.

"That fellow Reuben we saw when we first came in. What does he do here?" Lois asked.

For a moment, I thought Carter wasn't going to answer. It was an intrusive question for an *Englischer* to ask an Amish man about his business, but then again, Carter had threatened Reuben with firing right in front of us.

"Reuben worked roofing with Zeke. I like to think that he's moving slow today because he lost a friend, but I can't say for sure that that's the reason. If Reuben spent any time with anyone on the job, it would be Zeke."

I had never seen Reuben around the greenhouse in the many times I'd gone there since Edith and Zeke were engaged, and I knew he wasn't a member of our district. If he had been, I would have at least spied him at church. "Is he a member of a local district?" I asked.

"He's from a district over in Knox County, actually. He's one of a few men that a driver brings over each morning to work. He's the only bad egg in the bunch. The rest of them have been great. I hate to let him go because I believe *Gott* wants us to give everyone a second chance, but I have given Reuben over ten chances. It's started to affect the morale of the other guys too. I doubt he will be here much longer. He might even be gone by the end of the week. It's really up to the owner."

"Who owns the business?"

"Jeremy Swartz. He's a Mennonite, a liberal one at that. Looks and acts just like an *Englischer*. No offense," he said to Lois with a blush.

She grinned. "No offense taken."

"Is Jeremy here today?" I asked.

A strange look crossed Carter's face. "*Nee*, he's not here much at all. He will be in later, mostly to deal with Reuben, I'm afraid. Jeremy has many businesses across the county. He never visits any one of them, from what I've heard, for more than ten minutes at a time. Truthfully, we don't mind it around here. As long as we do a *gut* job and keep making money, that's all he cares about. That's why I think Reuben will have to be let go. He's starting to impact our ability to make money since some of my best guys refuse to work with him. Amish workers, in general, don't abide laziness, and Reuben is just about the laziest Amish man I've ever seen." He shook his head. "What do you want to know about Zeke? I promised my wife that I would help you as much as possible. Edith is a *gut* friend to her, and she is brokenhearted over the rumors about her friend."

"I am too," I said quietly. "Edith had nothing to do with his death. I'm certain of that." Even as I said it, I couldn't forget that I'd heard Edith mislead Deputy Aiden when she was questioned. I forced those worries to the back of my mind.

Just in front of me was a saw that held logs of wood as long as my house. The pieces of wood went through the machine and were shaved on either side until they came out the other end as perfectly flat boards. The blades of the machine were so sharp, it was as if they were cutting through butter and not hardwood.

Carter nodded at the machine and spoke up to be heard over the loud saw. "We take pride in planking our own boards. Not many construction companies are able to do that, but we want to make sure that if we put our name on something, it's done right. The only way to be certain of that is to do it ourselves. Swartz and Swartz Construction is well-known for making sturdy houses, barns, and other outbuildings. It's been owned by the Mennonite Swartz family for six generations. Jeremy took over the company about eighteen months ago."

An Amish man drove by me in a forklift, carrying what looked like roof shingles. I recognized him as a member of my community. A member of my district could drive a tractor or other equipment for work purposes. Only if he took the forklift out for a joyride on the road would he get in trouble with Bishop Yoder, or more accurately, with Ruth. She had, in many ways, assigned herself the position of her husband's enforcer.

The man driving the forklift stopped it close to where we were standing. He nodded at Lois and me and then said to Carter, "I can't find the Richards house blueprints. I've looked everywhere."

"They must be here," Carter said.

The other man pulled thoughtfully on his long, dark beard. "I would think so. I can't see a reason that Zeke would have taken them from the place. He wasn't one to do overtime." He smiled at me. "I'm so sorry to interrupt your conversation."

"It's no trouble," I said. "Are you talking about Zeke Miller?"

Carter's happy face appeared strained. "*Ya*, we were planning a new layout for a house. Zeke was doing a lot of the work on it."

"Don't you have it saved somewhere, like on a computer?" Lois asked.

All three of us looked at her.

"Oh, right."

Carter addressed the man on the forklift. "Keep looking. It has to be here."

His employee nodded and went back to his task.

Carter smiled at us. "Sorry for the interruption. It's a busy day here. Every day is a busy day, really, but I am feeling the pressure of Zeke's absence. He worked for the construction company for over ten years. Despite his less-than-cheerful attitude at times, he always showed up at work on time and did a quality job. I'm not looking forward to replacing him, even though there will be plenty of applicants. There are a lot of young Amish men in the county who would like stable work. Most construction companies in the area don't have the number of clients we do. It's not very often that we have no job to work on. As soon as Jeremy gives me the go-ahead, I will replace Zeke." He made a face. "I'm sorry if that sounds callous."

"Was there anyone that he worked with that he particularly didn't like or who didn't like him?" Lois asked.

Carter shook his head. "Not in recent memory."

"What about in less recent memory?" Lois asked.

Carter glanced at her. He was still wondering what she was doing there but was far too polite to ask. After a beat, he said, "He and Moses Hochstetler didn't see eye to eye on just about anything. I never knew why, but when I heard that Zeke was to marry Moses's widow, I thought maybe he'd had feelings for her all along."

That was an interesting thought, but it didn't

help me find a killer. I knew Moses was innocent since he had been dead for years.

"Anyone else?" I asked.

He shrugged. "Moses Hochstetler and Zeke made no secret of their dislike for one another. If Zeke didn't get along with someone else in the company, he wasn't as open about it as he had been about his dislike for Moses."

I felt my shoulders sag. It seemed that coming to the warehouse had been a huge waste of time. The only person that Carter thought might be a suspect was dead. I should leave the investigating to Deputy Aiden. That would be the best idea.

I smiled at Carter. "Thanks so much for your time. Lois and I will be going now. I know you have to get back to work."

"But?" Lois began.

I tugged on my friend's sleeve.

"There's nothing more for us to see here."

She narrowed her eyes as if she thought I was up to something.

"Can you ladies show yourselves out?" Carter asked. "I need to speak to one of my employees on this side of the warehouse before he goes to the next job site."

"Sure thing!" Lois said cheerfully and waved.

She and I left Carter. When we were no longer within earshot, she leaned in. "Is this the part where we snoop around?"

I shook my head. "There's no point in snooping

around when we don't even know what we are looking for."

"Speak for yourself. I can always find something when I sniff around. I have a nose for such things."

"So, you've solved a murder before?" I raised my eyebrows.

"Well, no, but I am a whiz at finding missing socks and keys. Ask anyone in my family. It can't be much different from that."

I shook my head and was relieved when Lois followed me out of the warehouse instead of wandering off to use her sleuthing skills. I wasn't sure what she would turn up at the warehouse, but I doubted it would have anything to do with Zeke's murder.

When we got outside, there was an *Englischer* standing with Reuben.

"Looks like Reuben didn't go back to work like Carter told him to," I murmured.

"That's Jeremy Swartz," Lois said into my ear. "I recognize his face from the billboards in Millersburg."

"Billboards?"

She nodded. "He's all over the place down there as a local businessman. He's trying to expand his house-building business. When Carter mentioned his name, I knew it was familiar, but I didn't put two and two together until I saw his face. He's a very powerful man and has a ton of money. I mean buckets of it. He is completely loaded. He is rolling—"

"All right, all right, I get the idea," I interrupted her. It was interesting that Jeremy Swartz would be at this warehouse, which according to Carter he never visited, just days after Zeke Miller was killed. Still, I couldn't see what any of it had to do with Zeke, other than the fact Zeke worked for Swartz. From what Carter said as his manager, Zeke had done a decent job for the company, so it didn't seem as though Jeremy would have any reason to want him permanently removed. Even if he had, murder wasn't the answer when he could have just fired him.

Reuben shook his fist at Jeremy. "You can't do this to me. You're only doing it because you're scared that he's back. Everything was fine for you until then."

"Don't say another word," Jeremy hissed. "Not one more word about it."

"It's okay to be afraid of him. Lots of folks are."

Lois grabbed me by the arm and pulled me around the corner of the building.

CHAPTER TWENTY-SEVEN

W ha—"

"Shh." She pushed me back behind the warehouse. "You don't want them to see us, do you?"

"Why does it matter?"

"Because we're eavesdropping. That's what Amish Marples do. You really need to get with the program, Millie."

"We don't even know that this has anything to do with Zeke," I whispered back.

"We don't know that it doesn't, either. I think it's best to gather all the information we can, and then sort it out later."

I wanted to argue more, but Lois held her finger to her lips and peeked around the side of the warehouse. Not knowing what else to do, I did the same.

"I don't have to listen to this," Jeremy said through gritted teeth. "You're fired. I want you out of here right now." Flecks of spittle gathered in his mouth.

"You can't fire me, you scared Menno. I know too much. Zeke was my friend, not yours."

I couldn't see Jeremy's face, but I saw his fist balled at his side. It seemed to take all his strength for him to keep from striking Reuben.

"Don't you threaten me. Do you have any idea of the power I have in this county? I could ruin you and your entire district."

Reuben laughed. "Threatening my district is no threat to me. They would be happy to be rid of me."

"I can see why."

"Besides, I don't live in this county," Reuben said with a smug expression on his face. "It would serve you well to remember that. Your power is not so great that it reaches outside of Holmes County."

Jeremy shoved Reuben in the shoulder, and the Amish man bounced back as if he was ready to strike, but then he laughed. The laughter had a sinister sound to it. "You will have to do better than that if you want to stop me."

"I want you off my property. Now," Jeremy said through gritted teeth.

"I'll leave gladly, but this is not the last you will be hearing from me, Swartz," Reuben spat back, tobacco-colored spittle flying from his mouth.

"Gross," Lois whispered into my ear.

Jeremy didn't say another word. He spun around and stomped toward the warehouse. Lois yanked me back around the corner of the warehouse just before he spied either one of us.

Lois grinned as if she'd come in first place at the county fair. "See, aren't you glad that we eavesdropped now?"

"What are you talking about?" I smoothed out my apron and skirts and made certain my pocket watch was in place.

She gave an exasperated sigh. "Clearly there are some nefarious happenings going on."

"Whether there are or not, that doesn't mean they are related to Zeke."

"But they could be!" Her enthusiasm wasn't dampened in the least.

"Even if that is true, which I am not saying it is, eavesdropping is still not something we really should be doing."

"I don't think taking any part in this investigation is something that we *should* be doing, but we're doing it."

She had me there.

"Who's back there?" a sharp voice asked.

I spun around to find Reuben glaring at us. I was dumbstruck under his furious gaze.

Lois was not. "Carter gave us a tour of the warehouse, and we were just walking around the outside to get a good look at it. It's a very impressive business. I have never been to a construction site quite like this before."

Reuben narrowed his eyes as if he didn't believe her. Honestly, I couldn't blame him. It was a very far-fetched story. There was really no *gut* reason I could think of that two mature women such as us should be wandering around the construction warehouse.

"I think you're here to make trouble." He leaned in closer to me.

I could smell the tobacco on his breath. It was a revolting scent, not only because it was so pungent but because of everything I had gone through with Kip and his illness. The scent made me sick to my stomach. I recoiled from him.

He took a step closer. "Did you tell Jeremy to get rid of me? Because it's not going to work. I won't disappear. I can ruin you all."

"Whoa, whoa, whoa," Lois said, inserting herself between Reuben and me. "Who said anything about ruining anyone else? Goodness, I thought the Amish were peace-loving people. Why are your feathers so ruffled? I think you need to take a breath and calm down, young man."

Reuben blinked at her.

"That's better. Take a breath," she ordered. "Also, while I'm giving sage advice, I would tell you to lay off the chew. It's an ugly habit and terrible for your health. Nobody likes it. Plus, you could get very sick and possibly die."

Reuben spat just an inch from her feet.

"Lovely," Lois muttered and then she shook her finger at him. "You need to learn to respect your elders a little bit better, young man."

Reuben glared at me. "Did Jeremy send you to spy on me? Is that why you are here, and why he showed up so quickly after you arrived?"

"Hey," Lois said. "We don't know any Jeremy,

so I'm going to have to ask you to calm down again."

I shook my head. What she was saying was mostly the truth. I didn't know Jeremy personally.

"We aren't here about Jeremy. We are here about Zeke." I folded my arms and stared him down with my best Amish-aunt face.

Beside me, Lois gasped, but I was tired of talking around the real reason that brought us to the warehouse. The only way I was going to get straight answers from the Amish was to ask straight questions.

"What do you know about Zeke?" I asked.

"I know that he wasn't who he pretended to be."

I stared at Reuben. "What do you mean?"

He laughed. "You think I am going to tell some old Amish woman and her crazy *Englisch* friend what Zeke Miller was like? I know who you are, and I know that you want to help Edith. Maybe you shouldn't be traveling around looking for answers and stick closer to home instead."

"What do you mean by that?"

"Ask Edith." His lip curled into an ugly smirk.

I felt a chill run down my back. I had known for the last two days that Edith was the one I needed to speak to the most about Zeke, but I hadn't had a chance to do so. Actually, if I was honest with myself, I was afraid. I was afraid she knew something, and I wasn't sure I would like what she had to say. I didn't know if I wanted to hear it.

I took a step closer to him. Just because I was an older Amish woman, I wasn't going to let him scare me. "You should give up tobacco just like Lois said. It's a bad habit. One of many I'm sure you have."

"What's going on back here?" a strong male voice asked.

Reuben looked behind him and saw Deputy Aiden and Deputy Little walking toward us. His face paled ever so slightly.

"Busted!" Lois said. "It's the cops."

CHAPTER TWENTY-EIGHT

Deputy Aiden and Deputy Little stood a few feet away from us with confused expressions on their faces.

Reuben hurried away across the parking lot. His movements were something between a fast walk and a jog. The way he moved triggered a memory. I pointed to his back. "That's him! That's the man I saw running away from the greenhouse. He was there the morning Zeke died." I had never been so certain about anything in all my life.

Deputy Little took off like a shot. I was surprised the deputy could run that fast. He hadn't struck me as a sprinter. A few yards away from us, Deputy Little jumped and tackled Reuben to the ground.

Lois's mouth fell open. "It's like watching one of the cop shows on TV. I didn't know it was really that exciting. Do you think he will zap him with his Taser?"

Reuben's lip was bleeding. "You hurt me. I will sue you."

Deputy Little snorted. "The Amish don't sue."

"I'm not like most Amish."

"I can see that," Deputy Aiden said, looking

down at Reuben. "You are nothing like most Amish I know since you fled when the police arrived. Can you tell me why you did that?"

"What's going on out here?" Jeremy and Carter came out through the open garage door, followed by a handful of curious Amish construction workers. When the workers saw the police, they turned around and went back into the warehouse. In general, my community was leery of law enforcement. Carter looked over his shoulder wistfully, as if he wanted to hide back in the warehouse too.

Deputy Aiden stepped forward. "We'd like to ask this man a few questions, but when we approached him, he ran away. Deputy Little stopped him. Running away from a sheriff's deputy is a serious offense."

Jeremy looked down at Reuben with disgust. "I'm not the least bit surprised that Reuben is wanted by the police. He has been nothing but trouble for me and for my company."

"He's not wanted," Deputy Aiden corrected. "We only want to ask him a few questions. Why would you assume that we had a warrant out for his arrest?"

Jeremy ignored Deputy Aiden's question. "Then take him away and question him. He shouldn't be here as it is. I fired him. I want him off my grounds."

"I take it you are Jeremy Swartz of Swartz and

Swartz Construction," Deputy Aiden said. "I would like to ask you a few questions as well."

"Me? Why would you want to talk to me? If it's about him"—he pointed at Reuben—"I have nothing to say. He doesn't work here anymore. I have a right to keep my opinions about former employees to myself."

"I used to work here until a few minutes ago," Reuben spat. "Until you fired me because I could tell—"

"Yes, he worked for me," Jeremy snapped. "But the man is clearly delusional if he hopes hanging around here will get him his job back."

Deputy Aiden raised his eyebrows at Carter. "Is that right, Carter?"

Sweat appeared on Carter's forehead. "*Ya*, Reuben has been a problem employee for some time. I knew that Mr. Swartz was planning on letting him go. I didn't know that it would happen today."

Aiden nodded. "Little, will you take Reuben to the car and ask him a few questions? Mr. Swartz, if it's not too much trouble, I would like a moment of your time."

"What about? I don't know what Reuben does when he's not here. I never really knew what he did when he *was* here, which is why I fired him. Nor do I know what you are doing here in reference to a minor employee."

"I'm not here about Reuben," Deputy Aiden

said. "I came here to talk to you about Zeke Miller." Aiden glanced at me. "It seems to me I'm not the first one to have the idea of speaking with you either."

Jeremy's gaze snapped in our direction. "Who are you?"

"I'm so sorry, Mr. Swartz." Carter was sweating. "They are—"

"We were just passing through. My friend Millie here was showing me around the county," Lois said as if she was chatting about the weather. "I have an interest in all things Amish."

"Why?" Deputy Aiden asked.

"Because I'm writing a book," she said effortlessly.

I tried to keep my face as neutral as possible, but this was the first I had heard of Lois wanting to write a book about the Amish.

"It's a novel," Lois went on to say. "I think the community is fascinating, and I felt that I needed to know more about Amish trades so that I could write about them. Of course, you have the largest Amish construction business in the county. It makes perfect sense for me to want to see the best example of Amish craftsmanship."

"You're researching a book?" Jeremy asked.

Lois looked him straight in the eye. "Research is important to me, and I feel I need to be exposed to aspects of Amish culture in order to portray it fairly in story form." She said all this as if she had really thought about it, and it wasn't something that she was just making up on the spot, even though I had a sneaking suspicion she was. I remembered that Lois had saved us both from trouble when we were girls because of her fast-talking ways and elaborate stories. I thought, at times, that my parents accepted her stories just so she would stop talking altogether.

Although I couldn't lie myself, I was grateful that Lois had jumped in.

"Carter, do you know anything about this?" Jeremy asked.

"They are friends of my wife's. I promised my wife that I would let them see the warehouse. I didn't see any harm in it. We give tours of the warehouse all the time to complete strangers."

"You need to clear things like that with me from now on. I don't want people moving around the warehouse who shouldn't be there. If they got hurt, we could get sued."

Carter turned pale. "*Ya*, okay, I will from here on out."

I frowned. The last thing I wanted to do was cause trouble for Carter and Iris. They were a young family and would struggle if Carter lost his job. "What Carter said is true," I put in. "His wife, Iris, and I are in the same quilting circle. Maybe you have heard of it. It's called Double Stitch."

Despite my corroboration, Jeremy narrowed his

eyes at his foreman. I had a feeling his discussion with Carter wasn't over. I also took his response as a no, that he hadn't heard of Double Stitch before.

Out of the corner of my eye, I saw the sweat on Carter's forehead getting more pronounced. It was time for Lois and me to leave. I couldn't put Carter's job any more at risk. I pulled on her sleeve. "Thanks so much for your time."

"I'll walk you to your car," Deputy Aiden said.

"No need," I said, waving the deputy away. "We know that you have many important things to attend to. Lois and I can show ourselves out."

"No, I insist." Deputy Aiden fell into step beside me.

Lois made a face. I felt the same way.

Deputy Aiden walked silently with Lois and me to her sedan. "This is your car, Lois Henry?"

Lois put her hands on her hips. "How do you know my last name?"

"I know who you are."

"How?" Lois asked, clearly surprised. Then her eyes narrowed. "Is this about some outstanding warrant for my first husband, because if it is, I haven't seen that man in fifty years."

Aiden opened his mouth, but Lois was faster and snapped her fingers. "No, this is about Rocksino-guy, isn't it? I can't shake that worm. What's he in the big house for?"

"Rocksino-guy?" the deputy asked.

"Husband number four. It's a very long story, how we met, but my relationship with him is all over. You can check the courts if you don't believe me."

The deputy shook his head as if he was trying to process everything Lois was saying and it wasn't coming together in his brain. I could understand that. I often felt the same way when Lois was speaking.

"I don't know anything about Rocksino-guy," Deputy Aiden said. "And I don't think I want to. I know of *you* because I visited the Sunbeam Café just a little bit ago and had a nice chat with Darcy."

"Lots of people go into Sunbeam in the morning to chat with Darcy," Lois said. "That doesn't mean anything. She does have the best coffee in the village. I believe she is doing the village a favor by having good coffee instead of that watered-down stuff the Amish drink all day long." She glanced at me. "Sorry, Millie, but you know it's true."

I didn't argue with her about that.

"Her coffee is good, and I did have some," the deputy said in measured tones. "But her coffee wasn't why I was there. I went to talk to Darcy about Zeke Miller."

"You knew about Darcy and Zeke?" Lois blurted out.

I sighed. If the sheriff's deputy had been waiting

for confirmation that the affair was real, Lois had just given it to him.

"It was a rumor going around the Amish community. I was able to pick up on it. When I told Darcy why I was there, she was quick to mention a visit from her grandmother's childhood friend who just happened to be Edith Hochstetler's aunt."

"I'm going to have to talk to that girl," Lois muttered just loud enough for me to hear.

"So what are you doing here?" Deputy Aiden asked. "And don't give me that song and dance about wanting to write a book about the Amish."

Lois narrowed her eyes. "But I do want to write a book about the Amish. I think I would do very well at it."

Deputy Aiden raised his eyebrows. "I'm sure you would, but I don't think that's the only reason you're here. Is it, Millie?"

"*Nee*," I said. "We want to find out what happened to Zeke."

Lois groaned at my honest answer.

Deputy Aiden shook his head. "You need to give me time to solve the case."

"If this situation isn't dealt with quickly, it might be too late to save the reputation of Edy's Greenhouse. Who is going to want to shop at a greenhouse where someone was murdered?" Lois asked. "Even more, who's going to want to buy flowers from a killer?"

"Edith didn't kill anyone," I said.

"I know that," Lois said. "Just like my Darcy didn't kill anyone, but this could ruin her business too, and it will be worse for her because it's a new business. My granddaughter has put her heart and soul into that café. If she loses it, especially after losing Zeke, I don't know what she will do. She's worked too hard to have it ruined."

"Well, now that you have Reuben in custody, things might be different," I said to the deputy. "I know he's the one who was in the greenhouse the morning Edith discovered Zeke's body in the cactus room."

"But you said you didn't know who that person was," Deputy Aiden argued.

"I didn't," I said, wavering just a tad. "But when I saw him running away today, I just knew in my heart it was the same person. It was how he moved."

Deputy Aiden pressed his lips together. "We can't convict someone of a crime based on how he moved. Did you see his face?"

I shook my head.

"You are playing a very dangerous game," Deputy Aiden said and then nodded to Lois too. "You both are. There is a killer on the loose and you are making yourselves targets."

Lois pointed at herself. "I'm not making me a target. I don't want to be a target. No, thank you."

I swallowed as I remembered my frightening ride early that morning on the way to the greenhouse. Could Deputy Aiden be right? And was that scary experience related to the murder?

"I understand your concern that everything is done right with the investigation," he went on to say. "And I know you care about your families. That speaks well of you, but you have to understand too that you are putting your own lives in danger and making my job investigating the crime even more difficult."

"I'm sorry if that's the case," I said. "We will do our best to stay out of your way."

Deputy Aiden pressed his lips together. "I guess that's the best I can ask for."

"Really, I don't want to be a target," Lois added.

CHAPTER TWENTY-NINE

We got into the car and watched as Deputy Aiden walked back to the warehouse. I glanced at Lois. "A book? That was the best excuse you could come up with for our being there?"

"I didn't hear you come up with anything better. Besides, when Bryan said he was writing a book, I thought, why can't I?"

I shook my head. "Who's Bryan?"

"Bryan back at the café!" She couldn't keep the exasperation out of her voice. "You met him yesterday afternoon. He's writing the great American novel, and I figure if he can do it, so can I. There's no time like the present, so I decided while we were standing there that it was just what I was going to do! Remember when we were young and used to love to write?"

Now that she mentioned it, I did remember Lois writing stories when we were girls. She loved even more for us to act them out in my family's cow barn. She said the hayloft made a great stage and the cattle a good audience. We performed countless numbers of her plays there until we were too old to see the joy in it any longer.

Lois grinned. "I can tell that you are remembering some of my old plays. My favorite was *The Pirate and the Lost Maiden*."

My face broke into a matching grin. "That was my favorite too."

"I know. You always wanted to be the pirate."

"Could you blame me? Besides, that maiden was missing for so much of the play, she was hardly on the stage."

"Good point." She settled her giant purse on my lap. I hoped it wouldn't leave a bruise.

"Even though you liked to write plays when we were children, I don't know how that translates to writing now."

"Are you kidding? I have the perfect material."

"What?"

"You!"

"What?"

"Just think of it, Amish Marple Mysteries. They would sell like hotcakes. I bet half the publishers in New York would be interested."

I scowled at her. "I don't want to be in a book."

"Don't you worry, I will change your name. It will be great!" She rubbed her hands together. "Of course, Amish Marple will have to have a brilliant yet slightly zany sidekick." She half bowed in her seat. "Ta-da, I'm perfect for the role."

I sighed.

The next morning, Lois's car rolled up my driveway a little before nine. She was late, just as she had been the day before. She hopped out of the car, and the goats ran to greet her. She was quickly becoming one of their favorite new friends.

I walked over to the trio, and Lois grinned at me. I noted that today she wore silver jewelry and pink eyeshadow.

"Where to next?" she asked when I reached the car and the goats began dancing around her.

"I think it's high time I had a heart-to-heart with Edith over everything that's happened."

She raised her fist. "To the greenhouse, it is."

At the greenhouse, Lois parked her car by the hitching post. There wasn't a single Amish buggy tethered to the post, and there weren't any cars in the parking lot either.

"I have a bad feeling about this," Lois said.

I did too. It might be Wednesday, but it was still May, the time of year when people bought the most plants. The greenhouse would have been open for several hours now, but there wasn't a soul in sight. I got out of the car. Despite the lack of customers, I had at least expected to hear the sounds of children playing somewhere on the property.

The only thing I heard was the rustle of the breeze in the trees and the mooing of a cow at a farm nearby.

Lois stood next to me and twisted one of the many rings on her fingers. "This is creepy. Where is everyone?"

I shook my head. I didn't know. "Let's check

the house." I walked up to the front door and tried the doorknob. It didn't turn. I knocked. No answer. The house was locked up tight.

I stepped back from the front door. "They still might be here. They're probably all in the greenhouse. Sometimes Edith likes the children to stay in there with her while she's working, so she can keep an eye on them."

"Wouldn't the children be in school?"

"You're right. I should have thought of that sooner," I said, feeling a little bit more at ease that there was some kind of explanation for the lack of people about. "The boys will be in school. Ginny most likely is with her mother. Edith wouldn't want her to be inside the house alone. I was here very early in the morning yesterday. My nephew Enoch is visiting. I don't see his car now though, so he must have left."

She held up her hand. "Wait, Enoch is here? I thought he was English."

"He is," I said. "He's back for a visit." I didn't say any more than that. Lois didn't know about my complicated history with Enoch, since he'd left the Amish community long after she moved away. I saw no reason to rehash it now, especially since Enoch had forgiven me. It was time to forget those difficult times in the past and move on to the challenges of the present. The first of the challenges being to find my niece.

"Isn't it strange the door is locked though?"

Lois asked. "Most Amish I know leave their homes unlocked during the day. Maybe not the ones in the village, but the ones living this far out from the touristy areas do."

"I think considering what happened to Zeke, my niece is just trying to be cautious."

Lois nodded and followed me to the greenhouse. I walked quickly. I wanted to see with my own eyes that Edith and Ginny were safe.

When we were within a few feet of the greenhouse, the five kittens that the children were playing with the day before galloped out from under the house. Peaches raced toward me and before I could stop him, he climbed up my skirt and tucked his little peach body into my apron pocket. "What on earth do you think you are doing, little one?"

"Oh my word!" Lois cried. "Aren't they the cutest things you ever saw? Is your niece going to keep them all or find homes for them? I think one of these little kittens would be just the thing to cheer up Darcy. She has always loved cats."

I patted Peaches's velvety head.

He looked up at me with big amber eyes and mewed, scrunching up his pink nose as he did. Oh dear, it seemed to me that the children might be right—the goats were going to have a younger brother. I had always been an animal lover. Anytime a runt had been born on the farm, I would beg my father to give it to me to nurse back to health. Peaches seemed to know that and had plans to come home with me.

The mother cat was a large, long-haired, white beauty, and she walked behind us, nervously glancing at my apron pocket. I wondered if she was considering taking the kitten from my pocket by force. I wouldn't have blamed her. If I was in her position, I would have felt the same way. I lifted the kitten from my large pocket and set him on the grass next to his mother among his white and orange brothers and sisters, who didn't seem to have the least bit of interest in me. That's the way it was with animals.

"There you are," I said to the mother cat. "He's safe and sound. He won't be leaving you for a while." I nodded to the little cat. "You have some growing up to do before you come home with me, little one."

"I knew you would decide to take the little kitten home the moment you picked him up."

"He's a *gut* match for me," I said with a laugh.

Lois rubbed her chin. "Maybe the matchmaker angle would be good to work into an Amish Marple book. It's like a mystery and a love story!"

I groaned. "Why don't we find Edith and you can plot your book later?"

"Fair enough, but I've got so many ideas."

"I'm sure you do," I said.

"This place feels spooky, it's so quiet," Lois said.

I swallowed. I wouldn't admit it to Lois but there was an unsettling feeling on the farm. I wouldn't use her word "spooky"; no Amish woman would. All I knew was I didn't want to go into the greenhouse.

Lois and I stepped into the outer part of the greenhouse, where the cash register and gardening supplies like soil, water hoses, fertilizer, and garden tools were kept. Through the archway that led into the rest of the greenhouse, I could hear running water. I was right: Edith was there watering the plants. I'd worried over nothing.

When I stepped into the greenhouse, the coolness of the room hit me. It was still much warmer than outside, but not nearly as warm as it would be at the height of the day when the sun was shining down on the building.

I wrapped my shawl more tightly around my shoulders. I had expected to see Edith or Ginny when I came into the greenhouse, but instead there was a man there, watering the tables of plants. I froze, and Lois walked right into my back with an "oomph."

"Millie, you can't stop in the middle of the road like that." She rubbed her nose. "Am I bleeding?"

I examined her nose. "You're fine."

Tucker Leham dropped his hose on the ground and the water sprayed Lois and me.

"Ahh!" Lois cried. "I can't get my hair wet—I don't have another appointment for a week."

It wasn't nearly so bad as Lois made it seem. The worst of the wetting was a splash of water on our shoes. I kicked water off the toe of my black sneakers. "Tucker, what are you doing here?" I asked a little more loudly than I intended, but there are few things I disliked more in this world than wet feet. I couldn't wait to get home and change my shoes.

He scooped up his hose and turned the nozzle off. "Oh, Millie, you scared me half to death." He blushed as he said the words. I'm sure he was remembering a man had died in the greenhouse. "Did I get you a little wet?"

"More than a little," Lois muttered. "Thankfully, my hair is okay. Had it been ruined, this would all go a lot differently."

Tucker stared at Lois with wide eyes. It was an expression that I had seen on many Amish faces when they looked at her. Her spiky red hair was very different from what we were used to in the Amish world.

"What are you doing here?" I asked for a second time.

He blinked. "Watering and pruning the plants, the same things I have been doing here for the last fifteen years."

"Wait," Lois said. "I heard that you were fired by Edith."

He looked at her. "Who are you?"

She put her hands on her hips and her large

purse thumped against her thigh as she moved. "If you don't answer our questions, I'm your worst nightmare."

Tucker looked like he might cry.

"Tucker, this is my friend Lois." I glanced at Lois out of the corner of my eye. She didn't appear intimidating to me. "She won't hurt you." I wasn't sure what I was saying was true, but Tucker seemed to need to be comforted.

"I'm also her driver," Lois said as if that gave her some kind of credibility.

It took all my strength not to sigh aloud. In a much calmer voice, I said, "I'm surprised you are here if you aren't working at the greenhouse any longer."

"I was not let go by Edith. Zeke was the one who fired me." He held up his hose as if to protect himself with it.

"Hey, watch where you point that," Lois said, gesturing to the nozzle.

Tucker held the hose nozzle listlessly in his hand. "I wasn't going to spray you."

"Tell that to my shoes. These are vintage Keds too. They had better come out just like new from the washer, or you will be getting me a new pair."

I looked down at Lois's shoes, which were white sneakers covered with a tropical bird pattern.

"Lois," I said as calmly as I could. "We need to concentrate on the task at hand."

"Right Amish Mar—"

I gave her a look and she stopped just short of saying my full code name. I think it said a lot that I had come to accept the fact that I even had a code name.

"I came over this morning to offer my help to Edith. Now that Zeke—" He swallowed hard. "Now that Zeke can no longer help her, I wanted to go back to work. I know she can use it. This is a big property, and there is a lot to do. Not that Zeke did all that much work before he . . ."

I wasn't the least bit surprised Tucker couldn't seem to say that Zeke was dead.

He swallowed again as if to regain control over himself. "I knew I needed to help her. The greenhouse is hard to manage all on your own, and Zeke had run off most of the staff."

I raised my brow.

"The more I hear about Zeke, the more that I dislike him," Lois said.

I said a silent prayer for Carolina Miller, Zeke's mother, hoping that she wasn't hearing poor opinions of her son now that he had passed. The only person we'd talked to who had something nice to say about the man was Carter Young, who said he was a skilled worker, but even Carter said that Zeke had a bad attitude at work sometimes.

He nodded. "I was the last person left, and Zeke finally got rid of me too. I suppose that a lot of those folks who left will come back now that he's gone. No one wanted to leave Edith; she's so sweet." He stared at his black shoes. "Or they will if she has enough money to pay them."

Lois looked around the empty greenhouse. "You're going to need customers for that."

She had a point. The flowers and other plants were lovely and well cared for, but they needed somewhere to go, somewhere to live, or they would die just as Zeke had.

"Where is Edith now?" Lois asked.

"Enoch took her into town." Tucker sprayed water on a row of petunias. "He said that she had to go down to the sheriff's office to give them her fingerprints."

I had forgotten. I should have remembered the fingerprints. I had wanted to go with my niece to the sheriff's department. There were a few questions I had for Deputy Aiden. However, I was glad that she wasn't alone, and Enoch did appear that morning to be the kind and attentive brother he had been when they were small. I prayed that this new Enoch would remain in Holmes County. I knew it was far too much to wish for him to rejoin our Amish district, but I knew it would mean a lot to his sister—and frankly, to me—if he was nearby. There were many people who'd grown up in Amish families living in Holmes County and they continued to be close to their Amish relatives even though they didn't belong to the Old Order. There was no reason in my mind that Enoch should have to run off again—to wherever he had been these last ten years. Since he was never baptized into the Amish church, he wouldn't have to worry about being shunned by our community. Although I knew there would be some, like Ruth Yoder, who would never be completely comfortable with his presence.

"And Ginny?" I asked. "Where is she?"

"They took the little girl with them. The boys are in school. They should be coming home in another hour or so."

I raised my eyebrows. I found it a bit surprising that he knew the boys' school schedule so well.

"I meet them at the bus with my buggy when Edith is away. It's a favor that I have done for her for a long time. We are like . . ." He trailed off and shook his head. "I like Edith's children. All three of them are kind and funny. Micah can be a troublemaker, but he means well."

I nodded, feeling marginally better that Edith and the children were accounted for.

"You saw Enoch?" I asked.

"I did. He's *Englisch*," he said as if he was telling me my nephew had some kind of dreaded disease. It seemed to me in Tucker's estimation being *Englisch* was a fate worse than death.

"He's been *Englisch* for a very long time," I said.

Lois bristled. "You got something against English, young man?"

His eyes wide, he said, "*Nee.*"

282

I smiled at Tucker. "Can you excuse us for a moment?" I pulled Lois away from him and walked toward the front door. "Lois, why don't you go outside and wait for me while I talk to Tucker?"

"What? You don't want me here? I'm supposed to be your sidekick." She held up her purse. "I have the gear and the muscle too, to back it up."

"I don't need gear or muscle right now, but I would like to hear what Tucker might know about Zeke's murder. He's not going to talk to me with you standing there looking so tough. He's scared of you."

She nodded knowingly. "I do have that impact on some men. Many times I wished I'd scared Rocksino-guy away, but he kept coming like a cockroach that would not die."

I grimaced at the image. "If you go outside, it will give you time to snoop around the greenhouse. Wouldn't you like that?"

She nodded. "I love a good snoop." She cocked her head. "But if you think that Reuben was the one who was running away from the greenhouse after the murder, why are we still asking questions?"

"I know he was here that morning, but I don't know for sure he killed Zeke, and I didn't see him in the greenhouse when I first found Edith with Zeke's body in the cactus room. I was looking everywhere for Edith. I know I would have seen him." I paused. "I think I would have seen him."

"Maybe he came back because he forgot something at the murder scene. Perps always come back to the scene," Lois said. "That's what all the cop shows have taught me."

"I'm glad to hear it." I saw no reason to trust anything on *Englisch* television.

"I'm sure Deputy Aiden Brody is asking him that right now at the sheriff's department."

I nodded. I suspected that Deputy Aiden was, indeed, doing just that.

"I heard from the early morning crowd at the café that Reuben was kept overnight at the sheriff's department," Lois said.

"Who said that?" I asked.

"Just about everyone who came into the Sunbeam this morning. It was the talk of the village."

I frowned. If it was the talk of the *Englisch* side of the village, then it most certainly was the talk on the Amish side too. Ruth Yoder must know about it. She'd left a message for me on the shed phone I shared with the Raber sheep farm, saying she'd organized a meeting of the quilting circle at my home that evening. I didn't hear the message myself. The phone was at the Raber farm, but Raellen sent one of her older children over to tell me. I guessed that Ruth would have a lot to say at the meeting about the current situation.

"Well." Lois tapped her chin. "Snooping can't hurt. It's clear he's not going to say anything interesting when I'm standing there. You're right—I *can* be intimidating at times."

"You really can be."

"And it will give me some time to gather information for my books."

"Exactly."

She nodded. "All right. You've convinced me. I'll be outside." She walked out the greenhouse door, and I gave a sigh of relief.

When I turned back to the interior of the greenhouse to speak to Tucker, he was gone.

CHAPTER THIRTY

I walked through the greenhouse and found Tucker standing in front of the cactus room. There were two long strips of yellow police tape, blocking the entrance. Tucker turned around and swallowed. "I was trying to see if the plants are all right. Edith wouldn't want any of the cacti to die."

I peeked into the cactus room. "They look all right to me. Edith told the police that they wouldn't need to be watered for a few days."

He nodded. "I just like to check. I want everything done by the time Edith gets home. I know she will be tired and upset after her visit to the police station. I wanted to go with her, but Enoch said no."

I studied Tucker for a long moment. I knew for certain now that he cared very deeply about my niece. How long would it take for Edith to notice? Did she already know? And if she did, why had she chosen Zeke over Tucker when it was clear that of the two men, Tucker was the one who truly cared for her?

A question struck me. "You knew about Zeke and Darcy. Did you tell Darcy about Edith?"

He blinked at me. "Darcy? I don't know anyone named Darcy."

"Darcy is Lois's granddaughter and the curly blond-haired woman you saw Zeke with."

He gasped and looked around the greenhouse.

"Don't worry. Lois went outside to see the kittens."

He relaxed just a bit. "I didn't speak to the *Englisch* girl."

"Did you give her a note?"

"A note?" he asked, clearly confused.

"You were torn about how you would let her know, but you clearly wanted Edith to find out about Darcy. If she knew, she would end her engagement with Zeke. That would give you a chance with her at last."

He looked away. "I've heard it is impossible to keep feelings hidden from a matchmaker."

I chuckled. "That is true. My advice would be to give Edith time. She's had a terrible shock, and with her brother back in the village, she might want to change some things."

"I know she will," he said under his breath.

Before I could comment on that, he went on to say, "Edith still doesn't know about the *Englisch* woman. I'm sure she doesn't. There is no point in telling her now. It will just be another way for Zeke to hurt her even after he's gone."

"If she didn't know about Darcy, why did she end the engagement?" I mused aloud.

Tucker shook his head. "I don't know." He looked away from me. "It wasn't because of me."

"Has Edith hired you back?" I asked.

"Not officially, but when I offered to water the plants, she didn't argue with me. She was very anxious about going to the sheriff's department. I said I would go with her, but Enoch said that I would be more help here." His brow creased as if he didn't agree with Enoch on that point. "Enoch had a car, so they should be home soon. They have been gone for nearly three hours."

"Tucker, do you know why someone would have a reason to hurt Zeke?"

He shook his head. "I need to get back to work. I don't want Edith to have to worry about anything when she gets back. That way, she can concentrate on her customers."

I looked around the greenhouse. That was assuming there would be customers. Lois and I had been at the greenhouse for over a half hour, and no one had shown up yet. I was afraid that rumors over what had happened had scared away customers, both *Englisch* and Amish alike. If that were true, what did Edith have to do to bring them back?

He swallowed. "I know business has been slow. I can see from your face you know that too, but it will get better now . . ." He trailed off.

I wondered if he was going to say that it would get better now that Zeke was gone.

A horn honked outside the greenhouse. Tucker stepped around me. "They're back." He removed his handkerchief from the back pocket of his trousers and wiped his damp forehead.

I followed him outside. I saw Lois speaking to Edith and Enoch, who was holding Ginny. I let out a breath. It was still surprising to see my nephew back home. I hesitated for a moment while Tucker kept walking toward the little cluster.

"Aunt Millie!" Enoch called. "We are surprised to see you back again so soon."

"Lois wanted to see the greenhouse."

"Oh, I did," Lois said, nodding with a little too much enthusiasm to be sincere.

He smiled. "I was just telling your friend how nice it is to be back in Holmes County. I'm surprised by how much I have missed it and this place." He gestured to the property and then looked at his sister, who was staring at her shoes. "I only wish I could have come at a happier time for the family. Edith, you should go rest."

"*Nee*," she said. "Working in the garden has always helped me, and that's what I plan to do. It's what our *daed* always did in hard times."

"Our father never had hard times like these," Enoch argued. "Let me take over for a few days, so you can relax."

She frowned. "Brother, I have been taking care of this greenhouse for many years through more difficult times than this. Just like any Amish person worth their salt, I need to work. I accept your help, but I can't sit in the house while there is work to be done. That's not the Amish way. That's not my way."

He looked around. "Work for what? The plants are cared for. I'm sure Tucker made sure of that. There are no customers. Zeke kept the customers away. We need to think of a way to bring them back. I can do that for you. I have had a lot of success in business in my English life. You've worked so hard for so long, and you have just been through a terrible trauma. It's all right to take a rest, Edith."

I raised my brow. "What are you suggesting?"

"Perhaps it would help to have a man take over the business again. You are the best with plants, Edith, but I can do better on the business side."

"That is the biggest load of cra—" Lois began, but I squeezed her arm. She snapped her mouth closed.

Edith stood even straighter and after glancing at her young daughter, who was listening to all of this, said, "I'm sorry you think I have done such a poor job managing the business, brother. However, I can assure you that I have done as *gut* a job as any man or woman could. What happened here on Sunday has temporarily scared my customers away, but they will come back. I'm so confident that they will return, I am holding the opening season bonfire just like our *daed* used to at the beginning of every growing season. I haven't done it since *Daed* died, but it's time to bring it back."

"You can't be serious," Enoch said. "What if no one comes? You will be the laughingstock of the district."

"That's just the risk I will have to take then. I'm not afraid of taking risks either, Enoch. It's something I have had to learn to do as a widow, raising three children on my own. I have my community to support me, but I can also be proud of what I have done."

I felt my mouth curl into a smile.

Lois started to clap. "You go, girl."

Enoch scowled. "Everyone coming will be talking about you. Do you really want to deal with that scrutiny?" He placed a hand on his chest. "I know what it's like to have the district against you. I don't know that it's a good decision for your delicate temperament."

Lois shook with anger beside me and looked as if she was gearing up to say something really scathing. I squeezed her arm in warning.

"I can face them because I have nothing to hide." As she said this her voice wavered, and I wondered if perhaps her assertion wasn't completely true. She shook her head. "Besides, brother, I don't know why you are so concerned. I'm glad you were with me today to go to the sheriff's department. That was very hard. However, I don't need you to hold my hand any

291

longer. I am a capable woman and have been since you decided to leave the family."

"Edith, that's not fair." He glanced at me. "What choice did I have?"

My heart constricted. I knew he meant to hurt me with his question. He might as well have said that my mistake had forced him to leave. Of course, the past still lingered. I'd been a fool to think he could forgive me so readily.

"What choice do I have but to ensure this greenhouse survives so that my children have a future? The bonfire is the best way to show customers that I'm still open and ready for their business." She lifted her chin. "I will be inviting all the *Englisch* and Amish in Harvest, and you cannot change my mind. The bonfire is this Friday night. I hope you will come to support my children and me."

"I think you are making a terrible mistake," Enoch said.

She looked up at her older brother. "It's mine to make, not yours."

CHAPTER THIRTY-ONE

E dith picked up her daughter and went into the greenhouse. Lois, the two men, and I watched her go.

"Wow, she's one tough cookie," Lois said.

I couldn't agree more.

"She's being ridiculous," Enoch said. "The greenhouse isn't in any financial position to host a bonfire. That's going to cost a lot of money, especially if she insists on inviting the entire community. How will she feed all those people?"

"I'm sure our Amish district will help," I said. "And many *Englischers* in the village will too."

He looked at me. "Yes, because the Amish district never judges the members of its community."

I felt as if I had been slapped across the face. Before I could say anything, he stomped away. To my surprise, Tucker followed him.

Lois put her hands on her hips. "What on earth was that all about?"

I smoothed my dress over my waist, not because it was wrinkled, but because I didn't want Lois to see the tears that had gathered in my eyes. "It's a very long story."

"I love long stories, and it might help me with my book."

"This story wouldn't, and as your friend, I

would ask you not to put it in your book."

She looked me in the eye. "If you asked me to do that, you have my word that I would not."

Some of the pain in my heart lessened at her promise. An old proverb came to mind. "Love always finds a home in the heart of a friend." Lois was my true friend, even with the great gaps in our lives together. She would still love me even after my story.

As we stood outside the greenhouse, I gave her the short version of what had happened ten years ago with Enoch.

"So you feel like it was your fault that he left your district."

"I don't feel it was my fault; I know it was. My brother told me as much, and he died without ever seeing his son again. That's what causes me the most guilt. He so desperately wanted to see his son just once before he died." Tears sprang again to my eyes.

She shook her finger in my face. "Nope, I'm not having that. Enoch could have come back anytime. It's clear he still had ties to the community here if he knew that Edith was running the greenhouse. He would have heard about his father's death. It was his choice and his choice alone not to come back."

"You can be very bossy when you want to be."

She grinned. "It's one of the many perks that comes with age."

I had to agree with her there.

"I wouldn't be too worried about the bonfire failing. If there is one thing the entire community of Harvest loves, it's a party," she said. "I will spread the word to everyone in the village, and we will blow it up."

"Why would we want to blow it up?" I asked, alarmed.

"It's just an expression. The young folks say it."

"Not Amish young folks," I replied.

"Yeah, probably not."

I knew she was right about Harvest coming out for the bonfire. I was constantly surprised by the high number of community activities and special events the little village organized. I knew a lot of that had to do with the force of nature that was Margot Rawlings, but the people of the village, both *Englisch* and Amish, had to be willing to chip in too. Margot couldn't do it all on her own. "Maybe I should call Margot."

Lois shook her head. "No, I think that might be taking it too far. From what I gathered of Edith's speech, she wants to prove she can do this. If you invited Margot to help out, she would take over faster than you could say Father Christmas. Invite her to come though. That will be good for Edith's business."

Again, I knew my eccentric friend was right. Lois might be a character, but she had a *gut* head on her shoulders.

"I'll talk to my granddaughter about providing some of the food," she offered. "I think it would be a great way for the two women to band together. Maybe it can be a fresh start for both of them after Zeke."

"That's a nice idea," I said to Lois. "I hate to keep you here much longer, but I would like to speak to Edith privately before we leave."

Lois seemed to note the serious expression on my face. "It's time for a big heart-to-heart, I take it. Go. I never got a chance to do my snooping, so this will give me the time I need. First, I have a question for Ginny."

"What's that?"

Her eyes sparkled. "You'll see."

Lois and I walked into the greenhouse together. Ginny played with a faceless doll on the concrete floor while her mother worked. The very idea of the child being so close to the spot where a man had died gave me chills.

Lois walked over to Ginny. "I heard that you have some kittens."

The little girl's eyes shone. "*Ya*. Five kittens. The peach kitten is for *aenti*. His name is Peaches."

Lois grinned. "She already told me about her claim on that one. I heard you were looking for good homes for all of them. My granddaughter would love a kitten, and I think it would be a very nice surprise for her. She could use a little happiness now. Would you show me the kittens and help me pick the right one? I promise I won't even think about the peach kitten."

Ginny jumped to her feet and clutched her doll to her chest. She looked at her mother for permission, and Edith gave a slight nod. Then Ginny took Lois by the hand and pulled her to the part of the greenhouse where the back door was. It was the same door that I had seen Reuben run through the day I'd found Edith standing over Zeke's dead body. I wish I could have stayed and been there while Deputy Aiden questioned him.

Edith walked down the rows of flowers with a tightly woven basket in one hand and a small pair of clippers in the other. She pruned and deadheaded the flowers to make sure they would look their very best when customers came back to the greenhouse. I knew they would come back. Our community was built on forgiveness. Whatever they might believe about Edith, they were compelled to forgive her. I also knew that she would recover from any financial mistakes that had been made. She would build the business back up just as she'd told her brother she would. I was very proud of her determination and dedication to hard work. Hard work was the Amish way. We never shied away from it.

"You are probably like Enoch and think I am foolish for having the bonfire." She clipped a dead blossom off an orange marigold and tossed it into her basket.

"I don't think you're making a mistake at all. In fact, I believe this is the time to hold your chin up just as you are. You can't cower. It will only make things worse for you."

"I'm not thinking of myself. It's for the children." She closed her eyes for a moment to hold back tears.

" 'A mother is a gardener of God, tending to the hearts of her children,' " I said. "That's how the saying goes, and I know you are doing this to take care of your children in the best way you know how."

She looked at me. "I am because I failed them before."

"What do you mean?"

"Oh, *Aenti*," she whimpered. "I wanted to tell you before. I wanted to tell you weeks ago and again when I helped you put your summer garden in. I could not work up the nerve. I was afraid."

"What, child? You never have to be afraid of me." I clasped my hands in front of me.

"I'm not afraid of you, but I didn't want to see the disappointment on your face, and now that Zeke is dead, it's so much worse that I didn't tell you before. I have made a huge mistake."

"Just tell me. You know what happened with Enoch and me all those years ago. I'm not in any position to judge another person's mistakes. Only *Gott* can be your judge and He looks on a repentant heart with kindness and love."

She placed her basket and clippers on a table beside a large, pink, potted rose bush. "*Gott* will judge me harshly for what I've done."

I felt my pulse quicken. Was my niece about to tell me she'd killed Zeke Miller? *Nee*, that wasn't possible. Edith may have taken a misstep, but she wouldn't take another person's life.

I heard Ginny's laughter float through the open back door of the greenhouse and I considered the possibility. But *nee*, Edith wasn't a murderer. I gripped my hands more tightly together. Unless it was to save her children. I shivered and felt worse than ever. "Did Zeke hurt the children?"

Her face paled. "*Nee*. It was nothing like that. He hurt their future maybe, but he never touched them."

I let out a breath. That was a great relief. "What do you mean when you say he hurt their future?"

She wouldn't meet my eyes. "I have been so stupid, *Aenti*. After all these years of managing this greenhouse by myself, I turned it over to the first man who asked, and stood by while he made one wrong choice after another. Zeke wasn't *gut* with money, his own or mine. I knew this before we were even promised to be married. I saw how he would spend and spend on things that he could never even use as an Amish man. He had a car, for one. Did you know that?"

I shook my head.

"He did, just because he wanted it. He fought

against the idea of the simple Amish life. He was greedy, and he wanted material things. He was also interesting and exciting, and I think I loved him in my way just as I loved Moses. Both of those men were flawed. Moses had his demons, and Zeke had his greed."

I started to speak words of comfort, but she shook her head. "*Nee*, please do not make excuses for me. I was swept up in the romance of an attractive, gallant man loving me or what I thought was loving me. I know now he didn't care for me at all. It was my money he wanted. He courted me with such attention and care, I was swept right off my feet. Then when we were engaged, he asked to be involved in the greenhouse. As an Amish man, he would be in control of the greenhouse when we were married, so I thought it was best for our future to give it to him. I turned over the ledger, the accounts, and all the money I had saved in case I ever needed it." She closed her eyes. "He spent it all. Every last cent, and then he began saying that we couldn't pay my employees. He let them go, one by one. Tucker was the last. I knew when he fired so many of my employees that things were bad. I tried to talk to him about it, but he refused to discuss it with me. He said he was in charge of the greenhouse and I should cook and take care of the children."

I felt anger in the pit of my stomach over how he'd betrayed my niece's trust, but I said nothing.

This was her story to tell without my commentary on it.

"I finally gathered up the courage to look at the numbers myself. He would be away for days at a time, and after watching him when he was here, I knew where he hid the papers. How stupid I was." She shook her head. "I had just found the proof I needed the morning I came to see you at your home. Even though I didn't tell you why, I did tell you that I was going to end the engagement."

"Where did you tell him it was over?"

She pressed her lips together. "Here at my home. Thankfully, Enoch was here. Zeke was so angry. I was afraid of what he would do."

"What did he do?"

She lifted her eyes to me. "Zeke told me it was the right thing to do." Tears sprang to her eyes. "He told me that he'd met another woman and she was *Englisch*. He planned to leave the community to be with her. He wasn't upset. He was relieved."

I raised my eyebrows. "You knew about Darcy?"

"Darcy?" she asked.

"Oh." I grimaced. Clearly, she hadn't known the name of the other woman. I wished I hadn't said it.

"That's her name, isn't it?" she asked. "I've known about her since Saturday, but I didn't know her name."

I couldn't forget the fact that Enoch had

witnessed the breakup. "Could Enoch have done something to Zeke . . ." I trailed off.

She scowled. "You have always thought my brother was trouble."

"*Nee*, I have not. I thought he made poor choices when he was young. I have no right to judge the man he is today. I don't know him, but I know he would want to protect you and the children. He came back here, didn't he, at your request? He did not come back to Holmes County for anyone else."

"Enoch didn't even know what I was doing. I went to the front yard and met Zeke's buggy. I told him before he even got out. He told me about the *Englisch* woman and turned the buggy around just like that. It was the last time I ever saw him alive." She cleared her throat. "Will you tell the police?"

"I will if I have to. If I can, I will keep this to myself."

"Thank you, *Aenti*. I'm sorry about becoming so upset over Enoch. I'm just so happy that he's home."

"Will he rejoin the community?" I asked.

She shook her head. "I don't think so. He . . ." She trailed off.

I would never know what she would have said next because Lois burst into the greenhouse holding a snow-white kitten. "Ginny and I picked the perfect one for Darcy. Isn't she a doll?"

I agreed that she was. The kitten was a fluffy snow-white ball with a bright pink nose. While Peaches had amber-colored eyes, hers were a piercing green color that reminded me of Charlotte Weaver's eyes. I sighed. I had promised Charlotte that I would think about a match for her. I owed her that too. She had warned me that something was going on at Swartz and Swartz Construction, and that's where Lois and I had found Reuben. She had been right. My fear, though, was that her perfect match wasn't Amish in the least.

After Ginny and Lois rejoined us, it was impossible to ask Edith anything more about Zeke because Enoch followed my grandniece and friend into the greenhouse.

I left my niece's house feeling both relieved and heartsick. I was glad that she'd had her reasons for breaking her engagement with Zeke, but now knew if the police learned what those reasons were, she would look even more like a suspect.

I recalled how she'd touched the bloody rock—the murder weapon, Deputy Aiden had called it. Surely her fingerprints were all over it. How long would it take for the police to determine the match?

I walked with Lois to her car.

"You look depressed," Lois said. Her large bag made a clack, clack, clack sound as she walked and the contents were jostled about.

I tried not to think about what those contents included.

"I am depressed," I said as I reached the car and opened the passenger-side door. "I am worried about Edith and her future."

A few feet away from us Tucker climbed into his buggy and directed it down the long driveway. I watched him go. "I'm sure he knows something he's not telling us."

She looked over the roof of the car at me. "Then we need to find out what that is."

"How?" I asked. "He won't tell us any more."

"There's always a way," Lois said with a twinkle in her eye. "Get in the car."

Frowning, I did as she asked.

Lois buckled herself into her seat and started the car. She drove down the driveway and turned in the same direction that Tucker had gone. It was the opposite way from my farm.

"Are you following him?"

She glanced at me. "You want answers, don't you? This is the best way to get them."

"How are we going to follow him in a car?" I asked. "His buggy moves so much slower. He is bound to see you."

"Let me worry about the driving, Amish Marple. It's why I'm here. It's time to give chase!"

Chapter Thirty-two

"This is a terrible idea," I said. "I'm sure he knows you're following him."

"You don't know that," Lois argued. "He headed to the center of the village. We have every reason to be going to the village too. That's where the Sunbeam Café is. That's where my grand-daughter is. That's where I live!"

"So that's our story. We are going to—"

The buggy in front of us stopped abruptly, cutting off my words. Lois hit the brakes hard, and the car's tires squealed. The fluffy poodle hanging from the rearview mirror swung back and forth like a pendulum.

My hand gripped my seat belt with all my might so it didn't pinch me in the throat as I was tossed forward in my seat.

Lois threw her arm out across me, hitting me in the chest.

"Ouch!" I cried.

"I'm saving you," Lois said. "It's called the mom arm."

Lois said a few choice words about the buggy in front of us. I didn't say any such words, but I was thinking a few.

"That nut could have killed us," Lois cried.

I rubbed my chest where her forearm had hit me.

Tucker jumped out of the buggy and marched back to us.

"That nut is coming this way," I said, dropping my hand and sitting up straighter.

Tucker stomped to Lois's window and tapped on it. His face was a mask of anger.

She lowered it just a couple of inches. "Are you trying to get yourself killed?" Lois wanted to know. "I almost rear-ended you. You could have hurt us, yourself, and your horse."

"If you ran into the back of my buggy, it would have been your fault. You would have caused the accident. If a car rear-ends another car or even a buggy, it's the car behind that's at fault."

She wagged her finger at him. "Don't you lecture me on traffic laws, young man. I'm the one with a driver's license."

"Lois," I said under my breath.

"I stopped because you were following me, and you need to stop." He shook with anger. "You have no right to harass me like this."

Lois pulled her neck back. "Harass you? Listen here, you—"

"Lois," I hissed.

Lois glared at Tucker through the window. "Following you? Don't you be ridiculous. Millie, have you ever heard a more ridiculous idea?"

I didn't move. I was staying out of the tale that Lois was about to tell.

"You could have gone around me at any time. You're in a car."

"I know very well that I'm in a car, young man. But there is no rule against driving slow. We were taking our time getting back to the village. We aren't in a rush like so many of you young folks are. I thought Amish young people were supposed to be different in that way. I suppose I was wrong." She sniffed.

His face flushed. "Oh, I—I'm so sorry. I should not have assumed that you were following me."

"You know what assume means, don't you?" Lois asked.

Tucker's face was blank.

Lois glanced at me. "I'm not going to tell him."

I leaned over the console between the seats. "Tucker, I'm sorry if we upset you. We would never want to do that. We're off to see Lois's granddaughter at the Sunbeam Café."

He nodded. He looked like he wanted to say something, but just shook his head. "I'm sorry. I—I don't know what came over me." He spun on his heel and ran back to his buggy. He leaped onto the seat, and a moment later, the horse clomped away, pulling the buggy behind it double time.

Lois smiled at me smugly. "See? Our cover story worked."

I rolled my eyes and settled back into the seat. "Now what are you going to do? Are you going to stick with your story that you are going to the village and not follow him?" I asked.

Lois waited a few beats before she shifted her car into drive again. "Let's see where he goes."

"You still plan to follow him."

"Of course I do. He would not have jumped out of the buggy like that, all high-and-mighty, if he didn't have something to hide."

She had a point.

We drove down the county road behind Tucker's buggy, but this time we stayed well back. It helped that Tucker had urged his horse to such a fast pace.

Lois glanced at me. "Don't you find his reaction odd?"

"It was surprising, I can say that. Tucker Leham never struck me as the type of person who would confront someone."

"He has anger issues," Lois said. "That much I know."

I nodded and Tucker just went up a notch on my suspect list.

Lois followed Tucker's buggy at the same distance and same pace as before. "This is working," she said.

It stopped working when we were almost at the village and Tucker's buggy turned off onto a side road. If we followed him, it would be obvious we *weren't* on our way to the Sunbeam Café.

"Drat!" Lois cried and tapped her long nails on the steering wheel. "I can't follow him now after we told him that we were going to the café!"

She continued straight down the road. "It was a good idea though. I think we shook him up a little."

The question was whether Tucker Leham was a man that we wanted to shake up.

Lois parked her car in one of the diagonal spots in front of Darcy's café. There was a small red vehicle in the spot next to us.

"Uh-oh," Lois said. "That car means trouble."

"What kind of trouble?" I asked, looking around to see if there was some threat. Apparently, I had been thinking about murder for too many days on end, and I was seeing danger everywhere.

She looked me straight in the eye. "Margot trouble."

"That's bad," I agreed.

She nodded. "We'd best go in and face it." Lois climbed out of the car, and I did the same. It was a warm May day, so I didn't bring my bonnet. I touched the top of my head to make sure my prayer cap was secure. The last thing I wanted was for my prayer cap to fall off when facing off with Margot Rawlings.

I followed Lois into the café. The same men I had seen there the first time I'd come to the café were still in the same two seats, working on their two computers. I was starting to wonder if they slept there. Bryan looked up from his computer and smiled at me.

I smiled back and looked around the café. It

was much busier than it had been the other times I had visited. Five of the tables were filled with *Englischers* eating a late lunch. Most of them were eating salad or soup. Everyone appeared to be enjoying the food.

At the counter, Darcy spoke with a short woman with cropped curly hair, which she continually patted as if to make sure it was in place. Perhaps she felt the same way about her hair as I did about my prayer cap. Margot's brown curls were her most distinctive feature. Since she was so petite, you usually saw her curls before you saw her face. She hadn't changed much since our younger days. Margot was another woman I'd known as a girl in the village.

Margot rested her hand on the counter. "I can see how this café could have potential in upcoming events at the square. You have done a wonderful job with the menu. Everything I've tasted has been absolutely splendid. Tell me your other plans for this place. There must always be new plans. You must always strive for more, bigger, and better." Margot stopped just short of holding her fist in the air as a show of strength.

Darcy was far less confident and licked her lips. "The café just opened."

"Don't think small, girl; think big!" Margot cried.

The *Englisch* tourists at the table looked over to see what the yelling was about.

"I have thought of expanding to catering. That's how I started cooking. I worked in catering. I can see how catering events on the square could benefit all of us," Darcy said in a quiet voice.

"Yes, me too. I'll bring it up with the committee. It would be nice to have a local business provide the main dishes at our events. Of course, Swissmen Sweets provides the desserts."

"Oh, I know," Darcy said. "That shop has been here for a long time, and I wouldn't want to step on any toes. I would happily work on the savory menus if they want to continue to provide the sweet."

Lois gave her granddaughter a thumbs-up sign behind Margot's back.

Darcy's eyes went wide.

Margot noticed—there was very little Margot missed—and spun around. Lois morphed her excited gesture into a yawn. "Goodness, I could use a nap. It's funny; when you're a child, you hate naps, but the older you get, the more enjoyable they are."

"Lois, how long have you been standing behind me?" Margot asked.

Lois feigned an expression of surprise. "Standing behind you? Millie and I just arrived. We wanted to drop in and see if Darcy needed any extra help around the café. Clearly, she doesn't and has everything well in hand. She has turned this business into one of the loveliest spots in Harvest."

I thought Lois was laying it on a little thick, but I just nodded. Anything I added to the conversation would make it sound even more false.

Margot pressed her lips together. "It's nice to see you too, Millie. I heard you were back in the village."

"I've been back for a few months," I said. "I've seen you around the square at different events, but you always seem to be surrounded by people who need your help."

"Being in charge of all the activities in the village is a full-time job, but it's one that I relish. It keeps me busy. Honestly, I don't know what I would do without it." She turned her attention back to Lois. "You will be happy to learn I think Darcy has done an exemplary job with the café. The place looks wonderful, and I can see much potential in using this space and Darcy's skills for future events in the village."

Lois grinned from ear to ear. "I'm glad to hear it. You couldn't find a prouder grandmother in the entire county than I am."

Margot patted the curls on the top of her head. "I must say that what you have here, Darcy, is quite impressive. I will leave you to it now. You will be hearing from me soon, and we will have the schedule for possible events we'd like you to partner with the village on."

"I would love that," Darcy said with a little bit of awe in her voice, as if she couldn't believe that this was actually happening.

"Good," Margot said, and turned toward the door. She stopped halfway there. "Millie, I was wondering if you had a moment to chat outside the café."

Lois and I shared a look.

"Want me to go with you?" Lois whispered. "I can be pretty tough."

"I don't need toughness to talk to Margot, just my wits," I whispered back.

She nodded. "Suit yourself, but dollars to donuts you come back in here having volunteered for fourteen if not twenty programs to be held on this square throughout the year."

I knew that was possible with Margot involved. I would have to keep my head to make sure it didn't happen.

CHAPTER THIRTY-THREE

Margot was already outside when I crossed the threshold and inhaled the sweet scent of hyacinths blooming in a planter just outside the front door of the café. Beyond the hyacinth planter and the sidewalk, on the other side of the street was the square.

The white gazebo had been freshly painted just before Easter. The needles on the pine trees around the square shone, and every blade of grass seemed to be pointed in the same direction. Not even the grass would have the nerve to do something other than Margot's bidding. If I looked hard enough, I could almost see the sign on the front window of Swissmen Sweets on the opposite side of the square.

A white-bearded figure moved around the square, picking up bits of litter from the grass. I realized that it was Uriah Schrock. I looked away, but not before he spotted me, and his face broke into a wide smile.

I guessed that Lois was right and I was going to end up volunteering for fourteen different activities on the square.

However, Margot surprised me by saying, "I have heard what happened at the greenhouse and wanted to know how Edith is getting on."

"Edith?" I asked dumbly. I didn't know why I

was surprised by the question. It's one I should have anticipated since Margot was just as nosy as Raellen. "She is as well as can be expected."

"Is she closing the greenhouse?" She cocked her head as if in concern.

I started. "Closing the greenhouse? Why?"

"I heard it wasn't doing well financially." She lowered her voice. "There have been rumors."

"She's not closing." I cleared my throat. "In fact, she has decided to bring back the Edy's Greenhouse bonfire that her father used to host every year."

Margot raised her eyebrows. "Really? I'm surprised, considering . . ." She waited as if she wanted me to fill in the blank. I stared back at her because I wasn't going to do that. I wasn't going to say anything that might reveal too much to Margot Rawlings about Edith's life.

"Well, I'm happy, for one, to hear that Edith is making a comeback of sorts. We have missed her flowers at the farmers' market. I was quite surprised when I heard she no longer wanted to participate."

"She said that?" I asked.

"Zeke Miller did. I suppose now that he's gone, she might want to do it again. Please tell her we would love to have her back. Her flowers were one of the best booths we had, and I haven't been able to find another nursery to replace her that I like as much."

My pulse quickened. "I will be sure to tell her. She'll be happy to hear the news too, and I think you are right that she will want to come back."

"Good." She paused. "You know I could help Edith plan for the bonfire. I do have some experience planning big events."

I smiled because I had been expecting this suggestion, and I knew it would be the last thing Edith would want. "That's so very kind of you, but Edith would like to do this on her own. It's important to her and she needs a project right now."

Margot nodded. "I can understand the need of a project, probably more than most."

"But we would love it if you could come. All the Amish and *Englisch* in Harvest are invited."

"I will do that then." She looked at the square. "I'm happy to see how much the village has grown in the last year. I promise you there will be many more wonderful things to come. Not to mention *Bailey's Amish Sweets* will be filming here in the summer, and the minister's wedding is coming up too. It will be quite a summer for us all. I have so much to do." She said good-bye and left.

I let out a giant sigh as she disappeared around the corner of the church. When I couldn't see her any longer, I turned around to go back into the café and ran into Uriah Schrock's chest with my nose.

"Oh, so sorry," Uriah said, holding me at arm's

length. "I didn't know you were going to turn that quickly. You are certainly still light on your feet."

I rubbed my nose and felt relieved when he let go of my arms.

He smiled kindly at me. "I saw you standing there with Margot and thought you would like to see a friendly face after your conversation. She has a lot of energy."

"She does," I said. For some reason, I didn't know what to do with my hands. I folded them, put them in my apron pockets, and then just dropped them to my sides as if they were useless things.

"Actually, I wasn't telling the whole truth. For the most part, I came over just to say hello." He blushed.

I found myself blushing too and wanted to pinch myself to make me stop.

Beyond me, Uriah looked into the window of the café and frowned.

"Is something wrong?" I asked and looked over my shoulder. Through the window, I saw Bryan watching us so intently that it made me feel ill at ease. I turned my attention back to Uriah.

"Nothing is wrong." He shook his head. "It just seems odd to me that that young man can sit in this window day after day just . . . watching. He's always watching. It's unnerving."

"What's he watching?" I asked.

"It's hard to say, but I know he's had his eye on Darcy. Any man could tell you that by the way he watches her."

I shivered.

"I'm so sorry. My wife used to say that I was given to an overactive imagination."

"Imagination can be a *gut* thing," I said.

He beamed at me. "I'm glad you think so, Millie, very glad."

I felt as if I had a wad of cotton in my mouth. "*Ya*, well . . ."

"I should be getting back to the square. There is going to be a concert put on by the local school bands, and Margot wants everything to be perfect."

I smiled.

He started to leave and then stopped. "Millie?"

My breath caught. "*Ya.*"

"I'm very glad our paths have crossed again." With that, he left.

"I'm very glad too," I whispered and then went back into the café.

Darcy let out a breath as soon as I stepped inside. "Oh my God." She winced and glanced at me. "Sorry, Millie."

I smiled.

"I just thought she would never leave. She was here for three hours and insisted on tasting every-thing. Thank goodness, I got that cheese I needed yesterday because she definitely ordered a grilled cheese. Two, in fact! She put them both away. I never knew that a tiny woman could eat so much."

Lois patted Darcy on the back. "You did well."

"Thanks, Grandma." Her face fell as grief settled back down on her shoulders. Adrenaline had kept her moving while Margot was here, but now that the older woman was gone, she deflated.

"Are you all right, my girl?" Lois asked and hugged her.

"Not right now, but I know I will be. I just wish . . ."

"What do you wish?" Lois asked.

"I know it's stupid. I just wish that Zeke was here to see it. We did a lot of this café together, and no matter how he treated me, he deserved to see how well received it has been so he could have been proud of this place too."

I bit my lip, trying to hold back the words, but in the end I said them. "I don't know if it's much comfort, but I do believe that Zeke cared for you."

She looked up at me with tears in her eyes. "How do you know?"

I told her about my last conversation with Edith, in which she'd said that Zeke almost seemed relieved she was calling off their wedding. "He felt that way because of you." What I didn't add was that it didn't excuse the fact that Zeke had brought the greenhouse to the cusp of financial ruin. Nor that he'd been carrying on a relationship with two different women simultaneously. Out of the corner of my eye, I saw that Bryan was following our conversation very closely. I tried not to think about what Uriah had said concerning the young *Englisch* writer.

"Thank you. That makes this a little easier to bear. I thought I wasn't worthy of being loved."

"Everyone is," I said. "Even Zeke."

She smiled. "I did love him. Maybe I fell for him too quickly. I know I did, but that doesn't make the feelings any less real."

I shook my head. "It doesn't."

"I'd like to come to the bonfire if you think that would be okay with Edith. Grandma was just telling me about it. I think I need to have some closure over what happened with Zeke."

"I think she would like to meet you." I would have said more but Deputy Aiden and Deputy Little stepped into the café just then.

"Millie," Deputy Aiden said. "I thought I would find you here."

What had I done now? I wondered.

CHAPTER THIRTY-FOUR

Deputy Aiden?" I asked. "You were looking for me?"

He nodded. "I was." He glanced at Lois. "I was looking for you both actually. I came by to tell you that you can stop poking your noses in the investigation."

"Now, you listen here just a minute," Lois began, coming around the café counter. "We have every right to help the ones we love."

He held up his hand. "I'm telling you because the investigation is over."

Deputy Little stood behind the senior deputy and nodded as if everything he said was Gospel. Probably Deputy Little thought it was.

"What do you mean?" I asked.

"It turns out that you were right. Reuben was the one running away from the greenhouse on Sunday morning. It seems that your recognition of the way he moved was spot-on."

"He was?" I could hardly believe it.

"More than that, we believe he had motive, and he has been arrested for the murder of Zeke Miller."

"What?" Lois cried.

Everyone in the café looked our way then. Deputy Aiden pressed his lips together and lowered his voice. "His footprints match the tracks that Deputy Little found Sunday morning running away from the greenhouse, and if that wasn't enough, we found a pair of denim trousers in his home that are missing a part of their seat. They were a perfect match to the piece of fabric your goat took off the man running away."

I blinked at him. Could it be true? Could it be really over? It just seemed too easy. Zeke's body had just been found Sunday.

Deputy Aiden could tell I wasn't convinced by what he'd said. "We found a wrench at the murder scene, and Reuben's fingerprints are all over it. His prints are in the cactus room as well. He would have no reason for being there."

"What's his motive?" I asked.

"That's right," Lois whispered in my ear. "Get all the details."

I waved her away.

"He told us that he, Jeremy Swartz of Swartz and Swartz Construction, and Zeke had been running a chop shop in the county. Zeke and Reuben stole the cars, and Jeremy unloaded them. I guess they had been doing it for years. Not many would look to the Amish as car thieves."

"That's how he knew how to fix my car," Darcy said in dismay.

"It seems," the deputy went on, "that Zeke had a change of heart recently and wanted to get out of the business. He said he met someone and wanted to leave both his Amish life and the life of crime."

Darcy gasped and covered her mouth.

Deputy Aiden nodded. "This will be the harder part for you to hear, Millie."

I wasn't sure how it could get worse, but I nodded for him to continue. "Jeremy said that he would let him out, but it could cost him money. That's what he did with all the money from Edy's Greenhouse. He used it to buy himself out of Jeremy's criminal ring, but Jeremy wasn't satisfied with the amounts that Zeke was giving him and sent Reuben to press the issue with Zeke. We believe that Reuben, who is known to have a short fuse, got carried away and killed Zeke while trying to pressure him to give Jeremy more money. He dropped the wrench while he was there, and he came back while you were there, Millie, to collect it before the murder could be discovered."

"Did he confess to the murder?" I asked.

He shook his head. "He blamed Jeremy Swartz for it. We brought Jeremy in too. He was going to be arrested anyway for grand theft auto. He said Reuben was the one who killed Zeke. Since we have no evidence to put Jeremy at the scene of the crime, it appears that is the most likely scenario."

"But"—I wasn't done just yet—"what about the note?"

"What note?" Deputy Aiden asked.

"The note that told Darcy about Zeke's being engaged to Edith," I said.

"I don't know anything about this," the deputy said.

I frowned. Darcy had never told the police about the note she'd received?

"Can I see it?" Deputy Aiden asked.

Darcy shook her head. "I burned it."

Deputy Aiden pressed his lips together. "You should not have done that, Darcy."

He looked as if he was going to lecture her more when there was a scraping sound as a chair was being pushed back from a table. "That was me. I wrote and gave her the note," Bryan said uncertainly.

"You?" I asked.

He nodded. "I knew about Zeke and Edith. I knew that Darcy deserved to know, but I didn't know how to tell her." His Adam's apple bobbed. "So I gave her the note."

Darcy looked at him, but instead of appearing upset by his news, she seemed pleased. Her eyes were shining.

Lois noticed too because she shook her head and then whispered into my ear. "Hopeless romantic. It's in our blood."

"We need to talk to you," Deputy Aiden said sternly and walked toward him. Bryan backed away. The deputies spoke with Bryan a few minutes in low voices.

"I wish we could hear what they are saying," Lois complained. "Do you think they would notice if I went over there to refresh Bryan's coffee?"

"They will notice," I said.

A few minutes later, Bryan sat back down at his laptop with a red face and concentrated on the work in front of him as if nothing had happened.

The deputies came back to us. "Darcy, I don't believe the note you received has any direct bearing on the case," Deputy Aiden said.

She swallowed.

Deputy Aiden looked over his shoulder at Deputy Little. "We should be going. Lots of reports to file."

"Deputy," I said. "Edith is having a bonfire Friday night at the greenhouse. We are inviting the whole community. We'd love it if you'd come."

He smiled. "If I can get away from work, I will. I know Bailey would enjoy it, but she left for New York this morning. She won't be gone long this time. She will be back tomorrow." His face broke into a bright smile, and the premature lines on his face smoothed at the very thought of seeing the woman he loved again. I knew he must be relieved that this case was closed before Bailey's return. She had been known to poke her nose in his investigations a time or two.

"You are welcome too, Deputy Little," I said. Had we been alone, I might have said something about Charlotte Weaver to the younger deputy, but I held my tongue.

Deputy Little nodded with a smile, and the two men left. After they went through the door, Lois said, "Wow."

"My thoughts exactly," I added.

She gave me a high five. It felt awkward.

"We solved the case. Great job, Amish Marple."

"Did we?" I asked, looking out the window. "I can't help thinking that something might still be missing. I don't doubt that Reuben was there in the greenhouse. I saw the wrench under the table and I saw him run away from the greenhouse, but I'm just not convinced that he was the one who murdered Zeke."

"Then maybe it was Jeremy Swartz," Lois said.

"Maybe," I mused, but that didn't feel right either.

"Does it matter now?" Lois asked. "We were looking into it because our girls were in danger of getting blamed for the crime because of their relationship with Zeke. Now, their names have been cleared. Shouldn't we be happy about that and move on? It sounds to me like getting ready for the bonfire will be plenty of excitement to occupy us for the next few days."

"You want to help?" I asked.

"Sure do!" she said. "I love a party. I should tell you about my trips to Vegas. They will knock your stockings off."

I wasn't sure I wanted to hear about those parties, and then I groaned as I remembered something.

"What? What is it? Do we have to keep investigating?" She sounded a little too eager at the idea for my taste.

I shook my head. "*Nee*, I forgot that Double Stitch is meeting at my house this evening. Ruth thought it was a *gut* idea to put our heads together to solve the murder."

"Won't she be disappointed that we already cracked the case?" Lois said.

I knew that she would. In fact, I expected to get an earful from the bishop's wife about not respecting her position in the community by not waiting for her help or some other ridiculous argument.

After a beat, Lois asked, "Can I come?"

"Do you quilt?" I asked.

"Not a stitch, but I can talk."

She certainly could. "*Ya*, you can come."

"Excellent," she said with a grin.

CHAPTER THIRTY-FIVE

I smiled at the members of my quilting circle. "*Danki*. Thank you all for coming. I know it has been a hard week for the community. The fact that you have taken time away from your homes and your families to come here and support both Edith and me, well, it means so much. It really warms my heart. This proves to me that coming back to Holmes County was the right thing for me to do, and despite what happened Sunday, I am glad that I did."

"It's been a much harder week for your family, Millie," Leah said as she smoothed her quilting over her lap.

"Of course we are here for you in your family's time of need, Millie," Raellen said. "You would do the same for us if we needed it."

"I would," I said. "I know coming out to my farm at the end of the day isn't ideal with all the work you have to do."

"Oh, this is a fine time. The children are off to bed and the husbands have had their suppers. This might be the best time to come," Raellen said. "We all want to know what we can do to find the killer." She pressed a hand to her cheek. "I can't even believe I said that."

"About that . . ."

"Don't tell me you don't want to learn the truth, Millie," said Ruth, who was sitting in a rocking chair beside my potbellied stove.

Before I could answer, there was a knock on the door. I got up from my rocking chair just as Lois let herself inside.

"Lois, what on earth are you doing here?" Ruth wanted to know.

"I invited her," I said. "Lois is going to be helping with the bonfire too."

"Also, I thought I would try my hand at quilting. If I am going to write a book about the Amish, I think I should work some of the handicrafts in. Quilting would be one of the top ones to incorporate. Who doesn't love an Amish quilt!"

"Write a book about the Amish!" Ruth shouted. "Millie, I thought we were here because you said Edith needed our help, and what's this about a bonfire?"

"Let's all sit down and I will tell you."

After they were settled, I said, "Lois and I have been trying to find out what happened to Zeke."

"Amish Marple and I have been all over the county looking for answers," Lois declared.

"Amish Marple?" Ruth asked with a wrinkle to her nose.

"That's my code name for Millie." Lois grabbed a cookie from the tray on my kitchen island and sat on the sofa between Iris and Leah. "I figured that you all can know it since you're her friends, but it doesn't leave this room." She looked each one in the eye by turn.

Ruth looked as if she wanted to say something more about that.

"Let's just focus on the task at hand," I said. "It seems that according to the police, Lois and I have cracked the case." I went on to tell about Zeke and Jeremy Swartz and Reuben and everything the police thought had happened leading up to Zeke's murder.

Raellen stared at me openmouthed when I was done. Finally, she snapped her mouth closed and said, "That is quite a story." She looked at Lois. "It would make a nice addition to your book."

Lois tapped her cheek with her index finger. "I think you might be on to something there."

"Please, don't encourage her," I said. I couldn't believe that Lois was still thinking of writing about the Amish.

"Are the police absolutely sure?" Leah asked.

"They seem to be," I said.

Leah cocked her head. "But you're not."

"Maybe not, but I have no reason to be unsure."

"Never doubt a woman's intuition," Ruth said. "If something doesn't ring true, it's not."

It was one of those rare times when I was in agreement with Ruth.

"What other suspects do you have?" Leah asked. "Maybe if we work through it, you will feel more confident with the police's findings."

I glanced at Lois. "Well, you all know about Darcy and Edith, but Lois and I can vouch for each of them, respectively."

"Just because you want them to be innocent, doesn't make them so," Ruth said.

"Darcy was working in the café," Lois said.

Ruth rocked in the chair. "All night?"

Lois frowned.

"Edith was home with the children," I said before they could exchange heated words. "I know this because I asked Jacob and he said she was there. He would have no reason to lie. He's only a child."

"Okay," Leah said. "If it's neither one of them, who else could it be?"

"Well, it could still be the suspect the police have accused. I can't rule that out," I said. "There is Reuben, and Jeremy, the young man we met at Swartz and Swartz Construction. I've already told you their motive."

Iris pressed her lips together. "Carter told me about your visit to the warehouse and the police coming and taking Reuben away earlier today. He didn't say anything about Jeremy. I wonder if he even knows yet." She bit her lower lip. "And I wonder what this means for his job."

I felt a tiny bit of guilt when Iris said that. I didn't want Carter to lose his job on account of me, but then again, Jeremy was the one behind the car stealing. It was really his fault.

"What about Enoch?" Ruth asked.

"You would love for the culprit to be a runaway Amish, wouldn't you?" Lois said.

Ruth scowled in return. "If Edith didn't marry Zeke and Enoch returned to the faith, the greenhouse would be his, but if she married before that happened, the greenhouse would have been her husband's."

This was something that I had thought of too, especially when it looked like Enoch wanted to tell Edith how to run the greenhouse when we were there.

"I still think you should have told us that Enoch was back in the village," Ruth went on.

"I didn't even know until just before Zeke died," I said.

"That's no excuse." Ruth sniffed.

I rolled my eyes. "I didn't know that I had to report all the movements of my family."

"A prodigal son coming back to the fold needs to be reported. I'm sure my husband would like to talk to him. The elders of the church will want to talk to him. One of our lost sheep is coming home."

"He doesn't want to join the church," I said quietly.

"What?" Ruth asked. "Then why would he want to come back? There is no other reason to come back."

"He told Edith that he was back because he

332

missed his family and wanted to get to know his niece and nephews. That doesn't mean he wants to live in the Amish way."

"Well, he can't be around the children if he doesn't," Ruth said decisively.

"Why not?" Lois said.

"We really shouldn't have an *Englischer* here. She doesn't understand our ways." Ruth said this in Pennsylvania Dutch instead of *Englisch.*

"I caught the word 'Englisher,'" Lois said, jumping to her feet. "I know you are talking about me."

"Ruth just said that we shouldn't discuss such things in front of someone who isn't Amish." I looked at Ruth. "Lois is my friend and she was your friend once upon a time too. Let's speak English while she's here so that no one is left out."

"Fine," Ruth said in *Englisch,* sounding much like a defiant teenager. "I still think some things should be kept close in the community."

"Now, why don't you think Enoch should be around the children?" Leah asked.

"Because his presence will corrupt the children and tell them that it's all right to go the *Englisch* way. I don't think that's very wise." She turned to me. "Millie, talk some sense into your niece and tell her why this is a terrible idea."

"Enoch is their uncle. He has a right to see them. He wasn't in the church when he left. He wasn't shunned, no matter the difficult circumstances that precipitated his leaving all those years ago."

She gasped. "Do you want him to lead the children astray?"

"Each child must make their own choice. Isn't that what *rumspringa* is about?" I looked her in the eye. "Edith's children will come to make that decision in their own time, and they can only fully commit to the Amish life when they know what the *Englisch* one is like. If they see the way the rest of the world lives and then commit to our ways, they are more likely to stay here. Wouldn't you agree that it is far worse to change one's mind after baptism?"

Ruth made a grunt-like noise, which told me I'd proved my point.

"But—" Ruth began again.

I knew she was going to change her approach. Ruth would do just about anything to win an argument. Most of the time she won because the person opposed to her view became too fatigued to go on. I thought that's how she'd gotten her position in the district, acting as bishop of sorts, on her husband's behalf. She just wore the church elders out.

"Ruth, stop it." I stood up. "Enoch left before he was baptized, so there is no reason that Edith or anyone in our district should shun him."

Ruth stepped back. "This is true, but I still don't think he should be around the children."

"Then that's your opinion."

Ruth sniffed. "I can see I am getting nowhere with you, Millie Fisher. You are the most stubborn woman I've ever known."

"Coming from you, I take that as a compliment. I thought you prided yourself on being stubborn."

"Pride? I have no pride. That is not the Amish way. In any case, as his *aenti*, tell Enoch that the bishop will want to talk to him now that he's back in town. Even if he decides not to join the church, it's important that he resolve the hurt left behind by his leaving all those years ago. He broke your brother's heart when he left, and he must answer for that."

"Umm," Iris asked in a small voice, "shouldn't we talk about how we can help with the bonfire now, since we no longer have to solve a murder?"

I sat back down. "I think that's a great idea, Iris. Edith will appreciate the help."

The ladies started listing the dishes they planned to make for Friday, and Ruth left not long after that. I was certain she was headed back to the bishop to report on all that she had seen and heard.

CHAPTER THIRTY-SIX

Friday and the bonfire finally came.

I was proud of Edith for continuing the tradition of the bonfire even when she was under so much strain. It was an annual event that her father had started at the beginning of every growing season. It was a celebration of the district and of a new season of Gott's creation.

Tonight, children ran around the yard, squealing, while their mothers shouted at them to stay away from the fire. The children careened by the flames, and a father chased them away from the danger. They didn't know that they were being protected and laughed as they were chased.

"I can't believe how many people are here," Edith said. "It just brings tears to my eyes."

"They are here to support you." I hugged her and watched as the lights from the fire played on the faces of my friends and neighbors. There had to be several hundred people there, both Amish and *Englisch*. They were all there to support Edith, her children, and the greenhouse. It warmed my heart.

"I can't believe it," she said again.

"Believe it. Look how many people from the district came to help you," I said. "When someone in the community needs help, we band together.

That is one of the best parts of being Amish."

She nodded. "I suppose I shouldn't be surprised they came out to help me, but a lot of it I owe to you and the Double Stitch ladies. You are the ones who got the community so involved."

I smiled. "We all helped, but you need to give the greatest amount of gratitude to Ruth."

"Ruth Yoder?" She placed a hand to her cheek. "But I thought she didn't approve of me at all."

"Ruth doesn't approve of most things, but she's still a softy at heart. I realize not everyone in this county believes that, but I have known her my whole life, and in my experience, when push comes to shove, Ruth always errs on the side of compassion."

She nodded. "Then I will be sure to thank her. I'll make a point to thank everyone from Double Stitch. I can't tell you how much this bonfire means to me. It's the first time I've held it since *Daed* passed on, and so much has happened since then. I don't think he would be happy with how I've handled things. He wouldn't like it that I gave Zeke so much control over the business when it was clear he didn't know what he was doing. And now that I've learned he used the money to pay off an auto thief, I can't even think about it."

I reached for her hand and squeezed it. "The police are trying, but you may never see that money again. It's best not to expect it, and move

337

on from here. We all make mistakes. It's what you do with those mistakes that matters. There is always a second chance and an opportunity to make better choices."

"I hope so." She smiled at her brother, who was showing her children how to roast marshmallows over the fire. "I am glad that Enoch has returned. He's told me he wants to work at the greenhouse again. He wants to stay."

"I'm happy to hear that."

"It's funny; the greenhouse would have been his if he stayed in the faith. I know that it must be hard for him to come back and have me as his superior in the family business."

"He made his choice, and maybe neither one of you has to be the boss; perhaps you can have a partnership."

"That's what I'm hoping for." The firelight shone on her hair, making her look even more angelic.

"Will he rejoin the church?" I asked.

She shook her head. "He said that he was too hurt by the church over what happened all those years ago." She wouldn't look at me because I knew it was impossible to think of that time without remembering the part I'd played in it.

"I am sorry," I said.

"You have apologized before to all of us. We can't ask you to do any more."

I wished that were true, but I felt I was still being

punished for a years' old misunderstanding—and I deserved it. The Amish have long memories, and I knew no amount of wishing it away was going to help them forget what I'd done to Enoch all those years ago. "I think I will have a chat with Enoch. He said he forgave me, but the last time I was here, I sensed there were still hard feelings. I want us all to be a family."

She nodded. "I think that's a very *gut* idea, *Aenti*. It's best to discuss it, and then let it go."

"I'll find Enoch and speak to him." Before I let her go, I said, "I do have one more question."

She frowned. "What, *Aenti*?"

"The day you found the body, why did you lie to Deputy Aiden about having watered the plants in the greenhouse when it was clear to me they had not been watered that morning?"

She looked down. "I should not have done that. I regretted it the moment I said it, but I didn't want him to know the truth."

"Which was?"

"I went into the greenhouse to hide from my children. I didn't want them to see me cry. Even though I had broken the engagement with Zeke myself, I was still suffering from a loss and a failure. I was crying over that and my stupidity of giving him access to my finances. I was prideful to want to hide that from my children and from the police. It was the wrong thing to do, but when I said the lie, I could not think of a way to take it back without looking even more suspicious to the police."

I hugged her again. "*Danki* for telling me. You go back to your party. Don't worry about me. This is your night and you should enjoy it."

She hugged me and went on her way.

I watched her go before turning in search of Enoch. I needed my nephew's full forgiveness, and I realized for the first time, I needed to forgive myself for what I had done.

I felt responsible for breaking my family apart. It was as if when Edith and Enoch's mother had died, their family had been held together by a thin pane of glass, and I took a hammer to it and shattered it into a thousand pieces. I knew that I wouldn't be able to put those thousands of pieces back together again. There was no way to rebuild what was shattered, but what we could make was something brand-new, something that was different but stronger than before. That's what I hoped for the very most. Edith and Enoch had lost both of their parents. I was the closest thing to a parent they had left, and they were the closest I would ever have to children. We needed each other. My hope was that Enoch would see that too. I wasn't sure he would.

I turned to the spot where Enoch had been with the children, but he was gone. The children were still there, sitting with some other adults, laughing as they squished their marshmallows into s'mores. There were other children from the community with their sticks in the fire.

Phillip and Peter stood a few feet away, so that they were clear of the flames but close enough to sneak a s'more when one of the children or adults around the fire got distracted. I shook my head. Those goats. I probably should warn the people making s'mores about my boys. I had started toward the bonfire when someone reached out and touched my arm.

"This is amazing," a voice said behind me. I turned to see Margot Rawlings standing there. She was holding a small paper bag full of Amish kettle corn. A few feet away Tucker was at the large kettle, popping the corn as he added butter and sugar to the mixture. "You should be very proud of yourself," Margot said.

"*Danki*, but it wasn't me. Edith did it almost entirely herself. My quilting circle helped get the word out, but she set up for the party and planned all the games for the children."

"How very impressive. This makes me want more than ever for Edith to come back to the farmers' market. I know her flowers would do very well there. This is a not-to-be-missed opportunity for her and for the village."

"I think she would come back if you asked her. She is eager to rebuild Edy's Greenhouse into what it was before . . ." I almost said before Zeke Miller got his hands on it. I'm glad that I stopped myself. There was no point in bringing up flaws in a man who could no longer defend himself.

"I'll do just that before I leave. I can't stay long because we are having a community meeting tonight about fall events in the village. I know that it's just May, but autumn will be here soon enough and we have to be ready. There are so many wonderful things in store for Harvest that I can hardly wait to see what will come next for all of us."

I nodded and said good-bye to Margot. I still needed to find Enoch. It was time for that talk. I walked around the yard looking for him and was surprised to see Bryan, the writer from the café, holding a plate of food and speaking to Darcy. Darcy laughed at something he said. Her blond curls looked like gold silk in the firelight. Bryan was relaxed and his pensive demeanor seemed to have melted away. Despite Uriah's reservations about Bryan, I sensed a match in front of me and a *gut* match at that. Yes, he'd given her the note that told her about Zeke's relationship with Edith, but he'd done it because he cared for her. I hoped that he would learn from the experience that there were better ways of going about showing your affection for another person.

I had to admit, I was slightly disappointed that Uriah wasn't there. I'd made a point, when I worked up the nerve, to tell him about the bonfire, but he'd said he was headed back to Indiana this weekend for a short visit. I told myself it was for the best.

Ruth Yoder walked over to me. I could tell from the set of her jaw that she had something to say. I was starting to wonder if I would ever be able to find my nephew. I plastered a pleasant look on my face. "What can I help you with, Ruth?"

"Nothing."

I raised my eyebrows. That was unusual for Ruth to say. She always wanted something. She had been that way since we were children. For her to say she wanted nothing caught me by surprise and made me suspicious.

"I was looking for Edith. I wanted to congratulate her on the bonfire. This is a very *gut* thing that Edith is doing. The bishop and the church elders are happy that the tradition is continuing."

"That's very kind of you to say," I said, pleased. "She's looking for you right now too, so I'm sure the two of you will run into each other soon. She wanted to thank you and the bishop for encouraging the other members of the district to come."

"It was no trouble, and I think we all feel quite a bit better that someone has been arrested by the police for Zeke's murder. The bishop, of course, is not happy that it is an Amish man, but at least it's not an Amish man from our own district. It sounds to me as if Zeke made a lot of poor choices, and they finally caught up with him."

"I would say that's exactly what happened."

She clucked her tongue. "To think he was stealing cars for so many years—it's horrible, and to be doing such things as an Amish man!"

"The police said he had a higher success rate than other auto thieves because he was Amish. Who would suspect an Amish man of stealing cars?"

"Will the cars be returned to their owners?"

I shook my head. "I don't know. It didn't sound as if they would be. Many of them are long gone or were taken apart right here in Holmes County. Deputy Aiden called it a chop shop."

"I'm sure the deputy is happy to have this case wrapped up, and the sheriff too. I am guessing Sheriff Jackson is relieved that an Amish man was found guilty of the crime. This won't make life for the Amish any easier in this county."

I had to agree with her on that point.

One of the children at the fire listlessly held his marshmallow to the side to cool. Phillip was prancing nearby and struck without warning, snapping off the end of the wooden stick. He swallowed the marshmallow, stick and all, and took off.

"Hey!" the child called and raced after the goat. Three more children joined in the chase, and Peter, clearly thinking this was some sort of fun game, ran after Phillip.

"Look at that!" Ruth cried. "I can't believe you brought those goats."

"I'm not asking you to believe it," I said with a smile. "And from what I can see, the children are having fun chasing the goats."

"Millie Fisher, you haven't changed a bit in all these years."

"I take that as a compliment." I held my tongue to keep from adding that she hadn't changed either.

"Why on earth would you bring the goats here in the first place?"

"They were here last week, working on clearing land at the greenhouse, so Edith's children invited them. As Micah said, it wouldn't be right to have the bonfire without Phillip and Peter. Considering what the children have been through this week, I thought it would be a nice treat."

Ruth made a grunting noise. She might appear tough, but when it came to children, she was a teddy bear. I had seen her with her grandchildren. She couldn't be stern with them the way she was with everyone else.

With the children off chasing the goats, a group of teenagers made their way toward the bonfire with marshmallows and hot dogs on sticks.

A moment later, Phillip and Peter ran back around the greenhouse at a fast trot. This time, Peter was the one to steal a marshmallow stick from a teenager. Instead of biting off the end as his brother had done, he grabbed the whole thing. He then tripped over the end and did a somersault in the lawn, much to the glee of the children and the teens and a *gut* number of the adults too.

Peter jumped back onto his hooves and shook his head. When he saw everyone looking at him, he smiled and ate the marshmallow.

Ruth groaned.

I looked away from the scene for just a second, which was long enough to see Enoch disappear by the back of the greenhouse.

CHAPTER THIRTY-SEVEN

In the commotion the goats had created, I was able to slip away and follow Enoch. I knew the bonfire might not be the best time to talk to him, but I couldn't wait any longer. I had to have some peace between us, not just for our sakes, but for Edith and the children too.

I walked around the side of the building. Light shone out from the greenhouse, which was lit up with lanterns for the night. Even though there would be no sales that night, it was important for the bonfire guests to see how healthy and well cared-for the plants were, so that they would come back and make a purchase. And Edith wasn't going to turn any customers away if someone asked to buy something that night.

The ambient light coming from the greenhouse cast a sickly pea-green glow onto the back barn, which was about twenty yards away. I knew the cat was hiding her kittens in the barn this night to keep them away from all the commotion. Part of me wanted to stop in and see how Peaches was doing, but I kept walking, looking in all directions for Enoch. I came to the other side of the greenhouse and still didn't find him. Had he gone to the barn or maybe already walked all the way around the greenhouse and was back in front of the fire?

I decided to check around the barn just to be sure. Then I would go back to the party. Maybe our conversation just wasn't meant to be tonight. Disappointment fell heavily on my shoulders.

"I don't know why you care that they are accused," a male voice said. "They broke the law. They deserve to be in prison."

"I know," another male voice said. This one was higher, and I recognized it immediately as belonging to Tucker Leham. "I know that, but they didn't kill anyone. Do you think Jeremy Swartz will go to prison for murder? It's not going to happen. He will do everything he can to find out what really happened."

"Then I will just disappear again."

"What about Edith and the children? I thought you came back to take care of them."

The first man laughed, and I now realized it was my nephew Enoch. "I came here to take my greenhouse back. Just because I left the Amish faith, I shouldn't be disinherited the way I was. This is my property. It all should be mine. I'm the only son."

"But you made the choice to leave the Amish." Tucker's voice came out in a whine.

There was the slamming sound of someone being tossed up against the outer wall of the barn. "I know that. Don't you think I know that? What choice did I have when everyone here thought I was a criminal? So I left and became what they expected me to be. The Amish are all about following the straight path, aren't they? And my path was straight to trouble."

There was a scuffle, and I didn't hear anyone speak for a long moment. I hesitated. Should I go and make sure Tucker was all right? But what match would I be for Enoch?

My heart broke for the boy, my nephew, for his innocence lost. I couldn't help but feel that I'd failed him. Not that my lack of faith in him as a boy excused his actions as an adult. Nothing condoned murder, but I couldn't help but think that if things had gone differently all those years ago, I wouldn't be hearing this awful confession today.

I took a step forward, but what I heard next stopped me in my tracks. "If you care about Edith, you will keep your head down and your mouth shut."

I heard movement behind me and spun around with my hands up to defend myself.

Lois cocked her head. "Do the Amish know karate?"

"Shhh!" I said and waited.

She inched toward me. "What are we shushing about?"

I pointed around the side of the barn.

"Oh! Are we sleuthing again? I thought you said that our investigating was over."

"Shhh!" I gave her a look.

"You made me do it!" Tucker accused Enoch.

"I didn't make you do anything." Enoch's voice was cold. "I just told you what would happen if Edith married that man. You made the choice to take his life."

Beside me, Lois gasped so loudly, I wouldn't have been surprised if they could hear it on the village square. I clamped my hand over her mouth, but it was too late. Enoch had heard us. He looked in our direction. I don't know if he saw us or just saw our shadows move as I grabbed Lois by the arm and dragged her into the bushes.

She yelped as the sharp branches poked at our skin and tore at our clothes.

The muffled sound of boots thumped over the lawn just outside the clump where we were hiding. The boots stopped a mere few feet from us.

"I didn't hear anything," Tucker said.

"I know I did." Enoch's voice was hard, harder than I had ever heard it.

"It's probably just a child or a teenager who wandered off from the fire."

"Are you a fool? Whoever it is might have heard what we were discussing."

"Oh," Tucker whispered. "See, this is what I was trying to get at. There is no way we aren't going to be found out. Someone will discover what really happened to Zeke Miller. Then you will have to give this all up again."

"Not if I can remove some of the variables."

"What do you—"

There was a yelp and then silence.

Lois whimpered. I covered my mouth. I believed that Lois and I had just overheard another murder.

There was a rustle of leaves and large hands pulled me out of the bushes. The branches scraped at my arms as I was forced to my feet. "Aunt Millie. I guess I should have expected you to be where you aren't welcome."

"Enoch Lapp, you let go of me right now," I said in my best angry-elder voice.

"Why? So you can go tell the police on me, just the way you did when I young?"

His words stung. "I made a mistake before, but there is no mistaking what you've done now. I heard what you and Tucker were saying. Where is he?"

"That doesn't matter."

I stared at Tucker's body on the ground just a few feet away and felt sick.

"If you want Edith and the children to be safe, you need to keep your mouth shut for once in your life," he said in that hard voice again.

"You'd hurt your own family?"

He grabbed my arm and wrenched it behind my back. "My family abandoned me when I needed them most. I didn't do anything wrong, but still I suffered for it. You caused that suffering. Maybe now I can even the score."

351

With my free hand I put two fingers in my mouth and whistled for all I was worth.

"What are you doing? Be quiet!" Enoch pulled harder on my arm. "No one is going to hear that over the commotion of the bonfire."

"I wasn't whistling for people to come," I said through gritted teeth.

"Wha—"

He couldn't finish his question because Peter ran at him full tilt with his head down. The goat rammed into Enoch's hip. My nephew cried out and before he could recover, Phillip hit him with his horns. Enoch's grip became weak enough that I was able to yank my arm free.

Lois popped out of the bushes like a jack-in-the-box.

Enoch swore. "What is going on?"

"The police are on their way," Lois shouted. "Deputy Aiden should be coming around the house any second now."

As if he heard her cue, Deputy Aiden ran around the side of the greenhouse with his gun drawn. "Freeze!"

Enoch held up his hands. "Don't shoot. I didn't do anything. I was just having a conversation with my aunt."

"He's lying." I closed my eyes for a moment because the scene was so reminiscent of what had happened all those years ago when I told the police where Enoch was when they were

352

searching for the stolen motorcycle. I opened my eyes again and found Phillip and Peter standing on either side of me like goat defenders. "Enoch was the one behind Zeke Miller's death. It wasn't Reuben or Jeremy. He goaded and encouraged Tucker to do it in order to protect Edith. What neither of them knew was she'd already ended her upcoming wedding to Zeke and protected herself."

"That's ridiculous," Enoch spat. "You have already arrested the persons responsible for Zeke's death. My aunt is tired. She doesn't even know what she's saying."

"I think Millie knows exactly what she is saying," Deputy Aiden said.

"How can you believe her as an eyewitness? She has made such mistakes before."

"Tucker Leham is lying dead behind us because of him," I said. "That's no mistake."

"Little, cover Lapp, and I will check on the victim."

Deputy Little walked up to Enoch with his gun drawn. "Please stand over there, ma'am," Deputy Little said to me.

I moved over to the bushes where Lois was standing, watching the proceedings with her mouth open. She wasn't the only one. I saw that at least half the people from the bonfire were peeking around the side of the greenhouse to get a look at what had happened. "How did you know Deputy Aiden was coming?"

"I had my cell phone, Millie. See, there are perks of having an English person as a friend."

I hugged her. "So many perks. Thank you."

She hugged me back, and the goats gently headbutted her.

"I think the goats are thanking me," Lois said.

"I know they are," I said and then I saw Deputy Aiden kneeling beside Tucker, looking for a pulse. "Poor Tucker though."

"I know," she said. "I know he killed Zeke, but maybe he really did think he was doing the right thing."

I glanced down at Tucker's hand; was it just a trick of light? I thought I saw his fingers move. Deputy Aiden was still searching in vain for a pulse as I knelt on Tucker's other side. I looked harder and his hand moved again. "He's still alive!"

Deputy Aiden looked up. "What is it?"

"He's still alive. I just saw his hand move."

Deputy Aiden started CPR. Breathing hard, he said, "An ambulance is already on the way."

As if he called the ambulance by just saying that, I heard sirens blare in the night, and the shouts of Deputy Little, warning the people at the bonfire to get back. I sat back on my heels while Deputy Aiden pumped Tucker's chest, and I prayed.

Tucker moaned.

"He's coming back to consciousness," Deputy

Aiden said as three EMTs ran around the green-house and took over.

The deputy helped me to my feet. "You did good, Millie."

I looked from my nephew, who was hand-cuffed and arguing with Deputy Little, to the cluster of EMTs around Tucker. "That's yet to be determined, Deputy Aiden."

"How we're all doing in this life is yet to be determined."

I stood amazed that he understood so well. If I didn't know better, I would have thought Deputy Aiden had some Amish in him.

EPILOGUE

Tucker Leham didn't die the night of the bonfire. He was severely injured after Enoch hit him on the head and would be in rehab for a long time to help him adjust to getting around without the use of his right side. Enoch was arrested and awaiting trial for the attempted murder of Tucker while Tucker was awaiting trial for the murder of Zeke. Jeremy and Reuben, though cleared of the murders, were awaiting trial for stealing cars, dozens of them according to reports. Reuben was in jail, but Jeremy, a very rich man, was able to post bond until trial.

A small part of me couldn't help but feel responsible for the way my nephew had turned out. Had my mistake all those years ago caused him to go bad? The very thought of it made my stomach turn. I could only ask *Gott* to take that guilt from me because I could no longer bear it on my own.

A proverb came to mind when thinking about my part in Enoch's life. "When you get to your wit's end, you'll find God lives there."

"*Aenti*!" Micah yelled as I pulled my buggy to a stop at the greenhouse. "It's kitten day. You get to take Peaches home."

I smiled at the boy as I climbed out of my

356

buggy and tethered Bessie to the hitching post. "I'm quite excited."

"Your *Englisch* friends are already here!" Micah shouted in a way only a child thrilled about animals could.

I saw Lois and Darcy standing outside Lois's car. Edith was holding Ginny in her arms and chatting with them.

"Has she seen her kitten yet?" I asked.

Micah shook his head. "But she will love her. How can you not love a kitten?"

"I have no idea," I said with a smile. "I'm sure the goats will be quite excited when I bring Peaches home."

"Do goats like cats?"

"These goats will," I assured him.

He jumped and ran to tell his siblings the news. I hoped I was right about the goats liking Peaches, but I supposed if they didn't, I could keep the kitten in the house. That would most likely make Phillip and Peter jealous, but that could not be helped.

Edith came to me. "*Aenti.*" She hugged me tight.

I knew that we were both thinking about the same thing. Enoch, the lost boy. I hugged her back. "Are you all right?"

She nodded. "*Ya*, I was just speaking to Darcy. She has no idea why they are here. Lois just told her it was a surprise."

"That sounds like Lois," I said. "She likes a surprise more than anyone I know."

"I'm glad that you found your old friend again." Edith smiled at Lois and Darcy across the yard.

"I am too." I swallowed. "It's a gift from a life lived long ago."

Lois clapped her hands. "Let's stop standing around here. To the kittens!"

Micah pumped his fist. "To the kittens!"

The three children took off toward the barn.

"I think I might have to watch Lois's influence on Micah," Edith said.

"She's harmless," I said with a grin.

Edith didn't look as though she believed me on that point. She shook her head.

"Kittens?" Darcy asked.

"I picked out a kitten for you." Lois held her arms up in the air. "Surprise!"

"What?" Darcy asked.

"You will love her," Lois said with complete confidence.

"Darcy, let me tell you about the kittens before you see them," Edith said.

Darcy smiled. "All right. I've never had a cat before. I'm not sure what to do."

"I've had countless cats," my niece replied. "That's part of growing up way out here. I can tell you what to do."

The two young women walked to the door of

the greenhouse, arm in arm. Lois and I stayed back and let them walk on alone for a bit.

"I think you made a match, Millie Fisher." She nodded at the two girls. "They are well suited for each other."

I smiled. "It's true. Not all the important matches in this life are romantic. A friend match is just as important."

"Like us?" she asked.

I grinned. "Just like us, Lois, just like us."

Books are produced in the United States using U.S.-based materials

Books are printed using a revolutionary new process called THINKtech™ that lowers energy usage by 70% and increases overall quality

Books are durable and flexible because of Smyth-sewing

Paper is sourced using environmentally responsible foresting methods and the paper is acid-free

Center Point Large Print
600 Brooks Road / PO Box 1
Thorndike, ME 04986-0001 USA

(207) 568-3717

US & Canada:
1 800 929-9108
www.centerpointlargeprint.com